Jenna's Flaw

Lee Tasey

Cover design: Ashley Cordier

Front Cover Photo: Shutterstock/Lario Tus

Back Cover Photo: ©iStock/da-kuk

To Western civilization

"From which stars have we fallen to meet each other here?"

Friedrich Nietzsche

Part I

1

On the day Coach Dixon found his star running back dead on the sandbars of the Platte River, an Amtrak delivered me to the Lincoln depot before vanishing into the jungles of corn leaves. I walked into the depot and swatted a fat fly from my face. In the corner, two elderly farmers with fresh blue overalls and red faces stood by a television.

"It's a tragedy."

"Kenny was a miracle."

"What happened?"

"Only God knows."

I lowered my body onto a bench and leaned forward with my elbows on my blue-jeaned knees, my satchel and blue suitcase at my sides. I'd heard about the discovery of the body on the long trip down. In fact, I'd heard about little else. Now I watched the breaking news story on the TV screen: Les Dixon, the football coach for Nebraska State University, stood at a podium in a conference room, shielding his eyes from the flashes of cameras. On the other side of a split screen, four paramedics muscled a stretcher up the bank of the Platte River, while an Adidas shoe dangled by a shoelace from a low branch of a cottonwood tree.

I brushed another fly from my face and ran my forearm across my forehead. Behind me, a fly buzzed against the window. My blue T-shirt darkened in the middle, sticking to my chest and the middle of my back. I pulled Nietzsche's *Anti-Christ* out of my satchel and began to fan my face.

Sad piano music began to play on the TV. On the screen, a Nebraska State Bison player ran down the football field, breaking tackle after tackle. He entered the end zone with a tattooed arm raised sky high, the football falling from his loose, taped-up fingers. At the bottom of the screen, his obituary scrolled lazily along. He was twenty-one years old. His name was Kenny Winslow.

The farmers walked toward the screen door.

"Don't know how it could've happened."

"With the corn crop dried up and now with Kenny gone, I wonder what'll happen next?"

"The football season is darn well over and it hasn't even begun."

"Kenny was a shooting star. Bright one minute and gone the next."

Ticket stubs and wisps of corn husks blew inside when they filed through the door, the depot now more full of flies. I sat for a minute, ignoring the news. It was a thirty-eight hour train ride out from Sacramento with the two transfers. I had known when I signed up for graduate work in philosophy at Black Forest University that football was God around here. I glanced at Nietzsche. And now it seemed that God was dead.

I needed to get myself settled. I walked to the ticket booth. A teenager was inside with a cell phone to his ear.

"Are there any cabs around here?" I said.

The boy looked up, his face red and flushed. "Say what?"

"Cabs." I tapped the ticket window with a knuckle. "Do you guys have cabs in this state?"

He lowered the phone. "Yes, sir. Should be waiting at the curb. If not, I can call one for you."

I snatched up my luggage. On the TV, the highlights of Kenny Winslow's career flashed on the screen—Kenny running down the field, his hair, long and gold like prairie grass streaming down his back, a razor blade tattoo on his left forearm, and Kenny charging into the end zone as the Husker players dropped like flies.

2

There wasn't a cab at the curb or for miles around, I guessed. I stood alone in the parking lot, Ray-Bans on, and studied my new home. Dust devils danced across the lot in a breeze that never seemed to stop. To the east, a cemetery of freight trains glowed in the afternoon sun, and high above the rows of quiet trains the Nebraska statehouse soared into the sky, big and tall and phallus-like.

I got out my Salems. I tried to light one but the flame blew out. I tried again. Then, hunkering down, again. Once lit, I took a hard pull and surveyed my new home.

So this was Nebraska.

To my left was a gas station with its windows boarded up and *We Remember #8* spray-painted in maroon on the garage— a sign that grief-based vandalism moved quickly. To my right, a junkyard with three pyramids of scrap metal. Three red cranes like gigantic beasts lowered their huge jaws and gobbled up car doors, small refrigerators, and silver pipes. I watched the beasts as they tossed the junk, on fire in the sun, from one pyramid to the other. A candy-apple-red locomotive, its hopper cars loaded up with coal, slunk past the pyramids and chugged off into the hillsides of sweet corn.

I sighed. I was beginning to understand why I'd been admitted to Black Forest University. Who wanted to live in Nebraska? I could probably still find cowboys and Indians here if I looked hard enough.

I pulled at my T-shirt, wet and sticky on my chest, and stared off into the great northern sky, over the grids of soybean and alfalfa fields and four silo farms. The Dakotas were up there somewhere. Canada, too.

I tapped my cigarette. "The Middle West. The Great American Desert as the pioneers had called it. A whole lot of nothing. Just football, beer, and religion. And me."

I puffed away on my Salem. The trains in the Burlington company locomotive yard were quiet and still, while the huge summer clouds like slumbering gods cast their shadows darkly against the rows of boxcars.

At least I'd gotten into a doctoral program. My plan was to finish in four years and then land a full-time teaching job in the Pacific Northwest or England. I saw my future with a godlike clarity: Dr. Carl Sorensen, professor of atheistic thought. I'd have tenure, summer vacations, and a heavy pension ready to kick in. For all that, I could deal with Nebraska for four years.

Of course, that was just a fantasy. Given the job market for PhDs in philosophy, I'd more likely wind up with an adjunct professor's job, making ends meet by painting houses over the summer. Oh well, at least I'd be doing what I loved.

Then I saw it. A small bus, sulfur white and blinding to the eyes, appeared out of nowhere. A young girl in a white tank top and short shorts was driving. She rolled down the passenger window. "You need a lift?"

"Are you a shuttle service?"

"We are."

"Could you take me downtown?"

"We can do lots of things."

The girl stretched out her arm to unlock the door, and I spotted a pink, rubbery scar on the inside of her wrist. The girl's gigantic black eyes were locked on mine. They were smiling, her eyes. Almost made me feel good about Nebraska. I tossed my suitcase in the back, then climbed in the front next to her.

As we left the depot, a local freight chugged on ahead of us, belching out smoke. A railroader stood at the guardrail, arms crossed, eyes barely visible under the bill of an orange hard hat. He waved. The girl waved back.

We drove through a suburban neighborhood that could have come from Hollywood in the 50s. Pink and baby-blue houses were set back on the dry lawns, strewn with old footballs and chrome dirt bikes. American, Husker, and Bison flags unraveled in the breeze, while the cottonwoods stood on either side of the street, trunks like the columns of cathedrals.

"Wow," I said. "This is small town life."

"You haven't seen this before?"

"Not in California."

"Then allow us to welcome you to Nebraska. It's the good life. Or so I am informed."

I looked at the girl. She looked twelve years old but she talked like she could have been forty. She had long, frizzy honey-blonde hair, like a girl out of an 80s music video. A pink bra and matching underwear peeked through the white, skimpy outfit.

Not bad. Maybe Nebraska was a blessing in disguise. It still didn't seem likely, but you never know.

We coasted down the street. Shirtless kids in cutoff blue jeans chased us on bikes.

"This is something out of a John Cougar Mellencamp video," I said.

The girl tapped her maroon thumbnails on the steering wheel and began quietly singing "Small Town," Cougar's famous song. She had a pretty voice, almost angelic.

She pointed at the satchel on my lap. "School?" But before I could answer, she held up her hand. "Wait, don't tell me." She closed her eyes and opened them. "Black Forest University."

I stared at her. "I'm going there in the fall."

"Hmm," she said dreamily. "The fall." She closed her eyes again and when she opened them her eyes were smiling more. "A doctoral program?"

"What are you, a psychic? If so, your skills might come in handy."

I told her about my doctoral degree—about the trainload of term papers and exams on the way, plus the lousy job market for philosophy. I explained that colleges and universities were relying on adjunct professors, part-timers, to teach most of the courses and that full-time positions were becoming few and far between, especially in the humanities. And this was happening everywhere, too. I didn't mention the dream of tenure. I was looking for sympathy.

Stabbing another Salem between my lips, I said, "All right, I'm off my soapbox now. But maybe you can give me the lowdown on Nebraska, on Black Forest University, on the local libraries . . . whatever I might need to know."

She seemed to consider my offer. Then she looked at me with big black eyes, and an invisible fire seemed to burn in them. "We could do that."

I was beginning to wonder about the first person plural. "Hey, can you turn the air off?"

"It's not on."

"It's freezing in here."

"Then roll the window down."

I torched my Salem, then hit the window's lever. My hair began to blow wildly.

"I was just joking when I called you a psychic," I said. "I don't believe in that junk. I studied it in divinity school for, like, a week. 'Paranormal Activity and the Spirit World' was the course's title. I dropped the class because the professor and the rest of the class were just way too credulous. Can you guess what I took, instead?"

The girl's eyes flashed over to mine. She seemed to know the answer.

"Medieval theology," I said. "It seemed more likely that I could figure out how many angels could dance on the head of a pin."

At a stoplight, the girl and I looked at each other. She smiled. I did, too. On the floor, I glimpsed a copy of *The Amityville Horror* and an issue of *Good Housekeeping*. Interesting combination. Unexpected.

"Do you like to read?" I said.

"I do."

"A lot?"

"Oh, yes. Whatever we can get our hands on."

That might explain the range of reading on the floor. I studied the girl's nice-looking legs, giving her the space to elaborate, but she seemed to be thinking of something else.

"Anyway," I said, tapping my cigarette. "All those right answers you came up with about me, that was just good observation and smarts. I mean, why else would a twenty-six-year-old guy move to Nebraska, if not for graduate school? So there you go, Ms. Psychic. Your two guesses accounted for."

3

The girl wheeled the bus onto Cornhusker Highway. We passed by Uncle Ron's, apparently a country music bar, and then a Phillips 66 where a boy attendant in blue overalls was pumping gas into a burnt-orange Chevy truck.

"Are you a student?" I said.

"Not anymore."

"Oh, that's too bad. I guess. What'd you study?"

The girl took a sip from a paper cup I hadn't noticed in the center console.

"Art." She put it back in the console and wiped her fingers on the white shorts, leaving dark wet marks.

"Ah, the humanities. Good for you. You may be driving a bus for the rest of your life, but hey, at least you'll have something meaningful to do when your shift is over, right?"

"Is that how it works?"

"You can't do much with a humanities degree."

"But your philosophy degree is going to make you the big bucks?"

"Good point."

She smiled. Her eyes wandered over to mine and then she averted them and blushed.

"So, can you tell me what I studied as an undergraduate?" I said. "There's no way you know this one."

The girl laughed and her overlarge eyes lit up like black flames. The bus was still freezing. I glanced at the dashboard. The air conditioning knob was really off. I crossed my arms.

"Okay, I'll tell you. Theology. You know, the study of God and salvation? I thought I might actually learn something useful, something that might help make sense of the world. Well, someday I'm going to write a poem about the whole experience. It'll be called 'DONE.'"

The girl grabbed a lock of frizzy hair. She ran her fingers down it as she looked into the rearview mirror.

"Do you know what I mean?" I said. "I mean, have you ever had high hopes for something, then reach the point where you get burned out and just say to hell with it."

The girl pulled at the lock of hair, now like flattened wheat. She was still looking in the rearview mirror with a peculiar smirk on her face. Slowly, I looked over my shoulder. The bus was empty.

I said, "What are you staring at?"

"Oh, nothing."

I studied her. What a weirdo. Smoking-hot body, though. I settled deeper into the seat, still unable to get warm. "But do you know what I mean about saying to hell with something?"

"Oh, we know exactly what you mean."

"It happened to me and a lot of my friends in divinity school. Some guys didn't even finish the program. One guy now runs a nightclub in Chicago, while another guy's an investment banker in Manhattan with a hot, younger wife." I looked out the window at a shimmering blue lake where a German shepherd trotted on the shoreline. "I don't know, maybe it was just a crappy lot of teachers. Did you ever take a theology class in college?"

The girl reached for the radio's dial, snapping it on.

"It's not a big deal if you didn't," I said over the news— more on Kenny Winslow's death. "Theology certainly isn't for everybody. It certainly wasn't for me."

The girl adjusted the mirror, and a silver chain-link bracelet slid down her wrist, past the pink scar. We drove on in silence as Lincoln, the Star City, came into view.

"So where are you from?" she said.

"Most recently from Massachusetts—undergrad at University of Boston. Originally, California. Sacramento."

"California." She said the word with a hint of longing.

"Have you been there?"

"In some sense."

I ashed my cigarette. "What's that supposed to mean? Either you've been there or you haven't. It's what philosophers call the law of excluded middle." I stuck my hand outside and sent the Salem into orbit, then crossed my arms, awaiting her reply.

"I've heard of it," she said. "The middle thing."

"Good." I was getting a little tired of the enigmatic stuff. It was like she was playing a game with me, and I'd had enough of that as an undergrad. "Because even though it's a law of logic, everybody uses it, every day. That cigarette butt that's rolling down the highway? It can't be both a Salem and an American Spirit. Not at the same time. Do you see where I'm going with this? So according to that logic, Ms. Psychic, you've either been to the West Coast or you haven't. So which is it? Yes or no?"

Her eyes were blazing now, though I wasn't sure with what. She bit down on her lips and her cheeks reddened.

"Okay, so you're not going to answer the question," I said. "You're just going to sit there—"

Without signaling, she crossed into the left lane and sped up, blowing past a taxi—they did have them here—and then a local news van.

"Let's just say it's complicated," she said.

When my breathing settled down a little, I inspected the stalks of blonde hair partially hiding her face. Her white nose stuck out prominently with a pretty dent in the bridge.

"Anyway . . ." I brushed the flakes of ash off my satchel. "Crap, I forget what I was going to say. Never mind."

"School?"

"Oh, right. I've got four years in this program, then I'm done. Ideally, I'll land a tenure-track job and life will be awesome."

"Oh, it'll take you longer than that. They don't finish in four years there. They take eight, maybe ten."

I let my head fall back on the headrest as the highway vanished under the bus. *Jesus, what's this girl's deal?* "You know the local scene pretty well, dontcha?" I inspected the girl's face, pale and sickly but also beautiful, and then noticed a batch of business cards next to the hardcover edition of *The Amityville Horror.*

I picked one up. "Are you Jenna McMaster?"

"I am."

"Any relation to John McMaster, the famous theologian? He was a professor of mine in Boston."

Jenna twisted up in her seat as the bottoms of her thighs peeled audibly off the vinyl. She thumbed the radio's dial, blowing through the stations.

"John McMaster is the most famous theologian in America," I said above the snippets of country music and mourning for Kenny Winslow.

Jenna rolled her window down, the hot air roaring into the bus, and a modern rock station blared through the speakers.

"Oh, look," she said. "There's the football stadium."

Off in the east, I saw Memorial Stadium, the landmark I'd read about in a Nebraska travel guide my previous roommate had given me as a joke. The stadium was an enormous art deco lump that could have been a hospital from the outside. In the parking lot, an ESPN van had stopped by the front doors, along with the local news crews.

"I hear the locals call the stadium 'God,'" I said. "Is that true?"

"They call it lots of things."

"Do you know what I heard about their old coach? The travel guide said that if he returns to coach the Huskers, it'll be as big as the second coming of Christ." I looked at Jenna, expecting her to laugh, but her eyes were fixed firmly on the highway. Both hands were on the wheel again. She wasn't smirking anymore. "Haven't you heard these things? You're from Nebraska, right? In some sense?" I looked past Jenna into the bus' side mirror at Memorial Stadium. Maybe I should try for the topic of conversation on everyone's lips. "It's sad what happened to that football player. He played for the Bison, right?"

"He did."

"What was his name again?"

Jenna inhaled through her nose, and I noticed her overlarge eyes now seeming to possess a black, smokeless fire.

"Kenny Winslow," she said.

"Do you know what happened to him?"

"In a sense."

We passed a minor league baseball stadium and then descended into the downtown area, stopping at a traffic light across from the Journal Star.

"So what happened?" I said.

"It wasn't a good situation."

"I might have guessed that from the fact he's dead. But how'd he die? Do the authorities know anything yet?"

Jenna shook her head.

"But you know, right?"

I waited for a follow up but of course there wasn't one.

The bus pulled up to the Pioneer Hotel amidst the large vans from the local and national news stations that were packed into the loading zone. Jenna double-parked, hopped out, dragged my suitcase from the back of the bus, and set it down gently at my feet.

"There." She patted the handle.

"Thanks." Now that she was out of the bus, I noticed the red high heels.

"It's our pleasure."

"Maybe we'll see each other down the road. I'm Carl, by the way. Carl Sorensen."

"Nice to meet you, Carl."

I shook Jenna's hand. It was cold. Then I handed her a ten-dollar bill, which she took with her small, child-like fingers.

"Thank you, Carl. Maybe now I can buy a book on mind reading."

"And after you do, we'll get together and talk about it. You can tell me about Lincoln. I'm certain this town has a lot going for it. Loads."

"We'd love to do that."

My eyes dropped to Jenna's upper chest—a constellation of dark red moles seemed to form a funny-looking face.

She leapt up into the bus and closed the door and stuck her head out of the window. "Oh, Carl?"

"Yeah?"

"There's something else you should know."

I picked up my suitcase. "Yeah?"

Jenna's lips parted slowly as a breeze lifted up her hair. "You're always going to live here."

4

The hotel lobby was swamped with reporters. I stood under the brick awning and caught bits of conversation: "Kenny Winslow" and "Heisman Trophy" and "death a mystery" came up a lot. A tall, skinny bellman in a pioneer outfit appeared, pulling a bell cart shaped like a covered wagon. He wore a bright-red crew cut and had a galaxy of red freckles on his face. I read his nametag. Avery.

"How do you like them apples?" Avery watched the white bus speed through the stoplight. "That was Jenna. She's an oddball but at least she's a drop-dead gorgeous oddball."

I was given to agree on both counts. "What's a girl like that driving a bus for?"

"It's the town mystery. Checking in?"

Twenty minutes later, Avery and I stepped into the elevator. Holding my suitcase, he pushed button number three.

"So I assume you've heard the story? A speeding train killed our star running back this morning. Coach Dixon found him before sunup while out jogging with his dog."

"Hadn't heard the train part."

"Well, just walking through the lobby now, you can absorb the latest."

The doors opened up, and Avery led me down a hallway, the carpet maroon and smelling of soap.

"It's insanity around here," I said.

"The hotel's booked up for a week. It doesn't get this crazy during playoff season."

Avery slid the key into the gold lock. It didn't open. He tried again. Nothing.

"The locks are brand new. Everything is changing around here—the doors, the locks, the carpets." He opened the door with a master key and hoisted my suitcase onto the bed's edge. "I'll be back." Three minutes later, he returned with a new key and tested it. It worked.

I decided I needed some decent coffee. "Where's a Dunkin' Donuts?"

"Illinois."

Oh. "Starbucks?"

"The first one arrives in September. There are other cafés, though, independently owned ones with lots of personality. Just go down to the Big Red Zone—that's the college strip."

After I thanked Avery and gave him a tip, I closed the door and threw back the curtains. Two blocks away stood the statehouse. An Egyptian sower stood atop a gold dome with a satchel of seeds slung over his shoulder. The Sower's right hand was pulled behind his body, ready to sow a handful of seeds.

I rested my forehead on the hot, dusty window. Of course. He's sowing the seeds of life, of possibility, of a better future, just as the sign at the Nebraska border said. "Nebraska: The Good Life."

I sprawled out on the single bed and turned on the TV. It was still Kenny Winslow, 24/7. On CNN, a woman reporter in a purple suit stood on a football field in Slippery Rock, Nebraska, wherever that might be. I turned up the volume as she spoke about Kenny Winslow and his sudden rise to fame: growing up in Red Cloud, Nebraska; sitting on the bench during his first two years as a Bison; and his steady climb to superstardom during his junior year, winning the Heisman Trophy and defeating the Miami Hurricanes in the Orange Bowl.

The lack of coffee and excess of Nebraska got the best of me. I drifted off.

When I woke up, *American Idol* was on TV. The Sower was barely visible in the sky, and a red light blinked at his bare feet. I looked at the alarm clock. Eight o'clock. I yawned, then snatched up my satchel and left for the Big Red Zone.

In the lobby, an old, hunchbacked doorman pushed open the glass door for me. Bellmen, like oxen, their bodies hitched to covered wagons, pulled the heavy loads of luggage as I stepped aside to let them pass. Reporters still stood under the awning and spoke on phones, making appointments for the next day.

I ate a decent roast beef sandwich at Bison Witches, a typical college-town diner I found in the Big Red Zone. While eating, I jotted down a to-do list, when the back of my mind noticed a contemporary rock song playing in the background. I'd heard it all summer long, a song about faith and doubt. At least that was my interpretation. I didn't know who the artist was, but now I wrote down snippets of lyrics, vowing to Google them later on. Maybe I'd even teach the song in class someday—it was the sort of thing the cool professors did. Make philosophy fun, and your students will love you for it.

After dinner, I walked outside into a light drizzle and ducked into Walgreens for some basics. A young girl rang me up. She had a brown ponytail and a nose ring.

"You're the first customer on my shift who hasn't bought memory cards or batteries," she said.

I remembered something I'd noticed on my way through the lobby. "The gift shop at the hotel has been invaded, too. It's madness. There's nothing left in the shop, just those little metal poles sticking out of the walls."

She scanned my items. "Are you new in town?"

I glanced at them myself: a map of Lincoln; a box of Benadryl; a small umbrella; and a postcard of bison on the flat, treeless prairie. It wasn't a hard guess. "I arrived today."

"You don't look like a journalist. Are you here for the school?"

"Black Forest. Graduate work in philosophy."

"Oh." She handed me a bag. "Good luck with that."

Back at the hotel, I turned on the TV but there was nothing on except the Kenny Winslow tragedy—the train angle evidently pushed it past a certain threshold. I swallowed a Benadryl to knock me out, brushed my teeth, got into bed, and opened up a Nietzsche biography, rereading the chapter on the "death of God." I found it strangely comforting to know that you could put together a view of life with meaning and purpose without resorting to the contrived, arbitrary, yet ironclad belief systems that passed for religion.

Every few pages, I looked out the window at the eerie-looking clouds, like dark riders atop their horses, torches blazing in the night. The Sower was barely visible. Only the red light was blinking at his feet.

I finished the chapter and webbed my hands behind my head. What a year. A useless degree in theology, meeting Nietzsche, and saying farewell to God. Explaining to mom and dad why I was switching to philosophy. And getting admitted to Black Forest University. Not Purdue or Rice or Cal. Not Yale or Duke or Emory.

BFU, the ultimate safety school.

5

At daybreak, I left the hotel with one thing in mind: coffee. What they brewed at Bison Witches wasn't terrible, but I needed something higher octane to get me started. The news teams were climbing into their vans and rental cars, departing for Slippery Rock, while I walked north toward the Big Red Zone. My body was already soaked with sweat by the time I entered the first café I saw.

It was a dark, artsy café with lamps burning dimly on the tables—the sort of place that would either serve nothing but chai tea or espresso you could peel paint with. Fortunately for me, it was the latter. I ordered a triple Americano and busted out my Nietzsche biography, reading a chapter on "life as art." It spoke of how, if God is dead, we must become gods for ourselves. We must become the artists of our lives, creating our own morality and meaning, since there is no God to do it for us.

I took meticulous notes. Occasionally I'd look up at a woman in a long black dress and a Chinese-schoolgirl haircut. She sat alone at a table stacked with the lesser-known novels of Virginia Woolf. She might have been a graduate student or perhaps an assistant professor of English. When I smiled and said hello, she glared at me above rimless eyeglasses, and I casually returned to my book. So Ms. Dalloway thought ill of me? Big deal. I had Nietzsche. I had better company. Friedrich Wilhelm Nietzsche—philosopher, psychologist, antichrist. He taught us the *übermensch*, the superman.

Before I left, I talked to the barista, a shaggy-haired dude with a grizzly beard and a Charlie Brown T-shirt.

"Where's a good place to live?" I said.

"The Ghetto."

"Is that as cheap as it sounds?"

"Oh, yeah. But don't let the name fool you. It's nice enough."

"Does it have studios?"

"Dude, it has everything."

"How much?" I said.

"Around three hundred a month. Four hundred will get you a really nice place."

You couldn't rent a closet in Boston or Sacramento for three hundred a month. I pulled out my map of Lincoln. "Show me."

I left the café. I wandered down the main street, admiring the old courthouse with its high clock tower, and then into the Haymarket with its maze of cobbled streets and dusty storefronts. At the main line track, I yanked up a piece of tall, dry grass and broke it in half, pushing the stalk into my mouth, telling myself I was doing it ironically. A Santa Fe locomotive grumbled toward me, blaring its horn while the dirt road shook under my shoes. Out west, the red cranes still hovered over the pyramids of junk, beyond which were the steel mills, the meatpacking plants, and, further west, the airport. Not an international airport, but a municipal airport.

Ten years, Jenna had said. I couldn't imagine it. I would finish my degree in four years if it killed me.

The locomotive throbbed by, vibrating something deep in my chest. I watched the line of old, creaky boxcars passing by just feet away, brown as coffins, with pink and baby-blue graffiti on the doors. Kneeling, I gawked at the big wheels as the rails sunk into the red rocks and rose up slowly. In the thickening heat, I listened to the pings and snarls of the train, sniffing the scent of burning oil and smoke, the rumble beginning to numb my body, so that it felt like I was floating.

Following the main line track, I passed over the Sioux Street crossing as locusts sprung out from clumps of goldenrod and blazing star wildflowers. I pressed on, my eyeballs on fire from a thick film of sweat, my face sticky from sunscreen and corn dust blowing over the tracks. Up ahead, a grain elevator rose into the sky like an Imperial Walker out of *Star Wars*. Near the top, two quarter-moons had been spray-painted, resembling a pair of sinister eyes. I studied my map. Then, shouldering my satchel, my eyes upraised, I watched the elevator's eyes watching me.

Soon, I found the Ghetto. The streets of this neighborhood were named after Nebraska Indian tribes—Omaha and Lakota, Otoe and Pawnee and Arapahoe—and each of the white frame houses had an unkempt yard with the seed-heavy heads of sunflowers drooping over the board fences. A seven-story tenement house made of red bricks dominated the area. The placard above the doorway said "The Guardian."

A bald man stood in a sandlot fixing the volleyball net. He wore cutoff blue jeans and a white T-shirt with drops of butter-colored paint splattered on it. A cigarette hung from his mouth.

"Are you the landlord?" I said.

"Sure am."

"Do you have a studio for rent?"

"Sure do."

He led me to the third floor and opened a battered door. The room was small, like a monk's cell. I walked across the pinewood floor, smelling of soap and lemons, and stood before a dusty window. On the sill were dried-up dead bees and flies. Outside, the dust devils were dancing by the outbuildings in the train yard, beyond which tractors and combines were grazing on a patchwork of brown fields.

"How much?" I said.

"Three hundred."

I still couldn't fathom it. "A month, right?"

"You'll find ones for two fifty, but you're better off here."

I signed the lease.

"Two other guys were supposed to look at your studio this morning," Craig the landlord said. "Both were no shows."

A Burlington locomotive appeared from behind the stand of cottonwood trees, pulling a line of sea-green boxcars.

I shouldered my satchel. "After what happened to Kenny Winslow, I guess some people don't want to live near trains."

"Could be." Craig squinted an eye and rubbed the back of his neck. "By the way, you're going to hear those trains at all hours of the day, but it's nothing to worry about. You'll get used to them after a while."

6

After lunch, I wandered the streets of downtown Lincoln until I found a used bookstore in a back alley. Behind the window, I saw a stack of old issues of *Time* magazine that looked like they were from the 1960s. The one on top had a plain black cover that asked, in blood-red letters, "Is God Dead?" I bought it, thinking I'd use it for my dissertation, after which I went down to the cellar where I browsed the biography section. Standing at the overflowing bookrack, I felt something brush my legs. I looked down as a black cat sniffed at my shins, then sprawled out on the carpet and stretched its front legs. Its big green eyes blinked at me.

The bookstore cat was apparently universal.

I knelt down and stroked the cat, then read the silver nametag. "Asmodeus?"

The cat blinked.

"Well, hello, prince of the demons. You're a neat little fella with the best gig in town. Take care, Asmodeus, demon of lust, and see you down the road."

Routine chores made the day blow by. I found a Walmart and bought a mattress and bed sheets, a folding desk, and a swivel chair. And a bike—a Trek, metallic blue and ready for the road. Feeling confident about the academic year, I pedaled back to the Guardian and waited for the furniture guy.

An hour later, he arrived. He helped me set up my studio, and after I tipped him, I brushed the bees and flies off the windowsill—now home to the collected works of Nietzsche in mismatched, used paperbacks, plus a manual on writing a dissertation. I stood by the front door and surveyed all I'd done.

"Perfect," I said. "My study. My cell. I'll be a secular monk, helping men and women survive the funeral of God. I'll help them to make their godless lives works of art, something they can be proud of without help from above or the comfort of an afterlife."

I pulled out *Twilight of the Idols* and sniffed its pages. Ah, the smell. My future office would smell like this book. My future house, too. Philosophy, literature, the arts, the humanities. The good life.

Outside, the combines were grazing in the far-off fields, like giant insects out of the Bible. The plumes of dust were spreading out over the pink gravel roads, and the skyline was bathed in a dark-red hue. I set Nietzsche back on the sill, then placed my palms on the window. I'll also make time for fun, I thought, since Nietzsche said to live dangerously and to get lots of experience in life. So I'll venture out of my cell and take risks, hammering and chiseling my life into the work of art I want it to be.

On that lofty note, I left my cell and hiked up the main line track, toward the Haymarket, under a blazing roof of stars. Kneeling down, I pressed the heel of my palm on the rail, still warm from the day's sunshine. Behind me, a freight train inched forward, its eyes boring through the dark-blue air. The locomotive blared its horn, and I stepped away from the tracks, watching the long line of oil cars like a snake crawling into its hole.

I pressed on. The dark, heavy rain-smelling air swept in over the train yard, ballooning my T-shirt out, cooling my body, and when I passed under a pedestrian bridge, a school of pigeons watched me from the heights.

By the time I entered the Haymarket, the awnings of the shops were flapping wildly in the wind. Then, about a football's throw away, I saw the Blue Note.

Even if it were simply named after the famous jazz place in New York, whoever named it had to at least know about the original. Worth trying out.

Inside, the bar was dark and smoky, with sawdust on the hardwood floor. A country and western song played on the jukebox. I went to the bar, unhooked my satchel, took a stool, and hooked the satchel's strap on my knee. An older man in a white shirt and with an apron stretched tight over his belly set a napkin down before me. He had wiry black hair and was balding a bit.

"What'll it be?" he said. A New York accent. Didn't sound contrived.

"Screwdriver."

"Large or small?"

"Large."

Above the three rows of liquor bottles, the wall was plastered with Nebraska license plates. HSKRLVR. NU X 5. BLKSHIRTS. SKERS. Some looked new, others as though they'd spent fifty years inside of a barn.

The bartender set the large glass on the napkin and spread his hands out wide on the bar. "You from back east?"

"I lived in Boston for three years. Kenmore Square. Two blocks from Fenway."

"Been there. What brings you way out here?"

"Graduate work in philosophy. Black Forest."

"Ah, a professional student."

"You could say that."

"Lotsa guys like you in town. Me, I'm from back east, too. Born and raised in Brooklyn. Moved to Nebraska at the end of '74." He wiped down the bar, making wide circles and leaving microbeads of water in its wake. "Nebraska's a good place. Got a lot to offer. Like I says to everyone who comes into the bar, 'youse ain't gonna think much of us at first, but stay a while and you ain't never gonna leave.'"

I sipped. Sure. Whatever. And "youse"? Was that for the tourists?

A man in blue jeans and a light-blue work shirt walked up to the bar and pointed to the TV remote. "Tony?"

"Yeah, go ahead."

Above the cash register, a TV blipped on. A woman reporter was standing in front of a small white house in, according to the crawl, Red Cloud, Nebraska.

Tony flung the towel over his shoulder and crossed his arms over his large belly. "Boy, what a mess, huh?"

"Ever since I arrived in town, that's all I've heard about. Kenny Winslow. The hotel where I stayed was at full occupancy—three hundred journalists and me."

"Jeez Louise, those news crews were everywhere. You gotta wonder what that kid was doing way out in the country at three in the morning."

"Didn't his own coach find him?"

"He sure did. Goes out for a morning jog with his dog and there's Kenny Winslow, his star player, next to alla that driftwood. Nearly every bone in his body was broke."

A photo of Kenny Winslow appeared on the screen. He was smiling widely with a big rainbow trout in hand, shiny on the fishing line. He wore maroon shorts and a white Bison shirt, cut off at the shoulders.

"You gotta wonder," Tony said, "did Kenny do it on purpose? Did he know his coach would be there and set it up so he'd find him?"

A few patrons entered the bar. While Tony tended to them, I turned on my stool. Outside, a napkin blew by on the sidewalk. Two college girls in faded blue jeans and red ringer T-shirts hurried by, arms crossed, hair blowing wildly and obscuring their faces. The sky began to grumble, and then a clap of thunder, like a gunshot, exploded over the town. Soon the cobbled street began to turn a dark red, and cool blasts of wind and rain were swirling into the bar, darkening the sawdust on the floor. The heavy rains continued to fall, and although the TV was no longer audible, I already knew the story.

Tony walked by, eying my drink glass. "Boy, that rain sure feels nice."

"It does."

"It won't do us much good, though. Too late in the season."

"If the crops are dead, what do the farmers do with them?"

"Feed it to the pigs. It's called silage."

I remembered the combines raising plumes of dust in their wakes. I wanted to say that, from my perspective, the destroyed crops had a strange kind of beauty, but I knew the local farmers and the people who supported them wouldn't share that perspective. Besides, I was taking some time off. I had a good buzz going on, and I wanted to keep it going. A philosophical argument would probably kill it.

I had a second drink, then a third. A crowd began to trickle in, mostly bearded young men in brown fedoras, tweed guitar cases in hand, heading for the stage. When the jam session got underway—genuine jazz, with no hint of country and western—I jotted down a to-do list and paid for my drinks.

"Thanks for stopping in," Tony said. "Don't let alla this get you down. Focus on school. I got high hopes for youse. High hopes. Now do good work and stop in anytime."

7

A week later, in early September, I matriculated at Black Forest University, a rural campus in the town of Sleepy Hollow, ten miles east of Lincoln. The land on which the school was built had a unique history. In the 1920s, popular meetings known as Chautauqua Meetings, after the famous rally in upstate New York that started it all, were held in the area. The meetings brought musicians, preachers, politicians, and social activists to entertain the locals. The most popular speaker was William Jennings Bryan, a Nebraska congressman, four-time candidate for president of the United States, and the central figure in the prosecution of John Scopes for teaching evolution in school.

Riding to campus, I breezed down Old Farm Road for ten miles. Nothing but a gray, drizzly sky and a two-lane country road up ahead. The farmland had been harvested on either side of the road, and I coasted between the hills of corn stubble, looking forward to meeting Dr. Duane Parsons, my advisor.

I parked my bike outside of Bryan Hall, which housed the Department of Philosophy and Religious Studies. But before going in, I lit up a cigarette and walked under a honey locust tree, where a bronze statue of the man himself—William Jennings Bryan—stood in the shade. He had a horseshoe of brown hair and wore a long overcoat and boots. His arm was held out, palm open, and he seemed to be asking me to join him.

I stared at Mr. Bryan as smoke tunneled out of my nostrils. I inspected Mr. Bryan's eyes, serious and unflinching. Four times he'd run for president and lost. Even at the famous

Scopes monkey trial, he'd won the case, but the verdict was overturned on a technicality. And he got a statue? What would they have done if he'd won something? I stubbed out the cigarette in Mr. Bryan's palm, blew smoke in his face, and went inside.

The conference room was full of philosophers—you could just tell. A dozen graduate students were chatting up the faculty, scrawny middle-aged men with rimless glasses and thinning hair. At the podium, two bearded young men in khaki pants and brown tweed blazers with elbow patches were in the midst of a philosophical debate, using big, technical words and gesticulating wildly. Others were sitting in folding chairs along the back wall with Styrofoam plates on their knees, eating.

I grabbed a plate of chicken-sandwich squares and chips, joined the wallflowers at the back wall, and small-talked it with the incoming students. Soon, a tall man in faded blue jeans and a black T-shirt sat down and set his backpack on the floor.

I eyed it, recognizing the angular bulges. "That's a lot of books."

"Yesterday I had a duffel bag, too."

"How many classes are you taking?"

"I'm done with coursework and exams. I'm writing my dissertation now."

"Really, on what?"

"Albert Camus."

Nice. One of the great French existentialists. "How's it going?"

"Writing a dissertation is like rolling a huge stone uphill for eternity. But you keep on pushing. You have to."

I introduced myself, as did he. Paul D'Angelo was the oldest student in the room. He could have been the father of all of us graduate students and could even pass for a tenured professor.

"How long have you been in the program?" I said.

"Ten years."

Jesus Christ. "Wow, a long time."

"Welcome to the madhouse."

The two bearded young men who had been speaking stopped in front of us. They continued their debate, something about Immanuel Kant and how the current unjust labor system in higher education would fail his ethical maxims.

"Why does it take so long?" I said.

Paul swallowed. "It's different for everybody in the program. For me it's a wife, two kids, and teaching part-time at three area colleges."

A side door opened up, and in walked Dr. Duane Parsons. He wore black slacks and a black turtleneck and took quick bird-like steps up to the lectern. He opened up a black binder and rubbed his black goatee as he moved a black mechanical pencil down a page of notes.

"Have you met Dr. Parsons?" Paul said.

"Just through email. He seems . . . dark."

"Yeah, the outfit's a little affected, and he's difficult to work with. But he does know his stuff, and you'll need him on your side if you want to survive here. I'll tell you more later on. For now, just one more little bit of affectation. His British accent? It's fake."

Dr. Parsons pulled off his black horn-rimmed glasses, inspected the lenses, and then put them carefully back on. Then he stood at the lectern with his hands behind his back, his bald head shining under the skylight. As the graduate students and faculty took their seats, the two Kantians continued their debate in hushed tones. Dr. Parsons cleared his throat and, spreading his arms wide, said in a semi-British accent, "It is my pleasure to welcome you all to Black Forest University. Over the next academic year, we shall embark on a most fabulous journey together, known as philosophy."

Dr. Parsons spoke on various topics: the strengths of the department (modern philosophy and existentialism), a list of recent faculty publications, teaching fellowships, assistantships, symposia, and First Fridays. When he fielded a question about First Fridays, Paul whispered, "I'd attend every First Friday, if I were you. That's where you build your future. It's not what you know, it's who you know."

When Dr. Parsons was finished, I walked to the podium to say hello.

"Why, Carl, it's so nice to finally meet you. Did you make it to Nebraska safely?" His accent seemed a little thicker and more British, up close.

"Yes, thank you, Doctor. Though I seem to have arrived at a bad time."

"Ah, yes, all of the hoopla in Slippery Rock."

"I'm not a sports fan, so it's easy to ignore."

"That makes two of us."

"Especially since I sold my TV on Craigslist before I began divinity school in Boston."

"I envy you. It's my belief that student performance in academics would improve if the football teams were cut out of the school budget. But let us save that discussion for another time."

We talked about my research interests within existentialism, mainly Nietzsche, Sartre, and Camus. When I mentioned a possible dissertation topic—Nietzsche's philosophy of religion—Dr. Parsons stroked his goatee, dyed black with a few gray hairs showing at the sides, bug-like eyes smiling behind the big black eyeglasses.

"Well, Carl, I'm thrilled that you've chosen Black Forest University to pursue your doctoral studies. I believe you'll make steady progress with few, if any, distractions. As they say, nothing ever happens in Sleepy Hollow."

8

Outside, Paul and I smoked under the honey locust tree. I pointed to the Great Commoner. "I didn't know Bryan was so foundational to the university."

Paul blew out smoke. "He was known as the Boy Orator of the Platte. There was more to Bryan than the Scopes trial, you know. He united the farmers and the poor, the women and the underdogs. If you were disadvantaged, Bryan was your man."

I looked at a nearby pond, black and mirror calm, and read the sign on the shoreline: "Chautauqua Pond."

"I didn't bother much with the school's history," I said. "I just applied to whichever schools I thought would accept me."

Paul scooped the cigarette butts from Bryan's hand. "Parsons would give you bonus points for not knowing much about Bryan."

As we smoked, Paul gave me the lowdown. Two years ago, Dr. Parsons had been awarded tenure and since then he'd been on a campaign to have the name of Bryan Hall changed. Doing so would reflect a more enlightened age, he said. Parsons had even met with BFU administrators and together they were looking for a donor who was an atheist.

My eyes rose to the Great Commoner, tall and proud in his long overcoat. "Does Dr. Parsons want the statue removed, too?"

"Who knows what he's got up the sleeves of that black turtleneck. The BFU campus is evolving." Paul noted that the administrators had developed a new strategic plan for the next decade, a plan that increasingly focused on science, technology, engineering, and math programs. STEM for short.

"While the STEM programs are growing, the humanities program is getting downsized. It's argued that the STEM degrees will get students better jobs, and yeah, maybe. How do you pay your electric bill by playing the flute or quoting Aristotle? Just look at the two parts of campus. One looks like the ruins of an ancient civilization, like Greece, while the other is out of the space age."

Paul and I entered the Black Forest that gave the campus its name—a three-mile stand of old forest where German immigrants had once wandered as they wrote poetry and had mystical experiences. We strolled under the dark canopy of oaks and pines as birds broke out in song and squirrels circled the big trunks, chasing each other.

Paul switched his backpack to his other shoulder.

"Don't let all of this get you down. Your goal is to be Parson's number one guy. He could pull some strings for you when you go on the job market, which is nonexistent as I'm sure you know."

"You said Parson's accent is fake? I thought he was from England."

"He got his doctorate at King's College, London, but he was born and raised in Ohio. Parsons likes to impress the incoming students, so he starts out the academic year with a thick British accent. By October, he's pure Dayton."

Two girls approached us, wearing pink sweatpants and gray tank tops, both on phones. Paul and I moved aside, allowing them to pass.

"What else should I know about Parsons?" I said.

"Agree with everything he says, even if you don't. That's something I learned early on. He can hold quite a grudge. So whether he's talking about socialism or global warming,

French expressionism or the problem of evil, just nod and say 'yes' a lot."

We crossed a bridge with a creek below it lined with mossy rocks. The sun winked through the treetops where a family of crows like defrocked priests eyed us from the great heights. This didn't sound encouraging. Still, getting on Parson's good side didn't mean I couldn't get a good education at the same time.

"What else?" I said.

"Parsons has a lot of disdain for religion, especially Christianity. He and Alvin Meyers are always slugging it out on Fox News."

"Alvin Meyers? Oh, God."

"Nobody in the department likes him, either. Ironically, they went to seminary together. Meyers remained a conservative evangelical, while Parsons came out an atheist. Parson's new book *How to Debate Christians and Win Every Time* was inspired by those debates with Meyers."

We passed through the south gates and back into the sunshine. Paul and I threw on our sunglasses. We moved down a serpentine path with hillocks of tallgrass on either side. Paul got out his phone and looked at it. I did the same.

"I need something else," I said.

"Talk openly and positively about Parson's published works. Attend his public lectures and debates. And hate on Bryan and Myers, too."

"Okay, that's not hard to do."

"Speaking of lectures," Paul said. "Parsons is speaking at a symposium next month. It's on suicide in twentieth-century philosophy. He's tieing in the death of Kenny Winslow, so it should be an interesting night."

Entering the quad, Paul and I strolled up to a lagoon, sea-green and speckled with pond scum. Three girls sat on the shoreline, sandals off, toes wiggling, and phones blazing on the sand. Two bronze mammoths waded in the water, their tusks big and terrible in the sky.

Paul tossed his keys up and caught them. "There's more I could say, but I have to pick up my kids at their grandparents'. Let's grab a beer sometime. Until then, stay focused. Don't get off track, which is easy to do. Over sixty percent of PhD students in philosophy drop out. And don't make enemies here, even though every graduate student in this program is already your enemy, especially with the budget cuts in the department, which means fewer fellowships and assistantships. They'll be even bigger enemies when you go on the job market. Be nice to everyone, including the departmental secretary—that's something I learned early on, too, be nice to the secretary. But Parsons is your guy. In a big way, your future is in his hands."

When Paul left, I fetched a copy of *The Mammoth*, the student newspaper, and returned to the lagoon. I kicked off my own shoes, my feet sinking into the sand, and sat atop a prehistoric stone above the green, scummy water.

A photo of Kenny Winslow graced the front page. His death had been judged a suicide—he'd thrown himself in front of a train. A symposium would be held in October at the University of Nebraska. There would be five speakers, one of them Dr. Parsons. After I punched the date into my phone, I watched the girls in tank tops and Daisy-Duke denims as gigantic gunmetal-blue clouds wafted over the campus, casting dark shadows in the quad.

*   *   *

At dusk, I soared down Old Farm Road to my cell. Black cows grazed in the stubble fields as the ditch weeds thrashed and hissed in the wind, while corn leaves slithered across the road. I was coming to see Nebraska would be a good place to think. Paul was right. Few distractions. I could write my first book here. My dissertation. As Dr. Parsons said, nothing ever happens in Sleepy Hollow.

Back in town, I saw Avery at the Pioneer. He was in full uniform, standing in the valet zone and playing with a yo-yo. I stopped my iPod and plucked out my earphones.

"How's school?" he said.

"So far, so good."

"Banged any hotties with bodies?"

"Best kind. Not yet."

"Fresh from the farms and straight into your arms. Speaking of which, your girlfriend just drove up in the bus."

I was watching the yo-yo, bobbing lazily up and down. "My girlfriend?"

"You know, Jenna? She just dropped off some college babes and their superhot moms. Go inside. The lobby is full of them." Avery caught the yo-yo. "What are you up to today? That's a sweet bike. I'm thinking of buying a Trek."

I wrapped the earphones around my iPod. "I'm looking for a job, preferably with lots of downtime so I can study."

Avery put away the yo-yo and picked a red maple leaf up by its stem. "You're in luck. Our doorman Lyle is leaving us. See those new motion-detecting doors? Lyle's been replaced by technology. He's decided to take an early retirement. He's moving to the Philippines to hand out Bibles." Avery studied the leaf, its edges brown and curling up. "It's a great gig, if you want it."

"Is there downtime?"

"Hell, yes. We're busy, like, three weeks a year—orientation, homecoming, and graduation. You'll also meet babes up the wazoo. Soccer moms. Business chicks. Call girls. You name it. They're all here, in the lobby, ready for the taking." He spun the leaf by the stem so that it looked like a fire wheel. "You'll even see Jenna. You interested?"

"I am."

"Step into my office."

9

The week passed. I'd gone to the student luncheon and applied for a job. I went to my graduate seminars on metaphysics, epistemology, and ethics—the three traditional branches of philosophy—and added to the collection of books on my windowsill. Now I was going to my first First Friday. There'd be a student paper reading, followed by drinks at the Sparkle Lounge, a bar in Sleepy Hollow's small business district—all two blocks of it. It was a chance to mingle with the very important people who'd help me to build my future in academia, brick by brick, the way the prairie pioneers had built sod houses.

During the student paper reading, I took notes and asked questions, mostly to impress Dr. Parsons. Afterward, I went out for a smoke while Paul spoke to Dr. Parsons about his dissertation defense.

Under the honey locust tree, the squirrels were at play in the grass, carpeted with tiny bright-orange leaves. I paced back and forth as Mr. Bryan's eyes followed mine.

"Your days as a dead man are numbered, too," I said. "Just thought I'd let you know."

Paul walked out of Bryan Hall and stood between the Greek columns. "Ready?"

"Let's go."

Inside the Sparkle Lounge, the huge speakers hovering above the dance floor thumped out "Hot Stuff" by Donna Summer. I walked through the semidarkness under the glittery silver globes and over to the pool tables. After I ordered a Jack and

Coke, Paul and I played a game of pool and discussed the paper we'd just heard, "On the Exploitation of Adjuncts in Higher Education."

Soon, Dr. Parsons advanced, beret on, goatee dyed black and neatly trimmed, martini in hand.

"Carl," he said. "When you have a free moment, may I have a word with you?"

While Dr. Parsons walked back to the elevated bar, Paul took the pool stick from my hand. "Your free moment is now."

When I slid into the bar stool next to my advisor, he was watching the TV and stirring the martini with a bright pink straw.

"Bradley and Vincent gave a thought-provoking paper today," he said.

I stared into my drink. Now was my chance. "They did make a good point, Dr. Parsons. The current academic labor system, which exploits its adjunct professors, can't possibly be compatible with Kantian ethics." I spoke eloquently of one of Kant's basic ethical principles—always treat human beings as ends, never as a means to an end. "But that's exactly what the universities are doing to their adjuncts—using them. Instead of paying adjuncts a living wage and offering them health benefits, the universities use the extra money to build huge, modern-looking buildings on campus, like the sports arenas, the student activity centers, the fancy dorms with high-speed Internet and, God help us, climbing walls for student recreation. Actually, they're using prospective students, too. When prospective students tour the campus, they say 'Wow, I want to go to school here. Look at all of this cool stuff.' They pay their tuition, then get less of an education because of the cool stuff that attracted them."

Dr. Parsons stirred his martini slowly. "Though I can sympathize with Kant's ethics, which, as you correctly note, places a great emphasis on respect for persons, I'm afraid things in higher education aren't going to change. Higher education is a business, and businesses never run according to Kantian ethics. Or, arguably, any ethics."

"Yeah, I guess you're right. But I liked the double standard that Bradley and Vincent pointed out. While the universities encourage their students to go out into the world and fight against social injustice, the universities' own labor system is totally unjust."

"It's quite ironic, though again I suspect the chancellor's office is immune to irony. But yes, it was a fabulous paper."

On the TV, a sportscaster listed off the college football rankings. The Cornhuskers were ranked number six in the nation. The Bison weren't ranked at all.

Dr. Parsons tilted his martini glass and stared into it. "The entire population of Nebraska will be in Lincoln and Slippery Rock tomorrow. It's quite a spectacle. I believe you said you aren't into football?"

"Nope. I feel like a black sheep."

"I share your sentiment."

"I read that when Memorial Stadium fills up, it's the third largest city in Nebraska."

"And when Slippery Rock's stadium fills up, it's the fourth. Here we have only football and religion, and I'm baffled to say which one is valued more." Dr. Parsons sipped from the glass, savoring the taste. "Carl, if I remember correctly, the president at your alma mater cut out the football team, did he not?"

"That's right. His logic was that it would improve academics and it worked. The students at the University of Boston are pretty smart."

"While eliminating football in this state would do wonders to improve academics, I suspect it might lead to a peasants' revolt. But let us save those topics for a more fitting time, shall we?"

For thirty minutes, we made small talk—about the department, my degrees in philosophy and theology, and our faith journeys, which were almost identical. The reason for our atheism? Good old-fashioned reading and studying.

Dr. Parsons stared at his empty glass. He turned it in half circles, his nails clipped short and perfectly manicured. His goatee was bathed in the neon-red light of the bar, while his ears perked up tall around the black beret.

"Carl, how would you feel about teaching a section of Introduction to Philosophy this fall? One of our graduate students has unexpectedly left the program, and we need somebody to cover his course. You could start on Monday. I've seen your transcripts, and they are quite impressive. Philosophy courses from Tom Schmidt and theology courses from John McMaster? You are most certainly qualified to handle our undergraduates."

Paul walked up behind Dr. Parsons, eyes on the TV, beer mug in hand.

"I do apologize for the short notice," Dr. Parsons said. "We have students leaving the program every year for nonacademic jobs, and this sudden vacancy means I would have to teach the class. Sadly, I don't have the time, what with my research load and all."

Paul looked at me. His eyes said, *Do it.*

Tilting my glass, I eyed the ice cubes glowing red at the bottom. "Sure."

"You mean you'll do it?"

I looked up. "I mean I'd love to."

"Oh, marvelous. You've just saved me weeks of headaches. Months. My secretary Betty will have you fill out the requisite paperwork. You can stop by on Monday before class."

10

It was official. I was a teaching assistant at Black Forest University—my first paying academic job. They would be giving me money to share the products of my brain. I'd hardly slept the night before, so excited was I about my lecture on Socrates, the father of Greek philosophy.

On Monday, I arrived on campus, and Mr. Bryan was there to greet me. I felt good and I looked good, ready for my first college lecture—ready to sting my undergraduates out of their dogmatic religious slumbers.

Standing under the honey locust, almost stripped bare, I looked at myself in my phone's screen. *You're the man, Sorensen. Authority. That's what you carry. You'll get attention, especially from the ladies.*

I'd dressed in a light-blue oxford shirt, brown slacks, an orange tie with white stripes, and black Converse shoes. I looked at Mr. Bryan, who smiled and offered me a handful of tiny golden leaves as though a small fire were burning in his hand.

"Wait, let me guess," I said to the Great Commoner. "You think it was God who got me the teaching gig, right? Your camel-loving, commandment-obsessed, pain-inflicting, child-killing, homophobic God decided to do me a favor. And now He expects gratitude. Well, that's not how it works."

I walked into Bryan Hall. Before I launched into the Western philosophical tradition, I had to lay the groundwork with my students, which meant Socrates. Besides, Socrates made for a good story, and when I'd called Paul for advice over the weekend, he said I should get them on the first day and I'd have them forever.

Standing at the lectern, I waited until the lecture hall was quiet.

"How many of you can read a book from cover to cover?" I said.

A boy in the back row, ball cap on, waved his hand like a windshield wiper.

I pointed at him. "Yes?"

"Who are you?"

"In a moment. So who reads books from cover to cover?"

No answer.

"That's what I thought. And why don't you read books from cover to cover anymore, if you even read at all?" I gazed out at the sea of blank faces. "Exactly. Because you're too distracted. You're on your cell phones or fooling around on Facebook."

I paced the length of the whiteboard, grabbed two dry-erase markers, and snapped them together, end-to-end.

"You're too busy messaging your friends or reading their status updates on what they just had for lunch. How can you be expected to read books, especially in the humanities, when your minds are wandering all over the Internet for hours a day? Why should you?"

I stopped in the middle of the whiteboard. Then, turning slowly and dramatically, I faced the class, arms at my sides.

"I'll tell you why. Because great ideas, the ideas that'll really change your lives, can't be compressed to 140 characters. You can't tuck them in between political rants and the latest viral video. They're built, chapter by chapter, piece by piece, and you can't understand them unless you do so from the ground up."

I scanned the room. The baseball players in the back row were slouched in their seats, faces red and guilty-looking, while the girls in the front row twirled their hair and stared at me. I had them. Now to bring it home.

"If you don't read books," I said softly, "you'll never expose yourself to new ideas. Think back to the world you lived in when you were six or eight years old, when you believed whatever your parents and friends happened to believe. If you don't read books, that's the world you'll live in for the rest of your life. You'll never be aware of the larger, more challenging, more rewarding world that'll open around you. You'll remain—and forgive the use of the technical term—stupid."

There was absolute silence in the class now. The hair twirlers had stopped, and the jocks were making eye contact with me.

"Do you think I'm lying?" I said. "Do you think the great minds of the ancient, medieval, and the modern worlds were staring at their phones every twenty seconds or updating their relationship status every hour? They could concentrate, they had attention spans, they could think. They could see the world in new ways and pass that experience on to others." I pointed to the student in the back. "So to get back to your question, who am I? I'm the one who's going to use the fusty old discipline of philosophy to open your eyes to the world around you. I'm going to stop you from being stupid and start you thinking. I'm your teacher." I stepped back behind the lectern and, in my friendliest voice, said, "So, shall we begin?"

Slowly, the phones on my students' desks began to disappear, while laptops, open and on at the beginning of class, were shut off and put away. I felt a bit light-headed and could feel a drop of cold sweat moving down my spine. But I was elated. I could do this.

"Not that digital culture doesn't have its pluses," I said, reaching for my first page of notes. "You can access works on your phone that you used to have to travel to a major university library to find. But use it responsibly. You won't have this opportunity again to study philosophy this in-depth. Now get her done."

For the next forty minutes, nobody moved. The bathrooms didn't exist, technology was a thing of the past, and there was no talking or flirting in class. Only one person mattered, and that was Socrates, the gadfly who stung the Athenians out of their ignorance and forced them to think about truth, beauty, and goodness. The man who taught us about the "other world," a world beyond our own, a spiritual world, one to which he'd go after the Athenians put him to death for being a rabble-rouser.

Midway through my lecture, I had an inspiration. I could use these students to help me write my dissertation. I'd toss out my ideas, and they'd give me feedback. I would be focus testing my thesis with laypersons, making sure that what I said was accessible and relevant rather than just technical academic word flogging. It would keep my thesis real.

After a small break, I tore through the second half of my lecture, amazed at how fast the class had gone by.

I swept up my notes. "Okay, next time we'll meet one of Socrates' students, Plato, who carried on his teachings. We'll see how Plato further developed his teacher's ideas and how, in my opinion—and in the opinion of other great philosophers, like Nietzsche—Plato got us into trouble with his belief in 'the other world'. And for more on that story, do the readings and stay away from *American Idol* and *Desperate Housewives*. See you Wednesday."

On the ride home, I got a text from Avery. He said to stop by the hotel. When I walked in, Michael Simmons, the front-desk manager, greeted me. He wore a white pinstripe suit and a glittery blue tie with a handlebar moustache slick on his upper lip. Michael flashed a row of bleached white teeth and invited me into the back office.

After the interview, we stood up and shook hands.

"I'm thrilled that you'll be joining our team, Carl. You're about to embark on a most wonderful journey at the Pioneer, Lincoln's oldest hotel. Now." He straightened his tie knot and brushed nonexistent lint off his sleeve. "Let's go grab your pioneer outfits. Oh, and here's a bag of goodies for you."

We left his office and went to the bell closet. Opening the door, Michael took a step back and rested a hand on his hipbone. "Avery, what have I told you about eating in the bell closet?"

I glanced past him, and Avery was on the floor, leaning against one wall, a sandwich in his hand, a Coke on the floor next to him.

Michael stepped over Avery's legs, muscled a covered wagon aside, and stepped up to a wardrobe. "So this is our uniform rack, m'kay? Find two or three you like. Oh, and don't forget your hat and holster."

As Michael walked out, he kicked the bottom of Avery's shoe. Avery yawned and turned a page of *The Touchdown*. "Mister, I need you on the lobby floor, pronto."

When Michael left, Avery chugged his Coke, his neck muscles working furiously, and then folded *The Touchdown* and tossed it aside as I went to the uniform rack.

"So you got the job, huh? Congratulations. How's life at the Big Fuck U?" I looked over my shoulder and Avery snickered. "That's what everybody calls it."

I lifted a uniform off the rack and held it to my chest. It was pure Roy Rogers—the west as imagined by early television. "Interesting. The Big FU."

"You'll love Nebraska. Most people think it's fly over country. It's not. We've got a lot of beauty here. You just have to look for it. And despite the cheesiness, the hotel rocks. The money, the babes, and free meals—not everybody gets a job like this." Avery rose up and swept the bread crumbs off his pants. He looked at himself in a mirror on the wall, inspecting his crew cut. "By the way, Jenna drove up earlier. She even asked about you. She's worth a poke or two, but she's not a callback."

I held a smaller uniform to my chest, then looked up. "A callback?"

"Yeah. After you bang her, you don't call her back." He shoved a batch of Colt .45-shaped flyers to give out to tourists into his holster.

"Right." I hung up the uniform. "A callback."

"You'll see her on Friday, too. Get ready. Bison fever and Huskermania are about to begin."

11

I tried not to drink on Mondays, but after my lecture on Socrates, and after suffering through a three-hour seminar on G. E. Moore with twelve ill-shaven, foul-smelling, and opinionated graduate students—plus my interview at the hotel—I needed a Jack and Coke, maybe two.

When I walked into the Blue Note, Tony waddled up to the bar with a big jolly smile. "Howya doing, High Hopes? Screwdriver?"

"Extra large, if you've got it."

I settled in at the elevated bar and Tony set down a napkin followed by the drink.

"How's school?" he said.

"Already got me gainfully employed. I'm a teaching assistant now. I'm also a doorman at the Pioneer. Not sure which is going to earn me more."

"Ah, the hotel. You gonna get a big dose of football on Saturdays. Red and maroon jerseys as far as you can see. You'd think the Platte River had turned to blood and overflowed on the plains." Tony dipped two mugs into the sink below the bar while I stirred my drink and took out the straw. "Drunken football fans, tips should be good, especially if the Huskers win. The Husker games are always sold out. Been that way for forty years, over three hundred games straight. I wish I could say the same thing for the Bison. They'll be lucky to make it to a bowl game." He raised the mugs and set them on a tray and then wiped off his hands with a dish towel. "Okay, so I gotta ask youse a question about philosophy."

Great. So much for being off the clock. "Sure, go ahead."

"Have you discovered the truth yet?"

I stifled a laugh and ended up coughing into my drink.

"That's what you're supposed to do, right? Find the truth?"

I touched my lips with a napkin. "Back in the day. Now it's more about living without it."

"You guys don't believe in the truth no more?"

"It kind of depends on what you mean by 'the truth.'"

"Ah, I knew you were gonna say that."

I poked at the ice cubes with a thin red straw.

"Here's the deal," I said. "Everybody has beliefs they think are true. I have mine. You have yours. The Jews, Christians, and Muslims have theirs. And so on. Even the atheists do. But as for which one of those belief systems is the Truth, well, we're still trying to figure that out." I stared into my glass. "Some philosophers have given up on the search for the Truth as a lost cause and are trying to figure out how to live with the truth—small 't'—that we've got. And to be fair, we've been searching for the Truth—capital 'T'—for twenty-five hundred years and haven't made much progress."

Two men walked into the bar. They sat down in a booth with a fan twirling above it and took off their denim jackets.

"Why's it so hard to find the truth with a capital 'T'?" Tony said.

I set the glass down. "Too many perspectives to choose from, I guess. Plus, every one of those perspectives can be defended and made to sound convincing. Which perspective do you go with?"

Tony pushed off the counter, the apron cradling his belly as it sagged below his waistline, leaving the edges of his belt visible.

"Guy comes into the bar. Says there's no such thing as truth. But if that's true, then there's at least one truth, which is that statement, 'There's no such thing as truth.'"

"Very ironic."

"Boy, ain't it?"

I sort of wanted the conversation to end. The class I taught was exhilarating, but I crashed afterwards. And G. E. Moore may be the single most boring genius to ever write in the English language. My brain was fried. But since I'd soon be a regular at Tony's bar, I had to be polite.

"There are facts that we can know," I said. "Alaska is the largest state in the Union. The sun is the nearest star to the earth. There are even small 't' truths that are pretty widely agreed on—'do unto others,' say. But as far as which religion is true or whether human beings have free will or not, those are things I don't think we can ever be certain about. Those debates go on and on ad nauseam."

Tony looked around for the waitress, then grabbed some menus and wiped them off with a towel. "So what happens if we can't find the truth with a capital 'T'?"

"We focus on the problems of the earth. We do what we can."

"Makes sense. God knows we got enough down here."

"That we do."

Tony paid the patrons a visit, menus in hand, while I polished off my drink and set the glass down. "That we do."

12

I realized the next day that my talk with Tony about capital-"T" Truth wasn't a waste of time. I'd be talking about Plato in my next class, and he was the one who invented capital-"T" Truth, along with capital-"B" Beauty and capital-"G" Goodness. I'd be able to tell the class that, for twenty-five centuries, philosophers and theologians had been talking about the Truth, but it was doubtful that anybody had found it or could ever find it. Humans were just too limited by their historical situations. I'd help them along in abandoning the 'other world' so that they'd focus on this world, on being faithful to the earth, just as Nietzsche had taught through his fictional character, Zarathustra.

So first thing Tuesday, I sent a group email to the class, updating the reading list.

On Wednesday, I walked into the lecture hall and was proud of what I saw: *The Death of God and the Meaning of Life* by Julian Young on my students' desks, with shreds of binder paper between the pages, growing out like buffalo grass. Their cell phones and laptops were out of sight. Everybody was seated. Nobody moved.

"Wow." I drummed my fingers on the lectern's side. "Looks like you're ready. So let's talk philosophy."

The hour flew by. I wrapped up Socrates and then launched into Plato, a true-world philosopher, according to Young. Plato believed our souls once lived in a perfect, spiritual world, a "true world," but had fallen out and had landed on earth. Now the souls were trapped in physical bodies. The goal of life? To return to the "true world," where our souls could once again gaze upon the eternal forms—Truth itself, Beauty itself, and Goodness itself.

"Does all of this true-world talk sound familiar? Most people in Nebraska believe some version of it."

Hands all over went up. "It sounds like Christianity."

"Islam, too."

"My neighbor is a Wiccan, and he believes we go to another world when we die—the Summerland. It's always sunny and seventy-five degrees there. Just like a Minnesota summer."

"I'm sure that's just coincidence," I said. "But ever since the Enlightenment, the 'true world' has been called into question. We'll look at these critiques down the road. But for now, know that many contemporary philosophers believe we're wasting our time on this 'true world' stuff, on trying to get out of time and into eternity. We don't know a damn thing about this 'other world'; it might not even exist. Instead, we should try to build a better future on earth for our kids and our grandkids. The American pragmatists, like James and Dewey and Rorty, would be sympathetic to this view. So would Nietzsche. But, as I say, more on them later."

After class, I fielded a few questions at the lectern, then a few more in the hallway. Dr. Parsons had stopped by the Coke machine and was talking with a group of administrators. He noticed the animated students around me, nodded, and smiled.

Back in town, the giant elms on the street corners of downtown were shedding their bright-yellow leaves, which were chasing the cars as they sped down O Street. At the hotel, I walked into the bell closet, which smelled of beef and cabbage from Avery wolfing down a runza sandwich. I stood behind a covered wagon and changed into my pioneer outfit. Avery brushed the bread crumbs off his pants and tossed the wrapper to the wastebasket but missed.

"Come see the girl who's about to walk by the hotel," he said. "Not Jenna, but wait until you see her rack. You'll have a religious experience."

Somebody knocked on the door. It was Michael.

"Avery, what are you doing?" Then, to me, he said, "Oh, hello, Carl. How are you today?"

"Well, thanks."

"Are you excited about your first taste of Nebraska football?"

"You bet."

"Good. I'm glad. It'll be a wonderful experience for you."

When Michael left, I strapped on my holster, shoving in a batch of Colt .45 flyers, and walked into the lobby with Avery.

Outside, it really was rush hour. The three lanes were full of traffic as Avery sucked on a mint and played with his yo-yo.

"Here she comes," he said. "See? With the yellow sunglasses?"

A blonde girl with big mirrored sunglasses strutted down the sidewalk with strips of hair the color of blueberries.

"She walks by every day at four o'clock," Avery whispered. "She works at the flower shop. Sometimes I stop in and pretend to buy shit."

As the girl grew nearer, the statehouse appeared in those big silver lenses. Her full chest heaved up and down in a loose white T-shirt as her flip-flops slapped the bottoms of her feet.

"Wow," I said. "That was . . . impressive."

The girl stopped at the street corner and looked at her phone. A sparkly blue Oldsmobile with huge tires and chrome rims cruised by. The number 32 was painted on the door, and the black windows boomed and rattled.

Avery caught the yo-yo. "The Bison are going to get killed this year. They'll be lucky to pull a winning season. I imagine you're not a sports guy. You just read books, huh?"

"Pretty much."

"Do you even know which conference the Huskers are in?"

"There are conferences?"

Avery pocketed the yo-yo. "I'd suggest you educate yourself about college football. You'll build camaraderie with the guests, which means you'll make more in tips, which means you'll be a happy camper. So allow me to be your professor, Mr. Future Professor."

We began to load up a covered wagon with luggage a cabbie had piled at the curb. A white bus drove by, tooting its horn.

"There she goes," Avery said.

I looked up. Jenna. The bus squealed around the corner and sped away as Avery took the briefcase from my hand.

"She'll be back," he said. "Do you have any questions about college football?"

"So in addition to knowing about the Huskers," I said, listening to the bus speeding away, "should I learn about the Bison, too?"

"It wouldn't hurt, but they're not serious contenders this year, especially with Kenny gone."

"Do they have any good players left?"

"Kenny was it. A one-man show."

A red Ford truck pulled up to the curb. A man in a tan cowboy hat got out. Avery handed him a ticket stub and took the keys.

"So this Kenny Winslow, he was that good?" I said.

"Dude, he was amazing. He broke every record ever set by a college running back." Avery jumped up on the truck's running board. "Kenny's final year was legendary. The Bison would blow out teams seventy to seven. Sometimes Kenny did it single-handedly."

A businessman and a blonde lady in a low-cut red dress and large sunglasses walked out of the hotel, arm in arm. I kept my eyes on the lady in red. "So last year the Bison won their conference and then went to the big game, which is the . . . Orange Bowl?"

"It was the biggest bowl game the Bison ever went to. The Hurricanes got their asses handed to them, too. ESPN had trouble picking the 'Play of the Game' since Kenny gave them about ten plays to choose from."

Avery got in the truck. I walked up to the passenger window, which was halfway down.

I said, "So after breaking all of those records, Kenny killed himself? How'd that work?"

Avery put the key in the ignition. "Why do you think there's so much press interest? Nobody can figure that out. If you watch the footage from last year's games, Kenny could outrun a train. And if you listen to what the forensics experts say, Kenny wasn't trying to avoid the train. He was running toward it."

13

Then I saw her. It was around ten o'clock, just after most of the guests had checked in, their bags carried up to their rooms and their cars parked in the garage for the night. A white bus pulled up to the curb. It seemed to come out of nowhere. I walked to the passenger window, whistling a Wagner symphony with my hands behind my back. Sitting inside the bus was a girl. She had both hands on the wheel. She was staring at me, her eyes big and smoldering, possessing the same black, smokeless fire I'd seen in them before.

"How's philosophy going?" Jenna said.

I stole a glance at her faded blue jeans and black halter top. One boob was slightly larger than the other.

Jenna cleared her throat. "Are you just going to stand there, Carl?"

"Actually," I said, "I plan on getting your number, so I can take you out for coffee."

"Oh, is that what you're going to do?" Jenna picked up a rubber band off the passenger seat and began to stretch it.

"And when I do," I said, "you can tell me about that book you got on mind reading. Did you get the book yet?"

Jenna pulled the rubber band into a triangle. "Since when do you end an English sentence with a preposition, Mr. PhD? And what makes you think we can read minds? We can't, silly."

"By the way, who are we? You always say that. *We.*"

Jenna looked at me through the pink triangle. She winked.

"That's for you to find out," she said. "But just so you mortals know, we can't read minds, though we can certainly read body language and draw conclusions. And we can see into your eyes, which are a gateway to the soul or, as you philosophers call it these days, the neural ganglia." Jenna smirked. She pulled the rubber band wider, so that the triangle lost its pinkness.

"Well, for your information," I said, "not all philosophers are materialists. Granted, I'm one. So was Hobbes. But others weren't, like Plato and St. Augustine. They were dualists, believing we had a body and a soul."

"I'm sorry to hear that."

"Sorry to hear what?"

"That those blockheads believed in a soul." Jenna's eyes, half-hooded, seemed to possess a vision of something only she could see.

I looked down the street. "You're obviously not a dualist."

"Nope."

"So, you're a materialist."

"Oh, no. It's far more complicated than that."

I waited a moment, then poked my head inside the bus.

"And what do you believe in, Ms. McMaster?"

Jenna shrugged. "That's easy. Nothing."

I climbed into the passenger seat. "You're cryptic. But I like that."

I studied Jenna's skin, ghoulish-white and baby smooth, her lips parting as her face glowed from my words, my praise.

"Oh, Carl, that's so sweet."

"I've lived on both coasts, but I've never encountered a girl like you. Your phone number, please."

"Hmm, I'm afraid my schedule is full."

"I'll wait." I placed a Colt .45 flyer on her thigh.

"Oh, look." She pointed at the gun's cylinder. "Look at those numbers. One hundred eleven. Hmm, I wonder what that could mean?"

A yellow light flooded the inside the bus. In the side mirror, a Honda Accord with a Nero's pizza flag pulled up in the loading zone.

"Hold on," I said.

A minute later, I was walking back to the bus, when an old bald man wearing an Army jacket and with a bedroll strapped to his back raised his hand feebly.

"Excuse me," he said.

"Can I help you?"

"Yes." He held up one hand while he caught his breath. "I was wondering if you could take me to the homeless shelter."

"Now?"

He looked at his hand and then rested it atop a knotted cane.

"How about I call you a taxi?" I said.

"Oh, I couldn't afford—"

"That's okay, I got it." Greatest good for the greatest number, a small-"t" truth. "Hold on, sir, I'll be with you in a second."

I got inside the bus. It was colder now, and Jenna looked out of her window as the old man shuffled by, pausing to glance at us, his blue, mystical eyes deep set in a nest of wrinkles.

"Okay," I said, turning to Jenna. "Where were we?"

"You wanted something?"

"Oh, right." I gave her a pen.

"Do you want my number, Carl?"

"Didn't I say that?"

"Not directly. You have to say yes."

"Come on, stop playing games."

"You have to say yes, first."

In my side mirror, the old man waited by the sliding doors, hands atop his cane, looking down.

"Jesus. Fine. Whatever." Then—"Yes."

"Okay," Jenna said. "We have to be sure." She wrote it down and handed the pistol back, and I got out of the bus, shoving the Colt .45 into my holster.

"And Carl?" Jenna said. "Whatever you do, don't do anything creepy, okay?" When I looked confused, she fired the rubber band at me. It hit me squarely between the eyes. She burst into laughter and drove away.

I bent down, picked up the rubber band, and tucked it in my pocket. "And she calls me creepy."

By the hotel doors, the old man was still standing in the same spot and seemed to have fallen asleep. I went in to call him a taxi, and when I came back out, he was gone.

14

The days passed like a speeding train. On Saturday, I walked out of the Pioneer at two o'clock, the Husker game about to begin. I stuck my hands into my hip pockets, stuffed with bills, mostly Lincolns. Downtown was empty. Not a car or a soul could be seen on the streets. You'd have thought the rapture had happened. Over at Memorial Stadium, the game announcer's voice, deep and ceremonious, boomed over the PA. A sinister bell clanged, and a song by AC/DC began to play. "Hell's Bells." The fans cheered.

The game was underway, so I could make my escape and study at the bell desk.

On Monday, I arrived on campus as though I were dynamite. I destroyed Platonic metaphysics in class and launched into Aristotle, the philosopher who grounded us in this world. Then I rocked my graduate seminar, putting my intellectual prowess on display, while scolding a graduate student with glee for his use of obscure language.

"Simplicity is best," I told him. "If you can't make your bartender understand it, then maybe you don't understand it either." Graduate students liked to sound smart, I reminded them, but if they wanted to be good teachers and wanted their students to appreciate the humanities, they had to speak in plain English. Otherwise, they'd isolate the masses from philosophy, like a lot of academic philosophers had done. Think Heidegger. Think Derrida. Or many philosophers in the academy today.

I was beginning to feel I could make a difference, make philosophy accessible by speaking in an idiom that everybody could grasp. Maybe I'd have an advice column in various national newspapers, "Zarathustra Says." There I'd take on the persona of Zarathustra, Nietzsche's fictional prophet, offering Americans advice on how to live godlessly. And my books, both popular and scholarly? They'd be written for a general audience, too. I'd follow in the footsteps of Bryan Magee and Father Frederick Copleston—masters of the English language who helped to bring philosophy to the masses. Like them, I'd introduce philosophy to nonspecialists, helping them to create lives worthy of living—works of art—and thus making sure the humanities would never die.

Arriving at my cell, I closed the door and leaned my back against it. The room was quiet. A train could faintly be heard through the walls as the sun's rays slanted in through the window, lighting up the floorboards in a blazing square of sunlight. My eyes burned in their sockets and my head began to ache, and when I looked away, that's when I saw it: Jenna's rubber band looped around the doorknob.

I smiled. I planned to shoot her with it on our date. It was pink and dirty with small cracks, as if she'd stretched it a thousand times, shot it a hundred times, striking her victims between the eyes. Now it was in my possession. Its nearness gave me comfort, eased my worries about school. I'd also taped the Colt .45 to my door. On the cylinder, Jenna had scratched out the number 111 and had written her phone number beneath it. The digits were scribbled in big, bubbly letters as though written by a third grader.

Next morning, I called her. I was walking down the main line track, sipping a Starbucks coffee—it had finally opened— when I stepped into the shade of a baby-blue grain elevator, the one with the sinister eyes on the side. Above town, the midwestern clouds hung dark and heavy, like big buffalo skulls in the sky, and a black cat lay in the shade of the elevator next to a blue puddle and stared at me with its green, mystical eyes. It yawned and licked its front paw, cleaning its claws.

Jenna picked up on the first ring. "Hi."

"You knew it was me?"

"Yes, through that transcendental practice of caller ID." She seemed to move into a quiet room. "You're up early. I, on the other hand, am getting ready for bed."

"Are you an insomniac?"

"Of sorts."

"I'm sure it ties into your interesting life. Isn't that right, Ms. I'm-So-Full-of-Secrets?"

"Absolutely."

A flock of purple pigeons flapped loudly off the grain elevator, heading north to the Haymarket, their shadows soaring down the dirt road.

"What are your plans for Thursday?" I said.

"Hmm, let me see. Um, I happen to have a gap in my schedule."

"Good. Because I thought we'd stroll through the University of Nebraska. I've heard it's nice up there, especially in the fall. They've got botanical gardens and dinosaur fossils and other cool shit. Maybe we can grab coffee, too."

"Did you say gardens? Oh, Carl, I love gardens."

The black cat rubbed its face against my leg. I remembered reading they did that to mark territory. "You do?"

"Oh, yes. Some of the best things in history have happened in gardens. It's the most exciting thing you've said so far. I like where this is going, Mr. Philosopher King."

"So you've read Plato?"

"Have I?"

"Well, you apparently know his ideal society would be ruled by kings who were also philosophers."

"Do I have to read a book to know something? There are different ways to know things, silly."

The pigeons landed on the eaves of an old redbrick building with its windows boarded up. The cat looked up at me and purred.

"Fair enough," I said. "What are you doing today?"

"Making plans."

"Oh, tell me one. No, wait—I like a little suspense in life. So tell me when we meet on Thursday, say in front of the university library. It's called the Garden, oddly enough. How's eight o'clock sound?"

"Divine. Or something. See you then."

During my seminar on ethics, I realized there was a problem: I'd just made a date with Jenna which fell on the same night as the philosophy symposium, the one on suicide, which Paul had told me about. But during the break, when I was out having a smoke with Mr. Bryan, I came up with a solution. Clapping my hands together, I slapped Mr. Bryan five. Bingo. Just show up, then leave before the symposium started. Say hello to Dr. Parsons, kiss his ass a bit, and take a seat. Then, bail. Besides, the ethics of suicide? I knew this topic inside and out.

After my seminar, I went to the library. I prepped a lecture on the Epicureans, the hedonists of the ancient world, for Wednesday—the students would love it. I thought of contrasting them with Hugh Hefner and wondered if that stack of old magazines I'd seen in the bookstore included any

Playboys. Of course, Epicurus focused on the mental pleasures, Hefner the physical.

And they did love the lecture. I answered questions for a half hour, then rode my Trek back to town and stopped at the Blue Note, where I ordered a screwdriver and shot the breeze with Tony, who asked more questions about the truth. It was nice. There wasn't any one God's-eye view of the world, though it was a nostalgic thought.

At twilight, I walked my bike down the main line track. I had a terrific buzz going on, and I stopped to watch a row of flat cars clacking slowly down the tracks. Across the Burlington yard, a pile of clouds pulled a cargo of rain, and below the evening stars came the almost-noiseless crashes of heavy metal objects, thrown by the red cranes from one pyramid of junk to the other.

15

Jenna was standing at the gates of the Garden. I saw her from a distance as I strolled under the oaks, past the soaring black trunks, hands in my blazer pockets, phone in one hand, and Jenna's rubber band in the other. A mighty rush of wind moved through the treetops, as the leaves spun to their graves on the grass. Buttoning up my blazer, I felt the chill begin to burn in my bones.

When I arrived at the Garden, Jenna was gone. Only the shadows of oak branches were furling and unfurling on the sidewalk. I turned my back on the dark wind, thick with the moisture of a thunderstorm, and got out my phone.

"Did you think I wouldn't be here?" she said from behind me.

I put my phone away. "Where'd you go? I saw you just a second ago. Did you just magically appear or something?"

"I'm fine, thank you. How are you, Carl?"

"Better now."

Jenna was wearing a brown leather bomber jacket and blue jeans that flared at the bottoms. Atop her head, tucked into the frizzy hair, was a pair of sunglasses, big and white, like the goggles a fighter pilot would wear. A red purse was looped around her shoulder.

"You look nice tonight," I said.

"Why, thank you." She held a honey locust seedpod and tapped it steadily on her finger, so that the seeds inside began to rattle.

"Shall we?" I said.

"We shall."

*   *   *

We walked down University Avenue, our bodies close, shoulders touching, my satchel bumping against my hip. The crickets sang darkly on the grass as we passed by Harleys and Hondas like steel horses under the half-naked trees.

"Oh, look," Jenna said. "There must be a big event tonight."

"There is. It's a symposium on mental health, ethics, and suicide."

"Shouldn't you be going, Mr. Philosopher?"

"I planned on it, but my plans changed." I nudged Jenna's shoulder and she looked up with big, lovely eyes.

"You skipped the event for me? Oh, Carl, that's so sweet of you."

Reaching the quad, we stopped and took in the view. There, under the lamp posts, scribbled on the blocks of concrete, were messages to Kenny Winslow, the fallen star. They were written in a rainbow of colors—Husker red, corn yellow, pumpkin orange, and John Deere green.

"Oh, look," Jenna said. "It's so pretty. What's it about?" She began to leap from message to message, like a frog. Then she lost her balance. "Look, I'm falling. Carl, help."

I lit a cigarette. "Be careful."

All across the quad, the students had written notes to Kenny Winslow. There were Bible verses and snippets of Arabic. There were passages from Whitman and Japanese haiku. And atop the student union steps, which rose like the steps of a temple, was a small portrait of Kenny Winslow framed in gold. Three candles pushed into tall red bottles burned on the step below it, while bouquets of roses lay atop the step below the candles.

A cold, wet breeze swept in from the plains. Jenna spun in circles, arms extended like a figure skater. Then she bent down, tucking the blonde ropes of her hair behind an ear, and traced a finger along the concrete but didn't touch it.

"Kenny Winslow, of course," she said. "Is this what the conference is about?"

I tapped my cigarette. "It is."

"Hmm, they must be talking about what happened, then."

I blew out smoke. "More about what it means, I think."

On the second floor of the union, a girl in a chair wrote on a notepad, while a boy in a baseball cap stared at his phone.

"Ready?" I said.

"If you are."

Jenna, still squatting, began to hum a song. It was the one I'd heard all summer but had never Googled. Thunder began to crash and roll like rifle shots as Jenna looked over the messages, pointing at them, even laughing at them. Then she sprang up as though she'd been branded.

"Jenna?"

Without a word, she clopped away toward the union steps. On the pavement where she'd been standing was a Bible verse chalked in emerald green.

Now she stood atop the union's steps, tall and proud as a god, facing the quad. She shook her frizzy hair, now a darker blonde, from her eyes and closed them.

"What are you doing?" I said.

In a voice that sounded strangely huskier than her usual voice, Jenna said, "Making it rain."

On the second floor of the union, a girl in a red blazer was staring out of the window, hand cupped to the windowpane.

Behind me, the bushes and treetops hissed as a black cat ran across the quad.

"You're not really doing this," I said.

"Watch me."

Then a raindrop went splat on my shoe. Then another. Then a third struck my shoulder and shattered into my neck. I hiked up the steps, past the portrait of Kenny Winslow and the red candles around it, each one blown out. One of them toppled over and clanked down the steps.

Then the rains came. The thunder rolled across the gray sky like a great ripping of gunfire, until the torrents of late summer swept across the quad in heavy, silver sheets.

For five minutes, the white, mystical spray moved like spirits across the quad. Jenna's eyes were shut, arms at her sides, while her nostrils flared in and out. The mane of frizzy hair was black now, and her nose was different too, though I couldn't say how.

When the storm ended, the portrait of Kenny Winslow had been blown into the quad, lying facedown in a puddle, and the messages to him were nothing more than a swirl of colorful chaos. Jenna surveyed all that she had done. She sighed.

"There." She clasped her hands together and rested them against her cheek and her shoulders went up. "All better."

Lifting my shoe, I saw a dry patch of cement. I laughed.

"Why are you laughing, Carl?"

"Do you know what you're going to do?"

"No, I don't," Jenna said. "But I can guess."

I looked at the water-beaded goggles atop her head. "You're going to give me a straight answer for once. None of this dodging the bullet stuff. Now what happened?"

Jenna scraped the corner of her lips with a fingernail. Then she flung back her mane of hair, which was slowly changing from black to brown to dark blonde as the long ropes spread out widely over her chest. Her nose looked normal now.

"Answer me," I said.

She began to tuck the white scarf deeper into the bomber jacket. "Carl, do you really think I can make it rain? We live in Nebraska, you know. We have a saying—"

"Yeah, I know. If you don't like the weather, wait twenty minutes."

"Well, it's true." She held out her hands, one underneath the other. "Can I have a cigarette?"

"They're in my blazer pocket."

She fished out the box of Salems. "Open."

I did, and eased one into my mouth, then hers. She lit hers, then mine. Taking a long, hard pull, I stared at the spot where Kenny's name used to be, now a lake of red, meaningless letters.

"Here's your lighter," Jenna said. She put it into my hand and closed my fingers over it.

"Thanks."

Jenna rose up on tiptoes and with a skeletal hand atop my shoulder whispered, "You're welcome."

16

There were few words between us. We walked the campus in the breeze, smoking our cigarettes as big drops of water fell from the black, spooky trees. The path was matted with oak and maple leaves, red and yellow and sparkly in the dark, and the stars shone hard and fiercely above Memorial Stadium.

"Maybe you're right," I said. "Maybe it was a coincidence. This is Nebraska. The weather changes every twenty minutes."

"You think?"

"What's the other choice, that you have supernatural powers? We don't live in the middle ages, when a cunning man could bring storms down on his enemies by dealing with the devil. Gods and devils, witchcraft and spells—it's so medieval. It's, like, so yesterday."

Jenna blew out smoke and held out her hand; I took the butt and dropped it into an ashtray full of dark, star-lit water.

"So yeah," I said. "I'm going with coincidence. And back to when you picked me up in the bus, your ability to guess about my life? Well, there's a natural explanation for that, too." I touched the small of her back and she looked up at me with her eyebrows furrowed. "I have to say, you were really something in the bus when you picked me up that day."

"Was I? I don't really remember."

"You don't? You guessed where I went to school, my major, and so on."

"I did?"

"Come on, you don't remember? You were pretty amazing."

"Oh, wait." She stuck out her arm and I stopped in front of it. "Oh. Oh!"

"Do you remember now?"

"Yeah. I was pretty good, wasn't I?" She flashed a row of perfect white teeth and then skipped ahead on the path, kicking her legs up high and twirling in circles with her arms out wide again. I hung back with my hands in my pockets, calm and cool, watching those perfectly sculpted legs in those blue jeans. She did look stunning. All the colleges I'd been to, the beaches I'd surfed on, the bars I'd crashed, I'd never seen anything like her. She was Plato's form of Beauty Itself. Or close to it.

Jenna stopped and shook her wrists as though she held pompoms.

"What," I said, "are you doing?"

She picked up a maple leaf and held it upside down by the stem. A big drop of water gathered at the tip, shining brilliantly. Then she tossed it aside and picked up a second, then a third, letting the water drop gather at the tip.

When she bent over to search for another one, I fired the rubber band.

"Good shot," she said as her hand vanished behind her, her eyes wild and excited and locked on mine. She picked up the rubber band and walked up to me, holding it before my eyes as she swung it from eye to eye as if trying to hypnotize me.

"Gosh, this looks familiar," she said and then laughed a little.

"Want it back?"

"No, I'd rather you had it."

"Why, so I can shoot you again?"

She grinned. "Only if you want to."

*   *   *

We walked deep into campus, Jenna on the left and I on the right, her arm drawn snugly around mine, so that my arm began to tingle. A cat ran out in front of us, followed by another, and then a third, who crouched low on the path and watched us and then scurried off into the bushes.

"There are tons of cats up here," I said.

"It's a wasteland for cats. A few escaped and nature took its course. I like to come up here to feed them."

"I always see stray cats at colleges. They usually just run from people. You actually feed them?"

"They seem to trust me."

"Is this what you do late at night, Ms. Insomniac?"

"Among other things. Like making plans."

"Plans," I said. "Right. We'll get to those later. But don't you get scared walking the campus at night?"

"Carl, welcome to Nebraska. You think I'm going to be mugged by a Holstein cow?"

"Yeah, I guess you're right. I guess you've got to go to the coasts to be baptized into the dangerous life. Speaking of Nebraska, are you going to give me the low down on the Star City?"

"Are you asking me to help you?"

"In a way, yeah."

"Well then," Jenna said and clung tighter to my arm, which was now feeling numb. "Perhaps I can help you."

We stopped at a ponderosa pine in front of a tall redbrick building. I read a sign out front, which listed the academic departments, one of them philosophy.

"Look," I said. "There's the University of Nebraska philosophy building. I understand those guys are into analytical philosophy, which deals with analyzing ideas and logical rigor."

"You say that like it's a bad thing."

"I'm more into continental philosophy. You know, where you talk about the death of God and all of those problems you then have to face, like loneliness, despair, and suicide. How do we live after God's burial with our heads held high and without fear and trembling? That's what I'm about."

"Have you figured out the answer to that, Mr. Philosopher?"

"It's coming. Give it time."

Somewhere a radio began to play, and Jenna eased her grip on my arm.

"Look," I said. "This building is called Oldfather Hall. I bet there's a story there."

Jenna snuggled into my side and then stared up at me. "It sounds like the name has a significance for you."

"It totally does." I told her how, in divinity school, nobody could believe in the old God anymore, the old father, the God of Abraham, Isaac, and Jacob. This was a God who intervened in the world, who parted the Red Sea, and who raised Jesus from the grave. This God, the old father, was no longer plausible.

"So what the theologians did was, they revised the old God and made him more compatible with modern ways of thinking. What was this new God like? Not a personal being. Instead, this God is creativity or an impersonal force or human potential or some nonsense like that." My arm was feeling numb as Jenna looked up at me as though in a dream. "Make sense?"

"So you reject the old deity and truth with a capital 'T'?"

"Pretty much. Hey, you seem like you're well read. Or did you not learn this stuff from a book, just like you didn't learn about Plato from a book?"

Jenna didn't answer, and I bumped her hip with my hip and she bumped me back.

"Seriously, I'm curious," I said. "Do you read a lot in the bus? And what do you believe about God and truth? Capital 'T', small 't'?"

Jenna released my arm. She looked skyward and pulled her scarf out, spreading it out and shaking it, so that the ends flailed in front of us. "In all honesty, I try not to think about it. It gives me headaches."

I rubbed the inside of my upper arm to get the blood flowing again. When Jenna pulled back her hair, I saw another pink scar, a rubbery line across her throat, and I looked quickly away from it. I had to remember to tread carefully here.

"Tell me, Mr. Philosopher, what do you think I think about it?" Jenna wrapped the scarf around her neck and then stuffed it with force into the bomber jacket. Then she felt the sunglasses atop her head as if to make sure they were still there. She lifted up a foot and looked at her boot and then brushed her thigh as if something was stuck to it. Then she put her hands into the jacket pockets. She wasn't looking at me, but past me, with her lips shaped into the impish grin that first caught my attention a month before.

I said, "For you I'd say the topic is complicated."

She peered over at me and broke into a smile and began to bounce up and down, clapping her hands and showing off those perfect white teeth. "Let's walk, Carl. Can we?"

"Was it something I said?"

She hugged me. "Uh-huh."

"Okay." I put my arm around her shoulder. "If that's what you want."

We walked in silence. My arm was feeling normal again, and when we passed by Memorial Stadium, I looked into Jenna's eyes, and they dropped to my lips as if she wanted to kiss them.

"That's so beautiful, Carl."

"What is?"

"What you said about the old father."

"You like it?"

"I do."

I smiled. "How much?"

She pulled down on my neck with her small, pink hands. "I think I want to marry it."

17

The symposium was well underway by then, and I didn't doubt my decision to ditch it. Not for a second. My date with Jenna was going well and it wasn't close to being over. We'd circled the campus again, and at times Jenna would hum that popular rock song I'd been hearing. Soon I found myself humming the song too. I recalled some of the lyrics I'd jotted down at Bison Witches but had forgotten most of them. Jenna, however, knew the song well.

I was tempted to ask her about it when we happened upon a prehistoric museum at the north end of campus. A big bronze mammoth stood at the entrance on a stone foundation with one of its front feet lifted up as though about to crush somebody.

"Look." Jenna skipped up to the mammoth so that she stood under its upraised foot.

"Be careful," I said.

"Ha. Maybe Mr. Crushfoot is coming for you." Jenna jumped up and down, unable to touch the big foot. "Shoot. Help me here, Carl."

I lifted her up by the waist and she thwacked the mammoth's foot with a palm.

"There," she said. "Patty cake, patty cake, baker's man."

I set her down as she wiped her palm down the side of her pants and then felt the goggles atop her head.

"Did that work for you?" I said.

"It did, thank you." She seized my hand with both of hers and pulled me locomotive-like to a bench. When she sat down, I ordered her to stand up. She obediently rose as if she'd done something wrong, and I got out a notebook, tearing out some sheets of binder paper and placing them on the bench.

"Sit," I said, and she did. Jenna's hands were atop her thighs as if awaiting the next order. I put additional sheets of paper on the bench and then sat down next to her, resting my arm on the backrest so that my fingers lightly touched her shoulder.

Pointing my shoe at the mammoth, I said, "We've got those at BFU, too."

"Nebraska loves its mammoths," she said. "Did you know, the woolly mammoths are the biggest mammals ever to roam the plains of Nebraska?"

"You know a lot about everything, dontcha, Ms. McMaster?"

"Well, that's what it says on that sign, right there."

Two students walked our way, hand in hand, their faces blue from the glow of cell phones. Somewhere on campus, a radio played.

"Talk," Jenna said. "Tell me more."

"No, I've talked enough about me," I said. "Let's talk about you for a change. I've been dying to know why you're driving a bus. I mean, as smart and as good looking as you are, why aren't you doing something else, like teaching or modeling?"

"Oh," Jenna said and waved her hand dismissively. "That's just something I do at the moment. I like the free time, the chance to meet people. I've done other things, too, lots of things."

A football player and a blonde girl emerged from a side path. They walked slowly in the shadows of trees through the heavy air, sweet and rotten with leaves. Jenna watched them with lowered eyes until the couple passed by, moving across the lawn to the dorms.

"May I ask what else you've done?" I said.

Jenna stared down the path, toward the temple-like stadium, her eyes seeming to peer into the other inscrutable world of hers.

"Jenna?"

"Huh?"

"What else have you done for a living?"

She looked at her lap and then raised a hand, curling her fingers and looking at her long nails.

"Legal secretary, health insurance agent, government aide, data entry officer. Stuff like that." Jenna turned her head a little so that her honey-blonde hair curtained her face. Only the tip of her pale nose could be seen.

"Oh." I remembered her various scars and felt as though I'd gotten too personal. Her hair blew out and completely hid her face. "So you're happy driving the bus?"

"I am."

"It sounds like you've had an interesting life." I rested my finger on her kneecap and made a small circle on it. "If you ever want to talk about your life sometime, I'd like to hear about it."

A breeze sighed in the black trees, and the full moon looked like a child's ball caught between the branches of an oak.

"Okay, Carl." Jenna rose up. "Let's play psychologist."

"What?"

"Here, you lie on the bench and I'll sit behind you." Jenna pulled out her scarf, folding it three times and making a pillow. "Okay, now lie down and tell me a secret. Ready?"

She spoke lightly, but there was an intensity beneath it that made me nervous. "Can we do this later?"

"Carl, you want to know me, and I want to know you. What better way than to play psychologist?" Jenna fished out a small notepad and pencil from her purse. "Okay, now lie down and close your eyes."

"You're serious, right? Because I'm sort of feeling the itch for coffee."

"Carl, lie down and tell me a secret."

I looked down the path, wet and shiny with yellow leaves.

"Let's make it quick, okay?"

I lay on the bench with my knees up and my hands folded atop my chest. The stars were big and twinkly in the sky, and the mammoth looked ten stories high, its mouth open and its teeth bared. I could feel my heart beat softly through my blazer's lapel.

"A secret?" I said.

"Big or small. Your choice."

My heartbeat was louder and faster and I took a slow deep breath and shut my eyes. I listened to the swish of branches blowing and water drops wetting the leaf-strewn path. Somewhere to the north, a train's horn blared.

"Carl?"

"Okay." *Jesus Christ, why was this hard? Just say something. Anything. Then leave.*

No, I knew why this was hard. The girl behind me, she was the one who should be on the bench. Not me.

"I guess you could say I'm worried about my future in the academy." As the pencil began to scratch its way across the notepad, I opened my eyes. "There aren't many full-time teaching jobs left, especially in the humanities. Most professors these days are adjuncts, part-timers, those who teach a few classes here and there, sometimes at four or five different campuses. It's the only way to make a living, but it doesn't pay well and you don't get any benefits, either. Nobody with a PhD wants that life. It's hell, the adjuncts are basically slaves, and it's only going to get worse."

My heartbeat was slowing down as I watched the eastbound clouds and listened to the pencil's tip, scratching its way across the paper. Then the pencil stopped. I moved my leg and then closed my eyes. I could sense Jenna's eyes looking down at me.

"I'm worried that I'll be a part-timer forever," I said.

The pencil continued on. "I see."

I opened my eyes. High above campus, a star fell from the sky and burned up in the earth's atmosphere.

"What's worse," I said, "is the alternative. I don't want to be parking cars at a hotel. Not with a PhD."

I listened to the scribbles and then turned my head and peered down the dark, empty parking lot.

Jenna crossed her legs. "So what you're saying is that your future isn't secure."

"It's the one thought that's been keeping me up at night." I spaced out into the star-splattered sky and then tilted my head back so that Jenna, her face curtained by her hair, came into view. "Are you happy now?"

Jenna ripped away the sheets of paper and closed the notebook, stuffing both into her purse. Then she got up and stood by my side.

"I am," she said.

18

After my therapy session, I suggested we grab a coffee, but it turned out Jenna didn't drink coffee. We were walking by the frat and sorority houses, my arm around her shoulder, when a bluesy guitar riff began to play. Jenna walked ahead of me, my arm falling to my side. She walked onto the lawn of a frat house and looked inside where a blood-red strobe light blinked on and off, and a ceiling fan's blades turned darkly on the wall.

"Carl, I love this song."

It was the song I'd been hearing all summer. I knew who it was now, too. Audioslave. "I do, too."

"I bought the album at Homer's."

"I've been meaning to buy it, too."

When the vocalist began to sing, Jenna joined in, and her angelic, choir-like voice soared over the streets, over leafless trees, and into the pitch-black night. Through a sorority house window, a blonde girl in a Husker T-shirt looked up from her desk, while her roommate in a pink jogging suit appeared in the window, grabbed a gold chain around her neck, and ran her finger along the inside of it.

I rested my hands atop the parking meter, blinking for coins. I wanted to tell the sorority sisters I'd never heard a voice like Jenna's, either. She should be in New York, not Nebraska.

"Here comes the chorus. Ready, Carl?" She spread her arms out wide, shut her eyes, and began to sing, this time louder. When the chorus ended, Jenna looked at me with a look of pure love.

"Did you hear that, Carl? You don't want to learn things you'll need to forget."

"Sure."

"Wasn't it beautiful?"

"If you say so."

Jenna walked up to me, took my hand, and placed it on her heart.

"I've even married it," she said.

"Good for you."

"Can we sing the chorus together?"

I squeezed her wrist and brought it close to my lips, staring into her eyes.

"We should probably go," I said. "You can do this on Halloween. You're scaring people."

Now I was the locomotive, pulling her onward by the hand. Jenna fought me, her leather boots creaking in the cold, but then she relented and followed my lead.

I looked back and smiled. "What's wrong?"

"You're no fun."

"We'll hear it again."

"But I want to sing it now."

I put my arm around her shoulder, and we walked toward the quad as the sprinklers spat and hissed on the lawns. Jenna still hummed the chorus, her eyes sneaking over to mine from time to time.

"So what are your plans for those papers?" I said.

"The ones I wrote on you as you lay on the bench? Oh, I'll just tuck them away someplace."

"So you've got a file on me?"

"I do."

"Well, that's very police state of you. Maybe next time I'll ask you the questions. Then you can tell me your secrets."

"Why don't you, then?" We entered the quad, her heels echoing in the dark silence. "We can create a file together. You and I. Us. *We.*"

"Sure," I said. "That'd be interesting."

"Oh, I can guarantee that."

We stood in the quad, inspecting the student union, the tree branches clacking away in the stone pots. On the second floor, the symposium was still in progress, while on the main floor, the revolving doors spat out students who hurried to their dorms, their eyes never leaving their phones.

"They're probably in the question and answer period now," I said.

Jenna closed her eyes. "Gee, I wonder what questions are getting answered? And which aren't?"

"Whatever they're discussing, it can't be more interesting than tonight. After what I've seen and heard from you . . . Jesus."

"Well, I'm glad you've enjoyed my company."

We ambled through Love Library, wandering the philosophy and literature bookracks, and then, twenty minutes later, arrived back at the Garden, standing at the big black gates. I looked through the rails at the library, its white cupola lit up in the sky.

"So," I said. "I guess we forgot to get something to drink."

Jenna took off her goggles and stuffed them in her cherry red purse, next to the yellow notebook. "Maybe next time."

"Do you want to stop over for a bit?"

"No, I'm okay."

"All right. If you change your mind, I live in the Ghetto, just south of the steel mill. My building is called the Guardian."

"I know just where it is."

"Okay, good. I'm in 301." I kissed her forehead. "Talk to you later, okay?"

She got in her Honda Accord and started the engine, then gave me a look.

"What?" I said.

"Remember, Carl, you don't want to learn what you'll only need to forget, okay?"

"Right." I tapped the car's roof with my hand. "Have a good night, and wear your seatbelt."

19

I woke up in the darkness of my cell. Somewhere in the train yard, an outbuilding's door slammed. It was unusually cold, so I spread a comforter over me but I couldn't get warm. I got up and cranked the heater but was still cold. Then I put my black robe on and climbed in bed and fell asleep.

In the morning, I stopped by Starbucks and then rode to campus. I dashed by the co-op grain elevator with its high, eye-like windows and the six crows perched at the top. Soon, I bounded over a pair of tracks, just as the signal began to clang and the white crossbar went down.

I peddled on, picking up speed on Old Farm Road, where the fields were harvested and left for dead. Hay bales were scattered on the hillsides, bound up with a light-green baling twine, while cows were crowded under a billboard, watching me pass by. When I passed by a cemetery, a gravedigger in a gray sweater and light-gray pants appeared and disappeared between the gnarly black oaks. He walked slowly with a shovel over his shoulder and work gloves on, as hunks of dark-red dirt dropped off the shovel's blade.

I got a text from Paul. *Good talk at Starbucks. More ways to survive as an adjunct.*

Tell me, I texted back.

In Omaha stuck in traffic. Have class. Just know there's no adjunct heaven, only hell and purgatory. Indulgences may be available.

Good to know.

I recalled my talk with Paul, whom I'd bumped into at Starbucks, just an hour before. There was a half-off sale on all drinks, and Paul was there to take advantage of the savings. "It's what you do as an adjunct," he'd said as we stood in line. He'd told me about a book he was writing, *The Adjunct's Survival Guide: Fifty Ways to Save as a Part-Time Professor*. This included shopping at Goodwill, crashing departmental events for the free food, using the copy paper in the recycling bin instead of buying reams of it at Staples, and buying women's deodorant because it was a dollar cheaper than the men's. "You'll have your own list, too," Paul had said. "Yours might even be longer than mine."

Arriving on campus, I circled Chautauqua Pond, saying hello to the mallards and swans, and then lit up and hung out with Mr. Bryan.

"Maybe if you were still alive," I said, "you'd have something to say about the inequalities in higher education. You'd unite the poorly paid adjuncts and help those who are struggling, like Paul." I looked into the Great Commoner's eyes, then dropped my cigarette and crushed it out with my shoe.

After my final lecture on Epicurus, a scrawny kid with a goatee appeared at the lectern. He wore tan pants and a pink Oxford shirt and had a backpack on, thumbs hooked on the straps. His name was Rob Loisy.

"Hey, man," he said. "Awesome lecture. You make philosophy fun. So many of the profs are old, passionless deadbeats."

"They should be in the archives, not the classroom."

"Totally agree. Though you said something on the first day of class that I'm not so sure about."

I slid a paperclip over my notes. "Regarding?"

"You said nobody reads books anymore. You called us a bunch of illiterates. And, yeah, there's truth to it, but a lot of people still read books. Like me."

"I was engaging in polemics," I said. "Nietzsche used to do it—make provocative claims, just to get a conversation going. But you see my point. We're distracted these days, and our attention spans are almost nil. Sure, you can read your Facebook feeds and Twitter updates, but can you read *Crime and Punishment* or Dante's *Inferno*? No wonder the West is dying."

"Totally agree. My roommates never read, and if they go to a café to study, they end up on the Internet, instead." Rob drew the straps of his backpack tight. "I wonder if Plato and Aristotle would have thought such profound thoughts or have written such great books if they were always goofing around on Google."

I shouldered my satchel. "Good question. Bring it up in class. Maybe it'd do those jocks in the back row some good."

"What'd Nietzsche say about reading books?"

"*The Anti-Christ*, aphorism fifty-nine. Nietzsche had praised the ancient world for inventing the incomparable art of reading well, which was the prerequisite for all systematic knowledge."

Rob put his hands in his pockets. "Hey, I heard you went to seminary."

"Divinity school—a distinction without a difference, really." Rob squinted his eyes, and I smiled at his bewilderment. "Let's get out of here and talk on the way."

20

Walking through the Black Forest, I told Rob about seminary and divinity school. Both trained men and women to be ministers, but in divinity school you'd meet students who were closeted atheists—and also going to be ministers. Rob confessed to being raised Catholic but leaving it behind a year or two ago. He'd even thought of becoming a priest at one time, but the more he learned about the Bible in college, the less convinced he was that it was true. And when he met his fiancée, Liz O'Reilly—also a Catholic and a sociology major at BFU—the priesthood dropped out of the question. He spoke intimately about his growing doubts about traditional Christianity, especially Catholicism. There weren't many liberal Catholics in Lincoln, Rob had said. You had to go to Omaha for that. Catholicism was by the book in Lincoln, and if Rome taught it, the Lincoln diocese believed it. Period. End of story.

When we left the Black Forest, we followed a winding path through the hillocks of tallgrass to the union.

"So where are you from?" I said.

"Sidney."

"No accent?"

"Sidney, Nebraska. A lot less exciting."

We had lunch at a sunny table with a view of the mammoths in the lagoon and chatted about divinity schools, where to apply if Rob decided to go, the art of writing a statement of purpose, that sort of thing.

"Who's writing your letters of recommendation?" I said.

Rob listed off the professors, including Dr. Parsons.

"He's my advisor, too," I said.

"What's your view of Darth Vader?"

I hadn't heard this. "That's what he's called?"

"Parsons is a science fiction guy. He's got a huge collection of comic books and cult movies from the 70s. And he always roots for the bad characters."

"Good to know."

Rob said that Dr. Parsons hosted a movie night at his condo in downtown Lincoln. All the philosophy majors would go. Last fall, they'd watched *The Matrix* series. This fall it was *Transformers*.

"What else about Darth Vader?" I said.

"He gives paper readings a lot. Last night he talked about Kenny Winslow at the University of Nebraska. Liz and I went. Did you go?"

"Sure did."

"Parsons totally got the crowd worked up, especially the fundies in the back row. He likes to give it good and hard to the fundies. I can't believe what he said about Kenny, though. Nobody could."

I rocked back on my chair's legs as Rob spoke highly of Dr. Parson's caustic remarks. Across the quad, the clusters of honey locust leaves, like small fires, blew across the pavement and vanished into the lagoon.

"Do you think Kenny could kill himself because he lost his faith in God?" Rob said.

My chair's legs hit the floor. "It's happened before."

"What's your take on Parsons' argument?"

I got out my phone. Great. Now I was trapped. "It was . . . interesting." I kept scrolling through my messages.

"You probably have to go, huh."

"I should probably study, but we can talk later on."

Rob stood up and shouldered his backpack. "I can't believe they've emptied out the lagoon already. Usually they do it in November."

"It's the crazy Nebraska weather."

"I know, right? It might even snow this weekend. Which isn't so bad if you're a cross-country skier. Liz and I go every chance we get. It's a blast. We should all go sometime."

I made some noncommittal noises, and he excused himself, pleading his next class. I stayed in the union and read an article in *The Mammoth*, then closed the paper and folded it. Was Dr. Parsons right? Did Kenny Winslow kill himself because, after losing his faith in God, he felt his life was meaningless and unbearable? I wasn't so sure. Half of my divinity school class lost their faith in the traditional God. More than half, in fact. But after the shock had worn off, they adjusted, and they went on with their lives without God.

But Kenny Winslow . . . I was trying to connect the existential dots of his life, while the honey locust leaves, those bodies of fire, blew across the quad, one after the other, each one meeting the same fate in the lagoon.

21

Before I rode home, I cruised through campus a bit. I toured the STEM area, which was heavily under construction, and then the Greek housing section, just in back of the old humanities buildings. Homecoming was around the corner, and the frat boys and sorority girls were gathered on the front lawns, making floats out of plywood and chicken wire and colorful paper. I rode past the Greek houses and then into the specialty houses—old farmhouses that housed various majors like history and political science, math, and physics.

And philosophy.

I rode by Philosophy House and there, on the front porch, were six graduate students.

Lowering my head, I pretended to shift gears. Their too-loud voices carried over the yard, sounding smart and smug. Big deal. They'd be in the program a year, maybe two, and then they'd be gone.

Soon they were out of earshot, thank god. Nothing was more annoying than grad student arrogance. They cut others down in class and spent every possible minute grandstanding, just to look good in front of the professors. Oh, well. Soon, the scythe of doctoral studies would cut short their academic lives, chopping each one down like a cornstalk. A good thing, actually, since in the humanities there were already too many mouths to feed.

Back in town, I set the copy of *The Mammoth* on my desk, then got dressed for work. In the bathroom, I looked at myself in the medicine-cabinet mirror, imagining what I'd say to

Kenny Winslow, should he have written me a letter for "Zarathustra Says."

"Hang tough," I said. "Life is suffering, but good things are down the road for you. You'll be drafted by the NFL, make millions of dollars, get married, and have a family. And after you retire, you'll be a coach, a sportscaster, or a consultant." I threw my dress shoes into my satchel and shouldered it. "There are plenty of worthy goals to pursue, even in a world void of God."

I left the Guardian just as a gray, brain-like ledge of cloud moved in over the train yard. I tried to focus on the Skeptics, the next philosophers I'd introduce my students to, but my mind couldn't let go of the dialogue with Kenny. There was something compelling about trying to help him through his existential crisis and keep his life from going off the rails.

At the hotel, the Demon Deacon fans had arrived. The lobby was swirling with black-and-yellow jerseys and jackets as Avery and I pushed a covered wagon into the elevator.

"Look at you with the grin," Avery said. "Did you meet a hottie with a body?"

"Times ten."

"How was she?"

"Platonic. It was just a date."

"Who dates anymore? You mean you hooked up. Even Plato got some sometimes."

"No, we didn't, really." I watched the numbers light up. "Jenna and I went for a walk and talked about life."

"What are you, entering the priesthood?" The doors opened and Avery walked out. "By the way, you don't get to know a girl like Jenna. You just bang the shit out of her. That's all she wants, too."

I smiled. "Maybe you just aren't doing it right."

We unloaded the luggage and rode the elevator down.

"You could have nailed her on campus, too," Avery said. "One of the football players boned her up there, right under a bald cypress tree. So did a baseball player. Not at the same time, but with a girl like Jenna such a scenario isn't out of the question. Are you going out again?"

"Probably," I said, not sure if I believed Avery. It didn't sound like the girl I'd gone out with. "If you bother to listen to her, Jenna's hella smart. We've got chemistry, it's a little toxic, but it's interesting as hell and I want to see where it goes. I just wonder what else she does for a living."

Outside at the curb, Avery dialed up Nero's Pizza, while a black hawk hung suspended in the air above the Sower.

Avery hung up and fidgeted with his phone. "If you're going out with Jenna again, you should talk to Quentin Smith. He works in the parking garage. He sports a big old moustache. And when you see that dickhole, tell him he owes me five bucks."

I spotted the moustache from twenty yards away. It was huge, as big as Nietzsche's, bigger even, and when I pulled a red Ford truck up to the ticket booth, I saw Quentin and turned away in fright. I held out the ticket, still looking away.

He took the ticket. "Doin' all right?"

I stole a glance at the moustache, then swallowed. Good God. A small animal could live in it. And perhaps did.

Quentin waved the ticket as if trying to get my attention. "What's going on, my man?"

I looked at the steering wheel. In my mind's eye, I saw Quentin's brown cowboy hat, the white Western shirt with brown arrows on the chest pointing down, and his eyes, big and brown and innocent like a cow's.

"New in town?"

"Sure am."

"Grad school?"

I nodded.

"Whatcha majoring in, music?"

"Close." I finally looked at him. "Philosophy."

"Gon' be a teacher?"

"That's my plan."

Quentin twisted the bar of his moustache. "Shit, you gon' bale hay for a living."

I inched the truck forward as Quentin crossed his arms and followed me. "Play in a band?"

How could he . . . "Used to."

"Guitar?" He pronounced it, "gee-tar."

"Yeah, but I don't have time for it anymore."

"Been wanting to learn to play myself."

The crossbar at the lot entrance stopped me. "There are lessons on YouTube."

"Whatcha think of Jason Aldean?"

"Who?"

Quentin slowly bent down with his hands on his knees, peering into the cab. "Where you from?"

"Out West."

"Well, you in Nebraska now, which means you gon' experience it." He ran the ticket through and the bar rose up. Pointing at the ticket, he said, "First truck you ever drove?"

I laughed. Hick. No wonder he worked here. Probably couldn't read or write.

"Ever baited a fishing hook?" he said. "Pitched a tent? Shot a rifle?" Quentin plopped down on a stool, his eyes barely visible from under the brim of the cowboy hat. "Ever held a rifle?"

I lifted my foot off the brake and gave the truck some gas.

"I don't believe in guns," I said over my shoulder.

22

After work, I stopped by the Blue Note. A man with a beard and John Lennon glasses stood on stage strumming an acoustic guitar, while I slid into a booth by the window and looked at my phone. Tony set a large screwdriver on a napkin and said, with a big, jolly smile, "High Hopes, how ya doing?"

"Better, thanks."

"Busy day?"

"The hotel was swamped. Good tips, though."

Tony eased himself down on a chair. "I wish I could say the Bison had a good one, too, but they suffered one of the worst defeats in the history of college football."

Outside, a car started up and then backed out of a parking space, its engine revving up, hot and mean, and then tore down the street, shifting through the gears. Two car alarms went off, and seconds later the alarms chirped and were silent.

"They're in for a long season," I said.

"Boy, you can say that again."

A barmaid wearing a Husker shirt breezed by. She looked at her phone and then slipped it into her apron.

"Okay, so get a load of this," Tony said. "You might enjoy this, since you're a philosophy guy and all. So last night, a guy from Winston-Salem comes into the bar, says he was a roadie for Led Zeppelin in the 70s. Guy says that all during the American tour, there was trouble in the Zeppelin camp, like a dark, nasty cloud was following the band on the road."

This was evoking some vague memories. "Didn't Robert Plant's son die?"

"Not only that, but his wife was in a car accident, too. Got hurt real bad. They ended up cancelling the tour. Guy says to me, 'Look, I don't mean to preach no doom and gloom to you Nebraskans or nothing, but the feeling I'm getting in the Cornhusker State is the same feeling I got on the road with Zeppelin.'" Tony twisted his torso from left to right, and his back gave a crack. "That's better. Guy says the guitar player, Jimmy Page, was to blame. Something about him dabbling in black magic. You ever study that stuff?"

"A little." Great. More religious talk. Stirring my drink, I forced myself to go on. "I've heard about that Led Zeppelin story. It almost ended their careers. And yeah, Jimmy Page was into black magic, but he didn't talk about it much. He also bought a mansion owned by Aleister Crowley, a famous magician."

"No kidding?"

"In Scotland, yeah. The house is on the shore of Loch Ness, where the famous monster is supposed to lurk. Jimmy also owned an occult bookstore as well as a lot of Crowley's possessions—clothes, manuscripts, and such. Apparently, evil spirits haunt the house. Or so people say." I took a few big drinks. "When Page went on tour, a friend of his would stay in the house, and even the friend would get freaked out. Like one night, while in bed, he heard a noise in the hallway, like a dog with its nose to the door, snorting. Then he heard growls and snarls, as if a gigantic beast was trying to get in. And a fair number of the owners of the house over the years either went mad or committed suicide."

Tony and I sat in the smoky bar. The stage lights had dimmed, and the ice cubes in my glass had turned a dark red.

"Sheesh," Tony said. "Stories like that give me the creeps. There's plenty of proof for ghosts and evil spirits. I know from personal experience. Do you think houses can be haunted?"

I stirred my drink. "I can't rule it out, but I'd bet science will eventually explain these so-called paranormal events. Soon we'll no longer have any use for gods and devils, ghosts and the like."

When a herd of Husker fans entered the bar, the barmaid stashed her phone in her apron and swiped up some menus.

"Gotta run," Tony said and got slowly up, cupping his lower back. "But if I was sleeping in that house you was talking about, and I heard a big beast out in the hallway, ain't no way I'd be a skeptic no more. God and devils, ghosts and spirits—it'd make a whole lotta sense."

23

Arriving at the Ghetto, I pulled a yellow sheet of paper off my door.

You, a yellow blanket, and me. Doesn't that sound warm?

Above me, the single light bulb, crusty with bugs, blipped on and off. I read the note again, the yellow page torn from a notebook. For all the coziness of the message, the sentences were written in a black, irregular scrawl.

Crazy girl.

I walked in and cranked up the heater, then called Jenna.

"You stopped by?"

"You were out, Scholar Boy."

"I also have a job, you know."

"But not a full-time teaching job." She breathed a moment, barely audible, as if she were expecting a response to this. When she didn't get one, she said, "So what are you doing now?"

I spread out on my mattress. "Thinking of how creepy you are. You know, I often wonder if you're hiding something."

"Carl, don't tell me you're back to thinking I have power over nature?"

"Oh, no. But there's something more about you than meets the eye. If so, you're the Form of the Lie Itself, to use Plato's language." I stared at the ceiling, dark and water stained, like a continent soaked in blood. "You there?"

"You pick on me a lot, you know."

"It's for your own good. And take your cigarette out of your mouth." I could hear her talking around it.

"It's not a cigarette. It's a nail."

Jenna's front door opened up—I could hear a car zoom by on the street. I rolled onto my side. "Are you outdoors?"

"I'm nailing something to my door. It's an old tradition."

"At three in the morning?" There was a silence, then bam, bam, bam. "You do have neighbors, right?"

"Uh-huh."

As the hammer blows came harder, I sat up. "And so you're just going to keep hammering?"

After a final blow, she closed the door and it was quiet again. "There. All better."

I stood up and unhooked Jenna's rubber band. "You're not the average Nebraskan, are you?"

"Would you have had as good a time the other night if I were?"

I laughed. "Good point. Good enough that I'm willing to overlook some things."

"Is that what you're going to do, Carl?"

"I am." I ran a finger down the row of Nietzsche books. "Hey, did you hear that? I'm starting to sound like you. You always say 'I am,' and I'm starting to say it, too."

"You are. We are."

"I bet you're going to take me over soon."

"We will. But only with your permission, Carl."

24

I didn't hear from Jenna for the next week. Every day after class I expected a knock, a note, or a text message. Nothing. It was late September now, and the winds blew steadily throughout the day, stripping the remaining leaves off the oaks and elms in the Ghetto, and I'd wake up each morning to the grind of ice scrapers on car windshields in the Guardian's parking lot. Cold weather was settling in, and it was barely fall.

I returned home from the café one evening, having prepped a lecture on St. Augustine, the great former sinner, when, at midnight, a soft, barely audible knock sounded on my door. I opened it.

Jenna stood in the hallway, three feet back. She clutched her red purse to her chest as she looked over my shoulder into my cell, and then lowered her purse and smiled. She was dressed entirely in black, from knee-high black boots to a black fishnet top over a lacy black bra. It looked more freezing than alluring.

"Hello, creature of the night," I said. "Where's the yellow blanket?"

"In my car."

"Seriously? Are we going somewhere at this ungodly hour?"

"If you dare."

The light bulb above us flickered on and off.

"Come in."

"Is that what you want?"

"That's why I asked. Oh, wait. I'm supposed to say, 'Yes, come in.' I always have to say 'Yes' before I get anywhere with you. In that case," I said, pushing the door open wide. "Yes, it would be my pleasure to invite you in."

Jenna's nostrils flared out wide, and, roping the red purse strap up her shoulder, she strutted into my cell, dragging a fingernail across my chest and unsnapping a button as she went. I closed the door and leaned my back against it as Jenna looked around my cell.

"Fishnets, huh?"

"I knew you'd like them."

"You know my animalistic nature."

"Do we ever."

I placed my palms lightly on the tops of her shoulders, the fishnets cold and prickly to the touch. "I have a big week coming up. Midterms."

Jenna bent her knees and slipped away, then walked to my windowsill and pulled out *Thus Spoke Zarathustra*.

"Why don't you live a little, Carl? Nietzsche said to live dangerously." She opened the book and ran a finger across the page. Then, as if taking a mental snapshot of it, she closed the book slowly and leered at me. "Well, Mr. In-Need-of-Experience?"

Outside the Guardian's front door, I buttoned up my Levi's jacket and lit a cigarette. When the black wind carried the smoke away, I saw Jenna across the sandlot, walking barefoot along one rail of the main line track with a long cigarette between her fingers. I walked onto the mound of red rocks, on which lay Jenna's black boots, toppled over, and a pair of black stockings, curled up. She took slow, careful steps, arms out for balance, moving south in her bare feet while peering at me over her shoulder.

"You're something else," I said.

"Just wait."

Inside the Honda Accord, the yellow blanket—there was a yellow blanket—was stashed under the emergency brake, folded up and glowing like an artificial sun.

"So where are we going?" I said.

"To a place I like."

"At two a.m.?"

"This is Nebraska. Besides, I'm protected."

I looked at the yellow blanket, folded up into a square as if done by ceremonious hands.

"Can you have me back in an hour?"

Jenna started the car. "We can do lots of things."

Fifteen minutes later, we arrived at what looked like the middle of nowhere. Jenna killed the engine, then the headlights. A line of black pines stood up like rifles before us, while dry leaves blew across the parking lot like great breaths of fire. The yellow blanket, radiant like a fake sun, was wedged between us.

"Are we going for a walk?"

"That's part one of this evening's entertainment. Part two is something you can use for your dissertation."

We climbed out, and Jenna took my hand in hers, soft and warm as if created fresh that night. Her other hand held the yellow blanket.

We entered the forest, the path strewn with pine needles and cones, and I closed my eyes, trusting her to lead the way. At times, she'd squeeze my hand.

"We're living dangerously, Carl."

"We sure are."

"You'll have a lot to write about."

"Whatever you say."

Soon we came into a clearing, and a great plain of grass stretched out before us under the full moon. At the center, an old church with a bell tower stood quietly by the cottonwood tree.

"Are we going inside?" I said.

"Of course. There's nobody in there. It's the best kind of church."

We walked up the meadow, side by side, our pinky fingers hooked together. Jenna held the yellow blanket, now dragging in the grass, and I looked back at the forest of rifles and the Sower in the distance, his light blinking red, like a beacon.

Jenna walked up the steps and pushed open the old sagging door. We walked in. The air was a century old, musty, and dead. As I coughed and sneezed, Jenna led us into the sanctuary, down the left-hand aisle, past the rows of empty pews to where the pulpit used to be. A sleeping bag had been thrown down, and a small radio stood atop a wood crate with a label.

"Nebraska AppleJack Festival?" I said. "I didn't know apples grew here."

"There are vineyards, too. For wine."

She spread out the yellow blanket. We sat down on it, and she handed me a beer, then pulled off her boots.

"So," I said, setting the can down and clasping her ankle and shaking it. "Do you come here often?"

Jenna leaned over and traced a finger on the floorboards, making a line in the dust. "As often as I can, especially in the fall. I love the fall. Everything's so alive and green. Then I get to watch it die."

Death. I was reminded of Kenny Winslow. "I've never seen such sports enthusiasm until I moved here. Are you into football?"

Jenna drew another pair of lines that intersected the other. "Football fever comes and goes, with me. Sometimes I'm into it, sometimes not."

I took a long, cool, deep drink of beer. "I haven't watched a football game in years, but when I moved to Nebraska, I couldn't avoid it. Plus you've got all that's happened to the Bison lately." I looked at the candles on the altar and then the beer can's faint golden glow. "What a lousy year they're having. Speaking of Nebraska, are you finally going to tell me about this place?"

"What's to tell? Nobody's home here, not even God."

We lay under the yellow blanket. Several beer cans were empty and toppled over as "Don't Fear the Reaper" came through the box radio.

"That's very perceptive of you," I said, watching the sleeping bats on the ceiling. "The adjunct situation at American colleges is like modern-day slavery. It really is. When you look at what adjuncts are paid and how they're abused by full-time faculty . . . Do you mind if I use your insight in a philosophy paper and present it at First Friday?"

"What we have is yours."

"Though, my advisor would throw a hissy fit if I mentioned a Biblical motif like slavery in a philosophy class, so I won't mention the Bible. I'll just—"

Jenna seized my hand. "Carl, I love this song." Through the radio's speakers, a train's horn began to blow. "It's called 'Express.' It went to number one in November of 1974." She turned it up, and the song picked up speed like a breakaway train, and Jenna stood up and began to dance to the disco grooves.

After we danced, I went outside to find a bush, then walked back in, keeping an eye on the bats above. I sat down and cracked open another beer as Jenna continued to draw on the floorboards.

"Great," I said. "Upside down crosses and pentagrams. I feel totally safe now. I'm in an abandoned church with bats all over the place and a strange girl drawing Satanic symbols. What could go wrong? Wait, that's right, you're protected, aren't you?"

"Uh-huh."

"So am I going to meet your protector, too?"

"If you want."

"Okay, but first we have to create your psychological file. Go ahead and tell me something, just one interesting thing about yourself. I already know you're an artist. But tell me something else. Something big."

Jenna traced a finger along the floor, drawing a "C" followed by an "S."

"Whenever you're ready," I said.

Jenna stopped drawing and bowed her head, her hair curtaining her off. The candles on the altar burned dimly as their shadows wavered on the wall.

"Well, I'm a witch." She wiped out my initials, leaving the floorboards smooth with dirt. Then she drew my initials again, only more slowly.

"A witch?"

She said it again as though she were describing where she went to school. "That's right. Have been for years."

I snapped off the radio. The speakers gave off a soft, barely audible hiss as the bone-yellow blanket glowed beside us.

"You know I think that's a load of crap." I clutched her ankle, and she kicked her leg free and rolled away, laughing. "I'll summarize that medieval and early modern nonsense in two words," I said. "Superstition and paranoia. Now get over here and stop writing my initials."

Jenna extended her leg out, then pulled it away. "Do you fear the reaper, Carl?"

"Not anymore."

"And, get over here? Is that how you win over all your girls?"

I hooked her ankle, reeling her in, until I pinned her wrists to the blanket. Under my palm, I could feel her pink, rubbery scar.

"Let go for a sec."

When I did, Jenna showed me the red splotches on her wrists.

"Look, Carl. Wounds. Do they remind you of anything?"

"You're nuts."

"You mean they don't?"

"Oh, wait. The Audioslave song. Duh. I rolled off her and reached for my Salems. "Christ, his nail-marked hands, the irrelevant church, and a boatload of other unbelievable bullshit. I've tossed all that overboard. But I like how your mind works, crazy girl. It's quite sexy."

"Do you really like me, Carl?" She suddenly sounded like she was about ten.

"I do."

"Can we build a psychological file together?"

"If you want."

"Yay!" Jenna took out a cigarette. "Carl, I should give you a gold star. You don't want to be married to God, the church, or to those stupid, worthless saints. You can be like us, instead. You can be married to nothingness."

We lay on half of the yellow blanket, snuggled together with the other half spread out over us. Jenna's body was like the Middle West, with my hand moving up and over the Rocky Mountains, then travelling across the flat, treeless prairie of Nebraska, until my fingers found the bluffs of Iowa, and wandered deep into the Missouri River, its banks strewn with burst-open fruit.

"I love how you talk to me," Jenna whispered.

I kissed the flesh of her upper arm. Do it, Sorensen. Danger is your business. The whole state is ready to watch football and the philosophy majors are arguing in cafés. Get experience. Live, teach and write. Your students are counting on you.

I fetched a Trojan, wormy and slick inside the wrapper, but Jenna plucked it out.

"What?" I said.

"It's so unnatural."

"Is there a better option?"

Jenna looked away. Then she peeled the top open and handed it back with her eyes closed.

"But it's so unnatural," she said.

*   *   *

When I rolled off, our bodies glowed like newly created beings. Half of the yellow blanket was spread out over us as we shared a cigarette, passing it back and forth.

"I guess you're protected," I said. "Nobody came."

"Funny, Carl."

"You don't get scared out here all alone?"

"Not anymore."

After we got dressed, I brushed the bits of dry grass off her fishnet shirt.

"I've never done it in a church before." I turned her around and kissed her forehead. "This is a night to remember."

"You think?"

"Do you know why?"

She hooked her fingers in my belt loops. "Tell me."

Bending down, I said, "Because what you did was so powerful it could have created the universe."

25

Next day, when I woke up in my cell, I recalled what I'd said about Jenna creating the universe—how her lips parted when I said it, how she dropped the yellow blanket, and how she smooched me hard, our teeth hitting, her lips mashed into mine, steamy and wet as her tongue wormed in and out. I recalled how she tore off my blazer and ripped off my oxford shirt, grabbing it by the collar and splitting it down the middle, the buttons flying off and clattering down the pews. My jeans were next. Then her clothes appeared to drop off her body, like magic. I recalled how she pushed me down onto the yellow blanket, already spread out, and, straddling me, galloped hard toward the final goal, her eyes to the ceiling and back arched as she yelled loud, unspellable blasphemies.

I yawned and turned in bed, facing south, my cell growing brighter with muted sunlight. Why did hearing that matter so much to her—to basically call her God? That was another mystery, lots of things were with her, but she seemed to revel in hearing those words, to have somebody acknowledge her place in the Great Chain of Being, as though she'd been longing to hear it her whole life, if not longer.

In the late afternoon, I drifted down the main line track, heading vaguely toward work, stopping to tie my shoelaces, loose in the dirt, when a Burlington Northern rounded the tracks, blowing its horn. I backed up, watching the brown, battered boxcars passing slowly and making me dizzy with their squeaky speech. In an aqua-colored boxcar, a bald old man in an army jacket with a bedroll at his side stared back at me.

In the bell closet, Avery was shaping his hair, iPod on, the ear buds dangling down his chest, a song coming through them, distant and familiar. I pulled my uniform off the rack.

"I always hear this song in shopping malls, especially in Abercrombie or American Eagle. Who's this band?"

Avery stopped. "Uh, Maroon 5? You need to get out more. Their guitarist is from Lincoln. It wouldn't hurt you to know this, either, since they're playing at Pershing next month and staying at the hotel." Avery scooped out gel. "What are you beaming about today?"

I stepped out of my blue jeans. "I had a date with Jenna."

"So, what? You had coffee and shook hands afterwards?"

"We shook more than hands."

"You hit it out of the park?"

"Try in the parking lot. She stopped by unannounced at two a.m. I couldn't believe it."

"I told you she's psycho. Have you talked to Quentin yet?"

"Not yet." I buttoned my shirt. "Something tells me we aren't an item, though. Jenna's . . . different. She may not be a callback, like you said."

Avery picked up his backpack. "Whatever happens, enjoy hitting that."

An hour later, when I pulled a black Cadillac up to the ticket booth, Quentin stepped out.

"Check out m'old guitar."

I handed him the ticket. "It's pronounced 'gui-TAR'."

"Not by me, it ain't. There she is. Look."

"I saw it."

"You didn't look."

Inside the ticket booth, an acoustic guitar stood on a stand. Quentin took the ticket.

"You gon' teach me some chords?"

"Possibly."

"Already got m'songs picked out."

"By Jason what's-his-face?"

Quentin, sensing my sarcasm, hooked his thumbs into a brown leather belt with a big, silver buckle.

"Aldean," he said.

"Hmm, seriously, I'm not sure. Between work, school, and my girlfriend, I don't have a lot of down time."

"Got a Husker hottie, huh?"

"Sure do."

"Gon' take her to a game?"

"Not if I can help it. She doesn't like football."

"My ass she don't."

"I doubt she has anything to do with your ass, either."

Quentin lowered his head, so that the brim of the cowboy hat concealed his eyes. He pulled at the bar of his moustache.

"She's from here, right?"

"Pretty sure."

"What's her name?"

I stared at the horn. "Jenna."

"The bus driver?"

"That's her."

Quentin knelt down on his haunches and picked up a matchbook, turning it over and inspecting it. "I ain't one to tell a man how to conduct his affairs but this Jenna's bad news."

"So you know her?"

"Of her. And she ain't with a guy for more'n two, three months. And if you ain't careful, you gon' have that look in your eyes. The same look all them dudes she dates got. A wild-eyed look." Quentin rose up and walked into the booth where he wrote on the matchbook. "Every guy she dates turns into a zombie, just walking the streets of downtown Lincoln with those huge, unblinking eyes, just like she's got. You seen her eyes, right? She's crazy." He handed the matchbook to me.

I turned it over. There was a local phone number written on the back in a tiny hand. "Good to know."

"Stop by the ranch sometime. We gon' grill some steaks, drink a few cold ones, and play us some guitar. And talk more 'bout that girl of yours, too."

26

I didn't call Quentin, nor did I plan to. There was a new trinity in my life—the PhD, the Pioneer, and Jenna McMaster. Nothing else mattered. In October, which grew darker and colder by the day, I'd return from the Loft, a café in the Haymarket, and Jenna would stop over, usually after midnight. She was like clockwork, like Kant strolling the streets of Prussia at his fixed hour. I'd be brushing my teeth and getting ready for bed, when I'd hear the click of her red high heels moving with purpose along the sidewalk. I'd open the door and there she would be, Jenna McMaster, in a black fishnet shirt and a skirt, as though she knew my weakness for them.

She'd never stay long. Before she'd leave, I'd try to play therapist, asking about her life, but she'd stare blankly at the ceiling or roll her head away on the pillow. "Jenna isn't here right now," she'd say or "Jenna's unavailable for comment." That was as far as it got. And while her file never grew, mine did.

One night in late October, I kissed Jenna goodnight, and after I'd come back upstairs, Rich Richardson, my new neighbor, stood in the hallway, beer can in hand. He'd moved in about a month ago, with his fellow failed frat boy, Bubba. They'd been kicked out of Nebraska Methodist University and were now attending a local community college.

"Sorensen," he said. "What's up, bra?"

"Not much."

Rich gulped his beer, his Adam's apple rising and falling like a piston, and I read the sticker on his door: "Life's Short.

Stay Hard." I could understand why they might not be welcome in a Christian school.

"So who's the honey?" he said, jabbing a thumb out the door.

"Just a girl."

"Your girlfriend?"

"Sort of."

Bubba walked into the hallway, catcher's mitt on, his lower lip puffy with tobacco. He knelt down and rocked from side to side, whacking his fist into the glove.

Rich scratched his head. "You know, me and Bubba always saw that girl at Nebraska Methodist University, before we got the boot. She got busted for dealing drugs."

I yawned. "You're sure?"

"She'd sit on a yellow blanket in the quad, and her clients would cruise on by. Don't get us wrong. She's a babe and a half with a golden hot ass on her, but you should know this about her. We're neighbors."

Bubba eyed me, rocking back and forth, while Rich polished off the beer, tossed it over his shoulder into his room, then pulled a fresh one from his pocket and cracked it open.

"Do you tell him," Rich said to Bubba, "or am I going to do it?"

Bubba looked at the mitt, rubbing the inside of it, and his eyes rose to mine as though I were a pitcher.

Bubba gave me the lowdown. It was last year. The Bison were in Colorado, ripping the Buffaloes a new one—it was fifty to nothing at half time or something insane like that. Coach Dixon had taken Kenny out of the game and put the second-string players in. There was a party on campus, and

Bubba had gone outside to slap more burgers on the grill. And who pulls up in the bus?

"Your girl," Bubba said. "So I go over to the bus, thinking I could score me a bag of weed. And when I get to the bus, she's in the driver's seat, speaking a foreign language. She looked at me with a wild, insane look, and keeps on talking gibberish."

My phone was ringing, but I didn't answer it. "And you're sure it's the same girl?"

Bubba whacked his mitt. "It's her."

Rich wiped his lips with the back of his wrist. "For what it's worth, bra, that girl's not playing with a full deck. We're just watching out for you, so no hard feelings, okay?"

27

I didn't listen to Rich and Bubba any more than I'd listened to Quentin. Jenna was just what I needed, especially after a long week of arguing at school. Plus, she was a lot more interesting than the fundies, the grad students at First Friday, and the football crowd at the hotel.

Next day, I pulled a second yellow note off my door. Jenna's address. Nice. I called her up and said I'd stop by after work. All afternoon, Avery and I checked in hundreds of Catholics for a pro-life rally. Priests, bishops, and theologians from across the United States had descended upon the Star City with seminars to give, papers to present, and self-righteousness to reinforce.

When I clocked out, I walked the windy backstreets to Jenna's, the leaves blowing over my shoes as I followed a small group of Catholics on the other side of the street. They met up with another small group, which had gathered at the steps of the statehouse. A bald priest in a black sweater was speaking at a podium in front of the Abe Lincoln statue while college girls held up a big white banner with a baby on it. "God is Pro-Life" it said, and, "Jesus, I Trust in You." I suppressed a couple of choice remarks, thinking they weren't worth the effort.

When I arrived at Jenna's duplex, a toy snake was there to greet me—nailed to the front door, hanging upside down with a large spike driven through the tail. I watched the purple-striped nylon serpent loll in the wind, its forked tongue dangling beneath it.

Jesus Christ.

I knocked. No Jenna. I texted her as a few Catholics walked by singing something with mournful words and an upbeat melody, then left.

She texted back a little after nine, and at ten o'clock, I walked into her duplex. "Where'd you go?"

Jenna walked away as I closed the door and locked it. I followed her to the bathroom, where she sat on the edge of an old claw-foot bathtub, blue jeans rolled up to her knees, with her legs in a foot of hot, steamy water.

"Where were you?" I said.

"Work."

"You had the day off, you'd said."

"They called me in." Jenna rubbed her calf muscle, then made circular motions in the tub, and the water flowed counterclockwise.

I noticed her hair was a different shade. "Nice. Did you go to a salon?"

"I don't let anybody cut my hair."

"Why auburn? It looks like a batch of goldenrod."

Jenna reached for a coffee cup on the soap dish and took several big gulps. She put it back and began to rub her calf again.

I examined the trim-and-color job. It looked pretty good to me. "So what, you cut your own hair?"

"Since I was twelve years old."

I sat down on the tub's edge, facing the sink. "Are you okay?"

"I'm fine."

I wasn't believing it. "Did you eat?"

"I had something at work."

She drank from the coffee cup again, and this time I heard ice rattle and could smell the hard liquor. Cutting her hair, drinking on an empty stomach. I'm no psychologist, but . . .

"Did something happen at work?" I said.

It was a minute or two before I got the story. Earlier in the day, Jenna had picked up a lady in the bus and began telling the lady about her paintings. But the lady had dismissed Jenna's passion as a fantasy and told her to get a real job.

"I hate it when they mother me," Jenna said. "The bitch needs to mind her own fucking business." Jenna dumped the cubes into the tub.

I watched the cubes bobbing up and down as they slowly disappeared. "What were you drinking?"

Jenna bent over and dipped the ends of her auburn hair in the tub. She looked at them carefully, then sat back up and squeezed the water out of the ends. The water turned faintly red.

"A suicide." She pulled a towel off the high silver pole, then got out and dried off.

"Is that what the bartenders call it?" I said.

"That's what I call it. I made it up." She flung the towel over the pole and, putting her hands on her hips, said, "But does that make sense what I just said? People need to mind their own goddamn business."

I rose up slowly and put my arms around her waist. "Your hair is pretty. I like the auburn, it's much more cheerful than the black." I pulled out a long strand and smelled it. "Or maybe your hair is black, but since I've gone without food today and have had insomnia and have had too many whiffs of your suicide, maybe I'm hallucinating. Maybe I've mistakenly thought your hair is auburn but it's really—"

"Carl." She touched the image of my mouth in the mirror. "Hush."

I held her, watching her dab at her eyes with a cotton ball, with my nose pressed into her nest of thick, dark, streaky-red hair.

"Where's the crazy, big-eyed, light-up-the-sky girl I know?"

Jenna threw the cotton ball into the toilet and leaned her body into mine, her small hands on my hands, pushing both sets of hands firmly into her stomach.

"Hey, I've had a long day, too," I said. "All those religious nuts were checking into the hotel."

Soon we weren't rocking anymore. Jenna looked away and, biting down on her lips, slowly pulled my hands away from her stomach and began to inch them down her hips.

"Are you okay?" I said.

"I'm fine, Carl."

I looked at her in the mirror. "Are you sure?" When she looked up, her eyes were cold and unresponsive, and I took my hands off of her and stepped into the hallway. "We can meet up tomorrow, if you want."

Jenna crossed her arms and looked at herself in the mirror.

"Jenna?" I watched her watch herself in the mirror. "Hey?" She nodded, still looking at herself, and I walked in and kissed her atop the head. Still smelling her hair, I locked the front door and left.

28

The next day, she was herself again. Whatever energy was absent from her body at her duplex had once again taken up residence inside her. This time, Jenna opened the door slightly, peeking through it with a single eye, heavy with black mascara and full of blacker fire than ever. Then she opened the door wide, and her lips were painted with lipstick the color of dried blood.

"It's a full moon," she said.

"The perfect evening for a witch."

I walked in. Jenna pecked my lips and closed the door. Then she leaned her back against it, spreading her arms out as though nailed to the wall. Closing her eyes, her head hung limply on her shoulder.

"What are you doing?"

"Something else you've tossed."

"You're obsessed with that song."

"It's the story of my life."

She led me into a small dark room that was apparently the living room. There was a lone high-backed chair in the corner and a mattress in the other corner. A gray blanket was in disarray, and two pillows were stashed against the wall. Across from the mattress was the kitchen.

"Did you just move in?"

"Last year, I think. In May or June."

A black iron pot was boiling on the stovetop, wisps of steam rising over the brim. Jenna picked up an apple and shaved it.

I pulled the bottle of red from the plain brown wrapper. "I brought us some wine."

"Okay, the glasses are up there."

Opening the cupboard, I took down two coffee cups—the only items inside—turned on the sink, and ran the cups under the flowing water.

"Your sink's a mess." At the bottom were orange and apple shavings, potato skins, slices of carrots, and a small knife. I turned the water off, then shook the cups. "Is your dish towel clean?"

Jenna fed me a slice of apple. "If it's not, use one of my shirts."

"To dry your dishes?"

"If my towel is dirty, sure, why not?"

I took a Starbucks napkin out of my pocket and wiped down the cups. "You need to be careful of germs, unless you're protected against those, too." I poured the wine as Jenna watched.

"My roommate protects me."

Roommate? There was barely room in the apartment for one. "Is she here?"

"It's not a she."

"So what, you live with a guy?"

"Probably not in the sense you're thinking."

We picked up our cups. "Is your roommate transgendered?"

"That's a little closer."

I set my cup down as Jenna drank from hers. Then, taking her cup, I set it down and picked her up by the waist and walked her to the mattress, placing her gently on it and, straddling her, pinned her wrists to the bed.

135

"You're messing with me," I said.

"We are."

"You think it's funny, too."

"We do."

"By the way, you're always saying 'we'? We who?"

"I've already told you."

I slid a pillow under Jenna's head. "So is this where you two sleep?"

"Uh-huh."

I looked into her smiling eyes, then looked away. "I'm sure this gets interesting."

"Trust us, Carl, it does."

Outside, a tree branch scraped against the shuttered window, and a passing car breathed asthmatically. I looked at Jenna.

"Shouldn't you have more stuff? You're a girl. It's been my experience that girls have stuff. The ones I know would never go for this . . . monastic existence."

"Diogenes and Thoreau liked simplicity. We do, too."

"Does your roommate have any stuff?"

"Lots."

My eyes roamed to the high-backed chair, one of the few items in the room. On the purple velvet seat was a black book with gold pages. An old Panasonic stereo with a dent in the speaker lay underneath.

"How old are you?" I said.

Jenna pushed me off and went for her wine cup. "Carl, you're never supposed to ask a girl her age. Besides, I'm not like other girls."

"You've got that right."

Jenna walked to the solitary chair, picked up the book, and sat down. She set the coffee cup on the chair's arm and the book on the other arm and then looked at me with her hands on her thighs.

"Are you sitting on your throne?" I said.

"I am."

"And is that the book of life in your possession? Speak, O Protected One, and reveal to me the mysteries of your deep, hidden knowledge."

She slid off the chair and crawled toward me with a familiar carnal grin. "You want mysteries? We'll show you mysteries, doubter boy."

Jenna slid off my condom and threw it on the brown carpet, next to the radio.

"I can put it in the trash," I said.

"Leave it."

She wedged a cigarette into her dark red mouth and, sparking the lighter to life, snuggled into me. "How's your philosophy program? Are you planning to be average or something bigger, like a star?"

A star. A philosophy star. I watched the side of Jenna's nose light up in the cigarette's glow. "Who doesn't want to be one of those?"

"That's what you want to be—a star?"

"It'd be nice."

"So why don't we begin your journey to stardom?"

A White Stripes song came on the radio as we lay under the thin gray sheet. The song was in a minor key, slow, and dreary—the sound of impending doom.

"What do I have to do?" I said.

"First, you must listen for the voice."

"And to whom does this voice belong?"

Jenna slowly let out smoke. "The Man."

I sat up. Jenna did, too. "The Man?"

"Do you want to meet him?"

This was getting a little creepy, or it would be if it weren't all superstition and posturing. But I decided to play along. "Is he the one who gives powers and protects you?" When Jenna didn't answer, I took the cigarette and pushed it into an empty beer can, then climbed on top of Jenna as she giggled and tried to push me away.

"You're a superstitious freak," I said. "But I like it, I really do. It's kind of hot, actually. I get to tell my colleagues at school about my psychologically unstable girlfriend. It's common for grad students to have those, you know. It's a rite of passage."

We wrestled and laughed out loud, our bodies slithering snake-like in the sheet, until I climbed on her and held her wrists securely to the mattress. Jenna smiled.

"So what happens after I meet the Man?"

"Then you go from Carl to Snarl."

I bowed my head. What are this girl's parents like? Not your typical Nebraskans, either, I bet. "So what, I'm going to become a wild animal?"

"You might like it."

"I'd rather leave a mark in academia, a legacy, something that makes me more than the average philosopher. So, the Man can help me?"

Jenna pulled her hands free and yanked me down by the neck, as though a gigantic weight were around it. "He'll do anything you ask."

*   *   *

Inside the bathroom, I washed my hands and dried them on my pant legs, then quietly opened up the medicine cabinet. There was nothing inside, just the rusty outlines of bottles on the shelves left by a previous tenant.

"Are you okay, Snarl?"

Closing the cabinet, I looked in the mirror at my growing hair and the black rings around my eyes. For the first time, it occurred to me to ask if I was okay.

"Are you getting ready for your big meeting?" Jenna said.

When I opened the door, Jenna was leaning against the wall in a light brown bathrobe, hands in pockets, with one big breast dangling out.

"Well?" she said.

I pulled the robe shut and tied the belt. "Why the hell not? This stuff's bullshit anyway. But if it happens to work, all the better. So yes, I'm ready to meet the Man."

29

It was after that when I began to see the faces. Evil faces, funny looking faces, and sad faces began to appear throughout the day.

The first time was in my cell. I stood in the kitchen in the dying light of day, cutting a long jalapeno on a plate. The blade split the pepper apart, and I saw an evil-looking face, just for a moment, in the white, seedy insides. Days later, a funny-looking face stared back at me from the square of sunlight on my cell's wall. And during my ethics seminar, I looked up at the rain-soaked skylight when a skeleton's face appeared with a big, goofy grin.

There were noises, too. Sometimes I'd wake up after midnight and would hear strange noises in my brain, like the shake of a rattlesnake's tail, only louder and darker and infinitely more deadly. As I lay in bed, I'd also smell sulfur and would check the oven to make sure the gas knobs were off.

By November, the days grew shorter and colder. My energy for my studies began to wither away as well. I spoke up less and less in my seminars, and when I'd teach my undergraduates, I'd walk into the lecture hall sleepy and cranky, and would show clips on YouTube, letting other professors do the teaching for me. I just sat in the back row, arms crossed and my eyes closed, taking stock of the changes in my personality, my physical appearance.

I was also spending more and more time at Jenna's duplex. It would be fair to say my only companions were Jenna, the funny-looking faces, and the otherworldly noises.

Then the visions began. There were many but one of them stood out. I was lecturing on Immanuel Kant, when a thick nasty black smoke seemed to fill the room. A dozen pink pigs, tails curled into dollar signs, hovered over the lecture hall and began to pee on my students' heads. But it wasn't urine that was coming out, it was gasoline. Then a huge pig with a cigar in its mouth lit a match with its tail and, dropping it, set my students ablaze.

I realized the lecture hall was filled with silence. I'd stopped speaking and the students, not one of them aflame, were staring at me. I shook my head and started again.

Minutes later there was another vision: pigs floating over a farmyard, like big pink hairy balloons, squealing obscenely and excreting on the green pastures, killing the swans in the pond and the baby lambs on the hillsides. When that vision ended, my students were gaping at me. I had the impression I may have been making incoherent noises.

After class, Rob approached the lectern. "Hey, man, are you okay?"

"It's called a heavy workload, plus insomnia. You'll understand when you get to grad school."

Later on at the hotel, I walked into the bell closet. Avery lowered the computer's screen, and I felt his gaze as I stood at the uniform rack.

"You were with Jenna last night."

"I was."

"What, did you screw her five times?"

"I did."

"Damn, she's putting the miles on you. You'll be an old man soon."

I unbuttoned my shirt. "She's the one with the miles on her. She's got thousands on that engine. I'd say it's been rebuilt. That girl knows exactly what to do, when, where, and for how long."

Avery set the computer aside. "I heard she's got the sucking power of an industrial vacuum cleaner."

"She must've started at an early age, especially with a technique like that."

Later I saw Quentin in the garage. I pulled up to the ticket booth, but he stayed inside, hiding behind the door with half of his moustache visible.

"Sweet Jesus," he said. "You look like you aged ten years."

I yawned. "Busy week."

"You been dating that girl."

"How'd you know?"

"You're gettin' that look, and if you ain't careful, you gon' be walking round town like a zombie, looking as lost as lost can be. Or worse."

That weekend, Jenna pulled her disappearing act again, and I stayed inside my cell. I didn't answer my phone, my students' emails, or even my door when Rich or Bubba knocked, demanding entry and wanting to party. And since I was too tired to cook, I ordered Nero's Pizza, letting my dishes pile up in the sink. It was nobody but me, alone with my books and the funny-looking faces, the heater on, trying to get warm.

On Sunday night, Dr. Parsons sent me a message. Could he and I please touch base before Thanksgiving break? He had fabulous news.

The next morning, the BFU campus shuttle picked me up at the Guardian. Along for the ride were several East Coast businessmen who had flown in for a campus visit. They sat in the back rows, dark-blue suits and sunglasses on, reading *Forbes* and the *Wall Street Journal*.

After class, I waited in the union for Dr. Parsons. The food court was a cultural hub where half a dozen foreign languages could be heard on a good day. I watched the STEM buildings grow bigger and taller, like spaceships taking off in the sky. When the sun through the windows began to hurt my eyes, I looked away to the other side of campus at the humanities buildings, old and crumbly-looking, in need of repair or resurrection, especially Bryan Hall.

Then I saw Dr. Parsons walking toward the union. Three dark-suited men were on his right, two BFU administrators on his left. The six men entered the quad as I held my fork to my lips, watching. After the men shook hands by the lagoon, Dr. Parsons walked robotically into the union, briefcase in hand.

"Hello, Carl."

"Hi, Dr. Parsons."

"I'm so excited about us having a coffee or, in my case, a tea."

"Me, too."

We got our drinks then sat down, and he fell into standard small talk. Was I enjoying my fall? How was being a teaching assistant? Had I run into any problems in class?

"Just medieval philosophy," I said. "Three lectures of nearly all superstition. God, what a chore."

"I wrapped up the age of faith in one lecture. No need to spend such precious class time on God, angels and demons, and other sideshows."

"Amen to that."

Dr. Parsons chuckled. "You're funny, Carl." He crossed his legs and looked out the window at the STEM project. "On a more modern and therefore relevant note, Peter and I are excited about our upcoming trip to England. We're hoping to purchase a lovely countryside church in which to spend our summers. I'll conduct research while Peter sells airline tickets and cruise packages."

"Sounds great."

We talked about his upcoming trip; about the scholars he'd meet at Oxford, including Richard Dawkins; and the lectures he'd attend, including one by Don Cupitt, an Anglican priest who was also an atheist. When our cups were almost empty, Dr. Parsons rolled his cup between his manicured fingers.

"Carl, would you mind teaching another section of philosophy in the spring? It would be a tremendous help. You'd also be building up your teaching resume. Search committees love to see teaching experience on an application."

"I'd love to."

"Super. This is going to work out for both of us. In the meantime, have a swell break and get some rest. You look frazzled."

30

Jenna texted me the following Wednesday, and I was at her door that evening. She opened it wearing a Halloween mask—a big-eyed skull with a creepy-looking smile. It was hauntingly familiar.

"Boo," she said.

"Take that off."

"Hi, Carl."

"Halloween's over."

Jenna put her arms around my waist, and I looked down into the skeleton's peepers where Jenna's eyes, cold and dead looking, gazed up into mine.

"I'm sorry, I'm not feeling so good," I said. "I just want to watch you paint or listen to you talk about yourself for once. Is that okay? Just tell me one thing about your life. None of this dodging the bullet stuff."

Jenna pulled down on my neck as her feet lifted up off the ground. She kissed me, and I tasted the skeleton's teeth.

"You're the one who has three silver bullets," she said.

"Excuse me?"

"Three. Silver. Bullets."

"So we're playing this game again?"

"We fight fair."

Fight fair? I looked into the skeleton's eyes. "Yeah. Whatever. Okay. Sure."

She showed me a painting. A young woman in a black vinyl bra and underwear with knee-high black boots, the kind Jenna wore. A gigantic lion cowered in the corner, away from her, its jaws bared. The girl's mouth roared wider than the lion's, her arm raised high, whip in hand.

"Ready for show and tell?"

"Whenever you are." I looked at my phone, and when I stashed it, Jenna was holding a whip by its cherry-red handle. "Where did you get that?"

"Okay, ask about my painting."

"I'd rather know about the whip."

"At Dr. John's. Now ask."

I looked at Jenna, who was still wearing the Halloween mask, and then over at the painting of a whip-wielding girl, towering above a male lion that was cowering in the corner, its mouth open in anger.

"The girl in the painting is you," I said.

"You're warm."

"It's a fantasy you've had."

"Even warmer."

I put my hands atop the chair. "You've had this fantasy for some time, too."

"You're getting hot."

I touched my forehead, throbbing in pain. "I don't know. A lion tamer?"

Jenna tore off the mask, and small, barely-burning fires seemed to burn in both her eyes. I wasn't sure if I was really seeing it, or if it was no more real than the pigs.

"You're on fire," she said.

I sat down in the high-backed chair as Jenna looped the spool of leather around my neck.

"That's what you want to be?" I said.

"We'll both be lion tamers."

"Where'd you get this idea? Nebraska has bison. Or buffalo. Or whatever."

She straddled my knees, pulling on the whip, so that our noses touched. It was suddenly very quiet. She whispered, "I've seen a lion."

"At the Omaha Zoo?"

She shook her head.

"Or maybe your invisible friend showed you a lion?"

Jenna tugged playfully on the whip, our foreheads bumping.

"Jesus, stop that." I raised the leather spool off my head and put it around hers. "So your invisible friend showed you a lion? What's his name—the Man?" Jenna bit down on her lips, and I squeezed her waist. "He showed you a lion, right?" I squeezed harder, bear hugging her.

She laughed. "Yes!"

I let go as she caught her breath. "I can only imagine what your other paintings are about."

Jenna got up, slipped off the whip from around her neck, and took my hand. "I thought you'd never ask. Follow me."

In the back bedroom, half a dozen paintings in frames were propped up against the wall. Each painting was of a solitary girl in a small windowless room. All of the girls were naked, and their heads were bowed, as if they were crying or helpless.

"Those are . . . interesting," I said.

She began turning them toward the wall. "Those will come later, on Thanksgiving, when you meet the Man."

On a green folding table, I noticed several Barbies standing in various poses. All of them were topless and had arms and legs missing. One was beheaded. And all of them had weapons in hand. Crowbars and butcher knives, chainsaws and two-by-fours.

"You're thirty-three and have a doll collection?" I picked up a blonde doll that was holding a long knife. "I didn't know they made psycho Barbies."

"They don't. Those are homegrown."

"So you put the knife in her hand?"

"Uh-huh." Jenna took the doll from me. "It's for good luck. Religious idiots have various objects on their tables and nightstands. We do, too."

We sat down at the table, and I looked around the room. "Okay, so what's the birdcage for if you have no birds?"

"It's for Jodie." Jenna extended the doll's hand. "Say hi, Jodie."

"The birdcage is for the doll?"

"Uh-huh." Jenna began to comb Jodie's hair. "She likes it in there, especially at night when I tuck her in."

I shut my eyes as the comb ripped through Jodie's hair. Even though I knew it was plastic, it sounded painful. "What else does Jodie like to do?"

"Hmm, let's see. She listens to my secrets. And, um, she can change into something else besides a doll."

I opened my eyes. "Like?"

Jenna braided the doll's hair. "Anything. A snake, a dog, a pig—"

"A pig?" I said. "Why does Jodie become a pig?"

"Why don't you ask her?"

"No thanks. Have you two been friends for long?"

"Ever since I was little."

I drummed my fingers on the table. This was getting a little weird, even for Jenna. "You two are perfect for each other."

"Can you guess what else she likes?"

"I'll pass." I held two fingers to my temple, then closed my eyes. "Look, I'm getting a headache, so let's call it a night. Oh, and if we ever go out in public, don't mention Jodie to my friends, okay?"

When I stood up, Jenna did too. She pushed her nose into mine, giggling like a child, and I felt the stab of Jodie's knife in my lower back.

"Hey, that hurts."

Jenna backed up, then held up the noose of Jodie's blonde hair to her eye and looked at me. She winked.

"I'm serious," I said. "This is embarrassing."

"Jodie's good at reminding me of things."

"Good. Tell that doll not to forget, all right?" Then I swiped up my coat, kissed Jenna, and left.

31

It was all over the news—a blizzard was sweeping over the Great Plains. In town, the Sun Mart was packed with people stocking before the storm hit. Paul had invited me to Thanksgiving dinner at his parents' house, as did Quentin, but I opted for dinner at Jenna's, after which I'd meet the Man.

On Thursday, the snow began to fall. I stood in the hotel's lobby watching the snowflakes simply drop in straight lines. By three o'clock, hardly a car was on the road.

When I entered the bell closet, Avery sat slouched in a covered wagon, legs stretched out, hands atop his stomach, eyes heavy with sleep.

"There's food in the kitchen," he said.

"I'm going to Jenna's."

"Damn, you're still laying pipe in that?"

"I'm surprised, too. From everything I've heard, she should have killed me by now."

"Give her time."

When I stepped outside, a Nero's pizza car drove soundlessly by. I was standing next to a flowerless pot, tucking in my scarf, when a man appeared in the street, looking lost.

"Excuse me," he said. "I was hoping you could give me a ride to the homeless shelter."

It was the old man with the army jacket and a bedroll strapped to his back. His ungloved hands were atop a knotted cane, and a Jewish prayer shawl was draped over his head like a shroud.

Pulling on my other glove, I stepped into the street, watching the old man's eyes, burning like blue flames.

"First of all, sir, get out of the street. Second, you have to be a hotel guest to get a shuttle ride. I told you that before." As I led him by the elbow to the curb, I nearly lost my footing and swore silently.

"Thank you," he said, catching his breath. His eyes were blue and cabalistic, and he looked kindly into mine. "The homeless shelter, I was wondering if—"

"I'll call a cab. Or maybe Avery can take you, but I doubt he's up for it."

The beggar looked at his hands. "I was hoping you could take me." The ends of the prayer shawl lifted up, while he shouldered a lime-green backpack, torn and stained from decades of travel.

"Avery will call you a cab. He's the tall, dorky-looking guy. He might even dish some food up for you, since we've got extra. Goodnight, sir, and happy Thanksgiving."

Long cords of blue snow whipped me like lashes, driving me onward to Jenna's duplex. The Sower stood invisibly in the gray, grainy sky and the squirrels sniffed about the oaks at the Governor's mansion, dimly lit under the torch-shaped street lamps. Moving deeper into a residential neighborhood, I passed by a white plank fence, when a German shepherd appeared, jumping and yelping as it went.

I stopped. "What's wrong, bud?"

The dog pushed its long snout through the planks, and I knelt to pet its head, its pink tongue warm on my face, doggie breath billowing out. Grabbing the collar, I looked at the tags.

"Hi, Beast. Did you have a nice Thanksgiving meal? I hope it was as good as mine's going to be."

Beast backed away and sat on his haunches and let go a volley of ear-splitting barks.

"You mean you didn't get any dinner? I'll bring you a slice of turkey, a scoop of stuffing, and some mashed potatoes. You'll be a happy camper."

Beast ran to the corner of the yard, looking south, ears perked up, barked loudly, and then looked at me.

"You look like the German shepherd in *The Hills Have Eyes* movies. His name was Beast, too. He killed those two cannibals, Mercury and Pluto. Pushed them right over a cliff." Beast trotted back to me, and I rubbed the base of his ears as he licked my cheek harder. "Did you get to meet Wes Craven, too? Good ole Wes. Okay, Beast, I'm out. Talk to you later."

The farther down the street I got, the louder Beast's barks got. When I looked back, the dog lay on his side. Then Beast looked up, let out a painful bark, and then lay his head down and was still.

Jenna opened the door. Between her teeth was a circle of hard red candy. She closed her lips and opened them repeatedly.

"Look, a Life Saver," she said.

"That's nice." I kissed her cheek, warm and perfumed, and then walked in. "I didn't know they made fire-flavored Life Savers."

"They don't. Jenna's teeth smashed down hard on the candy and the pieces began to rattle in her mouth. With my back against the door, I could feel the gusts of wind pounding against the wood.

"A white fishnet dress? Is that your formal attire?"

"For you."

"It sounds like we're getting married."

Jenna took my hands in hers, and I could smell the fire flavor on her breath.

"We are."

32

I dished up the food—Swanson turkey and stuffing TV dinners—then filled two gold goblets, bought at Goodwill, with wine. Then I stared at Jenna over the candles.

"We're eating together, Carl."

"That's what we planned."

"We're in solidarity."

"Nothing gets by you."

Jenna picked up a carving knife and leered at her reflection in the long blade. "We're not going to pray, are we?"

"I used to take prayer seriously. These days, though, I pray like Bart Simpson does." And in a nasal voice, I said, "Rub-a-dub-dub, God, thanks for the grub."

"Oh, Carl. That's perfect."

We ate, we chewed, and we swallowed. The lines of wax dribbled down the candles as we drank liberally from our goblets.

"Do you ever go home for Thanksgiving?" I said to fill the silence.

"Oh, sometimes." Jenna picked up her goblet and drank.

"Do your parents live in Nebraska?"

She nodded.

"In town?"

Jenna shook her head, still sipping.

I had never gotten this much information from her before and decided to push my luck. "What do they do?"

Jenna set the goblet down and stared at it.

"Do you go home to see them much?" I said before she withdrew entirely.

Jenna spooned up her potatoes and a huge pile went splat on my plate. "Eat."

I looked at my plate as steam rose from it, more interested in digesting the information I'd just gotten from her than the food. So she didn't go home much. Why? Poking a hole in the new batch of potatoes, I poured the gravy in, then looked up. "What does your dad do?"

Jenna had a hard time swallowing, then took a big drink and looked beyond me to the window. "Oh, look at the pretty snow. I wonder how long the blizzard will last?"

I drank from my goblet. I needed to stay on her, keep her talking. Leaning over my plate, I said, "What's your dad do?"

Jenna dropped her eyes. She lowered her fork and poked at a corn kernel so that the juice oozed out.

"My dad?" she said. "Hmm, I don't know. He's done lots of things."

"What's his name?"

Jenna mumbled something.

"Speak up."

"Lyman. His name is Lyman."

"Are you sure you're not related to John McMaster, the famous theologian?"

Slowly, Jenna looked up, and her eyes were dull and lusterless, like a reptile's. She threw her napkin on the table. "Do you want more wine? Because I want more wine."

When she returned, she picked up a strip of white turkey with her fingers and gnawed on it.

"So, Carl," she said. "Tell me what you did this week. Be specific."

Same old situation. I went through the motions, saying I was a graduate student and that my week was no different than the week before—reading, writing, and lots of stress.

When we were finishing our meal, Jenna placed a Life Saver in my hand.

"Desert." Then she held her own piece of candy to her eye, peering at me through its small hole. "Hi, Carl."

"No pumpkin pie?"

"Take and eat." She put the candy on her tongue as though it was a communion wafer, and after a few uneasy seconds had passed, I placed mine on my tongue, too.

As Jenna cleared the table, I sat in the high-backed chair, sucking on the red, spicy candy.

"So where's your invisible friend?" I said

"Running errands."

"Doing what?"

"Oh, you know. Things."

"Such as?"

Jenna shrugged. "Just things. He comes and goes as he pleases."

Outside, I could hear a car stuck in the snow. The wheels spun fast, then stopped. A car door opened and shut.

"It's a good thing you don't go out much," I said. "This dungeon of a duplex is perfect for you. Fishnets, lion taming, killer Barbies, and eating only the fire-flavored Life Savers. Remember what I said about us going out in public together? I meant that."

Jenna wiped off the counter with a T-shirt and dried her hands with it. "All done."

"Were you listening?"

"Uh-huh."

"Okay, good. Now tell your friend to hurry up. I've got homework to do."

Jenna stepped into the restroom, and a slab of yellow light pulsated on the carpet from under the door. Across from the bathroom was another door, halfway open, apparently to a closet. I reached in, found a string, and tugged.

A light bulb went on, and a pyramid of shoe boxes appeared on the floor. On the top box, I read my name, written teasingly in what looked like purple eyeliner. Slowly, I lifted up the lid and there, at the bottom, were the yellow papers. My file.

What the hell?

Below my box were more with other names, Chris Fisher and Bobby Long. When I picked up Bobby's box, I felt the blood passing through my heart.

The box beneath it was labeled "Kenny Winslow."

"There's a chair in my studio, Carl," she said from inside the bathroom. "Go sit down."

When Jenna appeared, I was sitting at the Barbie table as she flattened out the sides of her dress, looking pretty.

"I'm ready for the tour of your artwork," I said.

"I know you are, Mr. Man."

She showed me the first painting. In the Garden of Eden, a snake was crawling down a tree and swallowing Adam's head.

"A little over-the-top," I said, "but if that's what you're going for, you've succeeded."

The next painting was of Cain roasting his brother Abel over a campfire. Jenna turned from side to side, admiring her work. "Cain didn't like his brother."

"I guess not. Next."

In the third painting, an Egyptian woman held a small baby in a basket of reeds, the Nile River sparkling behind them.

"Pharaoh's daughter and baby Moses," I said.

"Try again."

I leaned in, then backed up. "That's not baby Moses in the basket. That's Satan."

"Isn't he adorable?"

The little Satan had a smirk on his face, thrilled to be going for a basket ride. "Are all of your paintings of this nature?"

"They are."

In the next painting, Jezebel was dumping a silver pail of hog slop into a trough, while a row of prophets knelt down on all fours, like pigs. The title was "The Troughets."

"Was this your idea?"

"The Man contributed, too."

"Let's take an intermission."

"Not yet."

Other paintings followed, all of them taking Hebrew traditions and turning them inside out, mocking them. As a reader of Nietzsche, I could appreciate the value of mocking religion, but this . . . the Israelites were in the Sinai desert having an orgy; King David was performing oral sex on his friend Jonathan; and Jezebel, a wicked Israelite queen, sword in hand, stood above the prophets Elijah and Elisha, both of them bound, blindfolded and kneeling on the temple floor, ready to die. There was genuine malice behind the paintings that tied them to the traditions as much as the deepest belief. Nietzsche had mocked religion to free men and women from it. These painting were revenge.

"There's more, too," she said.

"You mean the New Testament?"

"You'll love it."

As I might have guessed, each painting mocked a parable or a teaching of Jesus. Soon she showed me the Last Supper. There, at a table, in the middle of Jesus' disciples, a big red beast stood out obscenely, hands spread out, eyes bulging, with chunks of bloody meat hanging loosely from its fangs.

"Okay, stop the tour."

"It's over."

"A parody is one thing but this is . . . sacrilege."

"I thought you didn't believe in this stuff. Don't the Harvard students say that religion is, like, so passé?"

I got up and cupped her shoulders and turned her slowly around. "Look, I don't believe in religion anymore. It's bullshit. But the Bible helped to inspire and build Western civilization, plus there are two billion Christians on earth."

"Words, words, words." Jenna plunked down on a chair and picked up a razor blade and then a piece of wood shaped like a zebra. "It's not my fault if you can't have any fun."

"Most people wouldn't call it fun. They'd call it . . . well, evil. Most people—"

"How can there be evil if there's no God?" Jenna turned away from me and began to shave the zebra.

"Because people try to hurt each other for their own pleasure, which is evil enough for me. Were the Nazis evil? Hell, yes. Were Charles Manson and the 9/11 hijackers evil? You bet. Even if there's no God, there can still be naturalistic accounts of evil. Have you read John Stuart Mill or Kai Nielsen?"

Jenna brushed some wood shavings off her thighs and blew on them. When a penknife caught my eye, I realized how to make Jenna acknowledge the reality of evil. Fast.

I scooped up the knife and lunged at her. But when I raised it above my head, ready to bring it down in a mock murder, the weapon fell to the floor as though an invisible force had pried it from my hand.

Jenna blew on the zebra and then looked at me. "So. Now that we've had our tour, are you ready to meet the Man?"

33

I saw the Man, though I didn't meet him. I don't think. The memories are a little vague.

After the knife had fallen to the floor, I continued to argue with Jenna about evil, poking holes in her logic and even defending the Christian tradition, just for old time's sake, when the Man appeared in the corner of the room. He seemed to appear out of nowhere. He was tall and lanky, clad in a black suit and a black nineteenth-century preacher's hat. His hair was long and bleached bone white, and his smile matched Jenna's exactly. As I watched him, I felt my eyes grow bigger and bigger as he seemed to be walking on air and, unable to speak, I said with my eyes "Go away."

And he did. The Man just fizzled out of sight.

I left the duplex twenty minutes later, and when I got home, I locked my door and sat at my desk, cold and afraid, wondering what I'd just seen in her bedroom—if the Man was real or not. I was afraid I might be going crazy, but in a strange way I was also hoping for it. It was easier to believe that I was having hallucinations than that . . . something like that might actually exist.

Next day, I called Quentin and told him what happened.

"I told you she's batshit crazy," he said.

"She wasn't the problem. It looked human one moment and demonic the next. I couldn't draw a bead on it, because it was constantly changing."

"Be there at five. We gon' talk."

At five o'clock, a rusty orange Silverado roared into the Ghetto, its engine growling in front of the Guardian, and

Quentin waved me inside the cab. Twenty minutes later, we pulled off the main country road and onto the wet gravel driveway of Quentin's parents' ranch house. A row of deer antlers lined the sides of the gravel road leading up to the garage. Over the stubbled slopes sticking up through the snowmelt, the silos and water towers of the next town over were mute and black under a pink–cotton candy sky. We got out and walked up to the screened-in porch, the floor of which was covered with wood shavings.

"Excuse the mess," Quentin said. "Been teaching my boy how to whittle. Tucker's damn near carved up the barn and the house. His mama ain't too happy, but what you gon' do, right? He's a boy."

We opened a six-pack. On the barbecue, the flames leaped up high through the black iron grill, sizzling a pair of big, juicy steaks.

"It don't surprise me that she's friends with spirits," Quentin said. "One time she parked on the side of the hotel and went in, and I went over and stuck my head in the bus. Know what she got on the front seat? A book on witchcraft." Quentin swigged his beer and wiped his moustache. "Sounds like that book she got works. So the spirit you saw had big, smiling eyes, like hers?"

"Their smile was the same, too. And he wore a suit as though attending a church service or a wedding."

A warm wind blew through the screen, carrying with it the chill of snow, while the late November stars dropped one by one into the sky.

"Hope you got the sense to stay away from her now. I know you in graduate school, but that don't mean you got any sense."

When dinner was ready, we tore at the steaks, gobbled up the potatoes, the green beans, the rolls of wheat bread, the green salad, and, most surprising of all, bull balls—strips of skin off a bull's testicles, deep fried and smothered in ranch dressing. Rocky Mountain oysters.

Quentin twisted off the cap of another beer. "So you were talking 'bout a special meeting?"

"Jenna kept asking if I wanted to meet her roommate, the Man."

"And you obviously said yes?"

"Yeah. She said he could do stuff for me, like keep me from being an average academic."

"So?"

"What can I say, I want to be respected in my field. Plus, I don't want to be an adjunct forever. Jenna said my worries would be over, but only after a special meeting with the Man. I thought . . . I don't know. It was half humoring a crazy person, half hope."

Quentin looked away into the utter darkness of the barn lot. Semis whistled by far away on the interstate, and the Sower's red light blinked above the ribbon of light above town.

"Your girl was setting you up. Bet you ten horses that this Man fella is the one who gets them dudes she dates screwed up."

I told him about the lion tamer, the fishnets, the Barbie collection, and the shoe boxes in the closet pyramided against the wall.

"There was another box, too," I said, pushing my plate aside. "Guess whose name was on it? God, I can't believe I forgot to tell you. Kenny's box was under my box."

"Kenny Winslow? You sure you wasn't seeing things?"

"It was Kenny's, I swear. She had something to do with him, with his death."

Quentin got up slowly and walked to the porch screen. He took a gulp of beer as the warm breeze blew in.

"Reminds me of a story when we were kids," he said. "Selling your soul to the devil."

The legs of my chair hit the deck.

"You can't believe that stuff nowadays."

"Why not?"

"The devil? Old Scratch? What century are we living in?"

"Look, just because a belief is old don't make it false. And you saw something in there, didn't you?"

I realized that any hope that I was hallucinating was long gone. And while I wasn't willing to admit that what I'd seen was the classic red-suited, horned devil of Faust and Daniel Webster . . . what I had seen was something.

"Now if Jenna's dealing with the devil," Quentin said, "and if Kenny was dating Jenna, we got ourselves a story."

Betsy, Quentin's wife, pushed open the screen door and cleared the table, while Tucker appeared in blue bib overalls, small hands curled into binoculars.

"She was setting you up," Quentin said. "Jenna starts something and the Man finishes it. Maybe all of them shoe box dudes made their own deals with the devil. Wouldn't surprise me if they did. Not only does she got a shoe box for you, she's planning on putting you in a bigger box. A pine box. So count your blessings, partner, cuz you got out just in time."

I couldn't deny I had a sense of relief, of a near escape. But I still had to know.

What exactly had I gotten out of?

34

Quentin and I were quiet in the truck on the drive back to town. I was too busy connecting the dots—of my encounters with Jenna, to my vision of the Man, to Kenny Winslow's mysterious death.

I was also slowly becoming conscious of how much I had been shirking my duties as a teacher and a student. Whatever had been happening had kept me wrapped up good. When I mentioned this to Quentin, he told me to hang tough, that it wasn't unusual for graduate students to have a few rough semesters, especially with the demands and uncertainty about their future. He said he'd had one himself.

Before dropping me off at the Blue Note, I asked him what he'd majored in. It wasn't what I expected.

Philosophy. Not only that, but he'd been to graduate school, also in philosophy. I told him he was lying, to which he replied he didn't believe in lying, since he was a Kantian. He said we'd talk more later on, especially about why he dropped out and moved back to Nebraska to go to trade school to become a welder. He'd tell me all about that, too, once I got all of my horses saddled, he said.

I opened the Silverado's door and got out.

"Need you a drink, huh?"

"Or three."

"Gon' be thinking 'bout Jenna all night?"

"My weird girlfriend apparently wants me dead. How could I not?"

Inside the Blue Note, Tony stood behind the bar watching the president on TV, and I eased into a booth by the front door.

I studied my reflection in the window. I was tired and scared-looking in the dark glass.

Tony set down a large screwdriver without being asked. "You look like you've seen a ghost."

"You said a lot of the football players came in here. Do you know which ones?"

"Sheesh, the last time you were talking about philosophy and the truth. Now football? It looks like Nebraska is growing on youse. But yeah, lotsa players came into the bar."

"Did you ever see Kenny Winslow?"

"Sure did. Kid used to sit right where you're sitting now. Same booth. Same spot. He'd watch alla them girls walk by. He used to say with a grin, 'Those gals are so hot they could melt ice caps.'"

"Did he ever bring any of the hot girls into the bar?"

"Oh, sure."

"What'd they look like?"

Tony rubbed the back of his neck and squinted his eyes. "Gee, I don't know. They were all good looking, nines and tens. But one of them gals was an eleven. She was the first one I seen him with, too. Good looking gal. Great looking gal."

"What'd she look like? Specifically."

"On the shorter side with black hair and blacker eyes. They were alive, her eyes. And when I seen those two in this booth, it was a conversation you wouldn't dare walk in on. It was like he was asking her to marry him. Or vice versa. All the time."

A young man walked into the bar. He wore a denim jacket with a patch emblazoned on the back and tipped his fedora in greeting.

"So how come you're so interested in Kenny Winslow all of a sudden? You need to focus on school. That's what you're here for. The big degree."

I poked at an ice cube. "I hear you on that. I just got a little distracted."

"Easy to do. Lotsa guys say that, especially the grad students."

Up on the stage, the man in the fedora plugged in a guitar cable, and buzzing and static came through the public-address system. I could sense Tony watching me and he wagged the dish rag at me saying, "But something tells me you ain't gonna do it. You ain't leaving Kenny Winslow alone. I could tell youse til I'm blue in the face to forget alla this, but you ain't leaving this alone and that's the truth."

35

Then it was summer in December. The lagoon on campus was full of green water, while the mammoths were brown and shiny in the sun. Throughout the afternoon, the students climbed the prehistoric rocks to study in the dry heat of an Indian summer, while a male reporter from *The Mammoth* spoke to girls sunning on the sand, their phones raised up to block the sun's glare.

I sat by the lagoon, back at work again, drafting my papers for my metaphysics, epistemology, and ethics seminars. A street preacher had come into the quad wearing a sandwich-board sign over his chest with a list of sins hand-painted on it in red. The onlookers watched him with amusement but soon got up and left.

I typed away, cutting and pasting on my laptop, making my papers lean and mean and readable for a general audience. Men in hard hats with hammers hanging from their belts walked to the union, discussing the features in the new dorms: video game rooms, a Ping-Pong table, and a putting green for the golfers.

Any study lounges? Farewell to deep reading and concentration. I listened to the pounding of hammers and the whirring of drills, wondering if, by the time the renovation was complete, any students would care about philosophy.

The street preacher was almost shouting when Dr. Parsons walked onto the quad, black gym bag in one hand, in the other a briefcase with a gold symbol winking in the black leather—an eye in a triangle. He stopped next to me at the lagoon's edge and inhaled the strong, fresh air.

"My oh my, what a fabulous day to work out, and so off to the gym I go."

"It's nice, isn't it?"

"And what a beautiful new addition we have to our campus, is it not? Enrollment is on the rise. Soon you'll have bigger classes to teach—and more tuition to draw pay from."

I stared at the eye in the triangle; it looked as if it was from a lost Near Eastern civilization.

"Oh, and speaking of class, I've assigned Robert Loisy to be your grading assistant in the spring. I'm sure you'll find Robert's services to be an asset. And if you ever happen to be on the tenure track, you'll want to enlist the help of anybody you can, be it an undergraduate, a graduate student, or an adjunct. Remember, Carl, it's publish or perish in our field, so frame that motto on your door. It's a long, hard road to tenure."

When Dr. Parsons left, I mused over his last words. It was true. Whatever I'd seen at Jenna's, whatever it meant, I couldn't deal with it now. I had to clear away anything that could keep me from a tenure-track job. After I debated myself about it, I finally wrote Jenna a letter.

Dear Jenna,

Something freaked me out at your place the other night. I don't know if I saw a ghost, a demon, or if my brain was acting funny. Whatever the case is, it's best if we take a break from each other. I've got a big semester coming up, and I've got to stay focused.

I'll end by saying that if demons do exist—which is a big *if*—then you might want to sever your ties with them. Just hang out with your Barbies, instead. ☺

See you around,
Carl

Back in town, I slid the note into Jenna's mailbox and put my ear to the door. Silence. After a coffee at the Loft, I arrived at my cell and found a note on my door.

Dear Confused Carl,

The "demon" you saw in my room was the last trace of the conservative theology you once believed in. You expelled it. That's another thing you've tossed and need to forget. Don't you feel cleansed? No more conservative theology in Carl's life. So rejoice and be glad, like the stupid hymn says.

Your Crazy Big-Eyed Girl,
Jenna

I pulled the note off. "Nice interpretation, pretty girl," I said to myself. I went in and put her note on my desk, on top of the Kenny Winslow article, smeared with the dust of summer, and hammered away on my term papers.

Next day, I saw Quentin again. I handed him the note, but he wouldn't touch it. So I read it aloud. He said her reply was a smokescreen—that if Jenna was really in the service of Satan, she'd want to cover his hoof prints by trying to convince me he doesn't exist. It was one of Satan's oldest tricks.

"By the way, I seen her last night. She was at Russ' Market, talking to a bald biker on a Harley. Old biker boy looks twenty years her senior. She was just giggling and hopping up and down like daddy's little girl." Quentin strummed his guitar and a D chord rang out. "Bet she's got a shoe box for him, too."

A week passed. I submitted my term papers and my students' grades. Then I got ready to fly home for the holiday. On a cold, dark December evening, I stood in my cell, dumping my Nietzsche books into my suitcase and nursing a stiff Jack and Coke, when my thoughts suddenly turned to Jenna. What was she up to? I hadn't heard from her since our exchange of notes, though I thought of her often. I wondered if she'd thought of me. There were times at night when I'd wake up out of a deep sleep and I'd hear slow, heavy-booted footsteps in hallways of the Guardian. I'd once seen combat boots in her closet and wondered if she'd been spying on me.

Ah, let her. I hadn't worked this hard in school to be derailed by a girl, especially Jenna.

When I stepped out of the shower, I towel dried my hair in the misty bathroom when, in the medicine cabinet mirror, I saw a thick, black cloud behind me, then a human shape. A man. He was tall and lanky with a black suit and a preacher's hat.

I spun around. There, on the peg, hung my black robe. I sighed. "Just my imagination." I touched the robe's lapel. "Just my brain acting funny."

As I brushed my teeth, I kept an eye on the black robe as the thick shower of mist began to clear out of the bathroom.

Lying atop my bed, black robe on, I tried to read, but Jenna's rubber band caught my eye. I got up and unlooped it from the doorknob and lay down again, fingering the rubber band into a triangle. It seemed to have increased in pinkness. As the tonnage of a passing freight began to rattle the blinds, I got out my phone and scrolled to Jenna's number. *She loves me? She loves me not? Who knows, especially with her?* I contemplated deleting her number, then decided against it. Then, sliding the rubber band around my wrist, I texted Rob.

Have you found a senior thesis topic?
I wish.
Demon possession is huge these days.
Just saw the Emily Rose *movie with Liz. Scary.*
Ever thought of writing on it?
Pause. *Good idea.*
I'll check out some books for you on witchcraft and demon possession. Just read the pages I assign. I'll leave them at the circulation desk.
Roger.
Let's meet up in two weeks to discuss what you've read. Until then, I've got a doctorate to earn.

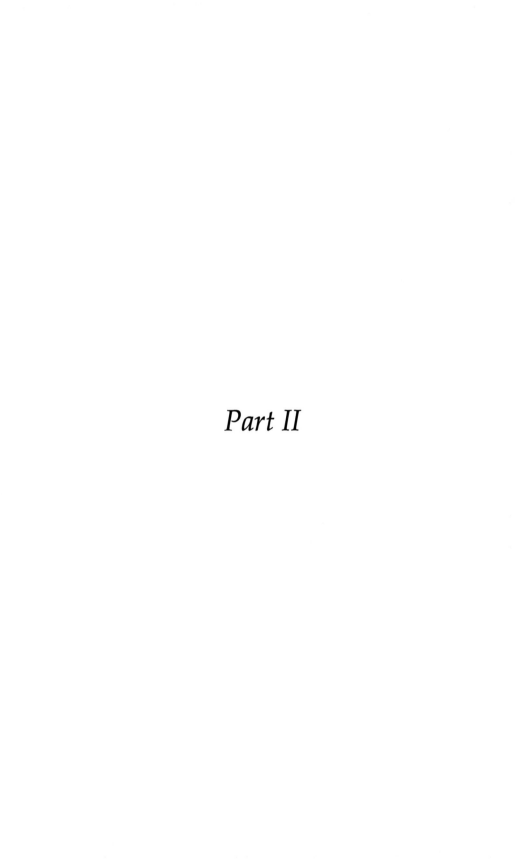

Part II

36

In early January, I flew back to Nebraska to focus on my next thirty years. Before my mom dropped me off in the city, I had been sipping Irish-creamed coffee on the sun porch, leafing through the *San Francisco Chronicle,* when a headline buried in section two caught my eye: "Locals see ghost of Kenny Winslow." I boarded the Southwest Airlines plane still thinking about Kenny. When I fell asleep on board, I dreamed of him, and when I woke up in Omaha, his presence seemed to hover above the jet as it taxied on the tarmac.

Back at my cell, I put on a country and western station and began to unpack when "Shout at the Devil," a song by Mötley Crüe, began shake the walls. Then a fist pounded on my door. I opened it.

"Bra."

"What's up, Rich? Bag any babes?"

"Lots. You?"

"I sent them your way."

"My favorite thing to hear, bra, my favorite thing to hear. Say, you still dating what's-her-face?"

"Not really."

"Scared you off, huh?"

I pressed a finger on my cell's door, still sticky from Jenna's last note. "Did Jenna stop by while I was gone?"

"If so, she was invisible."

At that point, I wouldn't have put it past her.

After dinner, I chilled at Rich's pad. Three of us guys—me, Rich, Bubba the catcher—and a tall hippie girl named Hazel kicked it on beanbag chairs and watched *American Idol.* A copy of *The Dirt*, the autobiography of Mötley Crüe, lay atop a Valentino's pizza box.

"I didn't know the Crüe had an autobiography," I said.

"Tommy Lee was in town not long ago," Hazel said. "He was, like, a student at the University of Nebraska. They've turned it into a reality TV show. Tommy even took a class with us, and we read *The Dirt*."

"In class?"

"Yeah, it was sweet."

Opening the book, I saw the four Crüe members in colorful costumes standing in front of a pentagram tapestry on the wall. "Who taught the class?"

"Eric Tanner."

I flipped through the pages. "Any good stories in it?"

Rich crushed the beer can and tossed it over his shoulder. "Just your typical rock star behavior. But there's a lot of freaky stuff too, like when the Crüe dabbled in the occult and weird shit began to happen."

Bubba smacked his catcher's mitt. "That's why they wrote 'Shout at the Devil.' It's not about worshiping the devil. It's about fighting him."

Rich blew through the TV channels and settled on watching Hannity interrogate a Muslim cleric.

I closed the book. "Can I borrow this?"

"*Mi casa es su casa*," Rich said. "You'll love it. It's the only book we didn't sell back to the bookstore."

37

A week passed. New students had moved into the Guardian, and the hallways were noisy with Keith Urban and Eric Church. I took note of the new country music. It had a different vibe than the old stuff—harder and more gritty-sounding, like 70s rock 'n' roll with a banjo or a fiddle thrown in. More shocking were the male vocalists, who looked like frat boys in black T-shirts and blue jeans with model-quality good looks.

With this commentary, I was ready to impress Quentin.

On the Sunday before the spring semester began, I cracked my cell's windows for some fresh air. As I listened to Nebraska public radio, an Italian cardinal came on the airwaves, offering a short commentary on the Pope, who'd vowed to purge the Catholic church of its liberal wing. "There will be a purer, smaller Catholic church," the Pope had said. He also had another mission: to re-evangelize Europe, which was slipping into philosophical materialism, low birth rates, civilizational exhaustion, and existential despair. God was dead in Europe, and the Pope was ready to bring its Christian culture back to life.

Later that night, Rob and I met at the Loft. He reported back on the books I'd assigned, offering me details of God throwing Lucifer out of heaven and also of Lucifer's goal on earth, which was to get revenge on God by taking as many humans to hell as he could. Then Rob spoke of the three types of demonic activity: infestation, oppression, and possession—the latter being the rarest and most dangerous.

When he finished, Rob looked up from his notebook. "Do you believe this stuff?"

"I'm ninety-eight percent sure it isn't true."

"It's all boogeyman crap. I feel like I'm seven years old."

"I'm not arguing with you."

"How come you're so interested in demon possession? If God's dead, the devil is, too."

"Good point."

I got up for a second cup of heavily creamed coffee and then confessed to Rob about Jenna.

"Oh," he said.

"Yeah. It may be boogey man stuff to you and me, but she believes it."

"Have you told Dr. Parsons about this?"

"Are you crazy?"

"Good. He'd crucify us."

We got up and put on our jackets and Rob handed me a book, *Gods' Man.* I flipped through it and scowled.

"My little niece wouldn't look at it," Rob said.

I dropped the book in my satchel and handed him *The Dirt.*

"Awesome. Tommy Lee was just in town."

"So I'm told. Find the parts on the occult and Satanism and then report back to me. I'll make it worth your while. I promise."

38

Paul had good news. He texted me that he'd learned of an adjunct position.

Interested?

You bet.

I'll tell you more tomorrow.

Pick me up at Starbucks. One of my students is a barista. Free drinks.

See, you're already thinking like an adjunct ☺

On Monday, Paul pulled up to Starbucks in a faded blue minivan. I jumped in, handing him a venti mocha. "I just saved us ten bucks."

"Nice work."

"Make every dollar last."

Driving to Sleepy Hollow, Paul told me about the adjunct gig. His friend, Eric Tanner, had gotten into an argument with the division chair, calling him a pansy and suggesting he was unnaturally close with his mother before he quit on the spot. So, suddenly there was an adjunct-sized hole in the roster.

After school, Paul drove me to Nebraska Methodist University, just north of Lincoln. Thirty minutes later, I'd landed my first adjunct gig. I was moving up, and my resume was getting longer. I immediately went to the Loft, where I typed out my syllabus and was finished in an hour, on the dot.

Next day, I told Dr. Parsons.

"Your drive and determination never cease to amaze me, Carl. Of course, you don't want to adjunct too much, especially after you earn your doctorate. Beware of the adjunct trap. With that caveat in mind, allow me to offer you my warmest congratulations."

We left the seminar room and started wandering the hallways. He told me of his holiday trip to England, the lectures he'd heard, the Indian restaurants at which he and Peter had dined, the growing Muslim population in London and elsewhere, and the empty churches for sale. The most breathtaking ones, Dr. Parsons noted, were perched atop England's dark green hills like something out of a Blake poem.

"Peter and I viewed some fabulous pieces of property, and should the stars in heaven align, we shall purchase our countryside church this summer and not a moment later. Fingers crossed."

We stopped in front of the departmental office. Dr. Parsons stood in the doorway, facing me in the entrance. He held his briefcase by the handle with both hands, while the eye in the triangle shone dimly in the gloom. "I'd love to chat more, but I must utilize my precious hour of free time at the gym. Is there something else on your mind?"

When I asked if Eric Tanner had been a doctoral student at BFU, Dr. Parsons took a slow, deep breath. "I see you are becoming acquainted with our academic culture. The person to whom you are referring is no longer a student here, nor shall I divulge to you the exact nature of his departure." He looked at me directly. "But let us content ourselves with the following truth: he has moved on and so has the department."

I fled into the stairwell. Paul was climbing up with a Kinko's box tucked under his arm like a football. When he saw me, he slowly set the box on a window ledge and, crossing his arms, rested a black boot on a step. "Wow, look at you. Those grad students can be ruthless."

"It wasn't them." I leaned against the wall as the chatter died off in the stairwell. "It was Parsons." I told Paul what happened, then pushed away from the wall. "It was a fair question," I said.

"To you, yes. To Parsons? I need to give him a copy of my dissertation, but I'll let him cool off first. In the meantime . . ."

I slid down the brick wall and sat on the landing as Paul gave me the dirt. Eric Tanner, it turned out, had once been a doctoral student at BFU but had transferred after a blowout with Parsons. Paul, who'd witnessed the event, said that Tanner had stood up at a departmental meeting and accused Parsons of chronic whining and intellectual obfuscation, not only in his published works but also in his seminars. Eric had verbally opened fire on the other faculty members, too, listing their intellectual sins. But his main target was Parsons.

"It was brutal," Paul said. "Eric was fed up with academia then, and he's even more fed up with it now. He's been an adjunct for a decade and still can't find a tenure-track job. It finally broke him. He's a great teacher and he loves Nietzsche, like us, but he's tired of rolling rocks uphill, and so he's leaving that task for others to do."

"So what's he up to now?"

"Looking for a job with the state. He's tired of being on food stamps."

39

When I got home, I forgot about Eric Tanner. A yellow note with familiar handwriting was taped to my door.

You can still be a star, you know.

I went in, ripped it up, and flushed it down the toilet.

Next day, I saw Craig, the landlord, pushing a snow blower down the walkway. He wore dark-orange coveralls and a black ski mask with a cigarette poked through the hole.

"A young lady stopped by your studio last night."

"What'd she say?"

"Not a word. Just taped a note to your door, then left." He turned the blower off and pulled the cigarette out. "Strange thing is, I'm not sure if she was real or a figment of my imagination."

"What do you mean?"

"Okay, this is weird. I walked over to the fire escape door, where she'd gone out, and the three flights of stairs were covered in snow. Not a doggone footprint."

I pulled out my box of Salems, tapped a cigarette out, then lit it. I took a long, thoughtful drag and looked across the train yard at the snow-coated pyramids of junk.

"Oh, well," Craig said. "Maybe I'm just getting old." He started up the blower, then turned it off. "Oh, and have you by chance seen a pig on the loose?"

"A pig?"

"Yeah. There are cloven hoof prints all over the back lot."

"Show me."

When we arrived, Craig dropped his cigarette in a hoof print. "I'm not imagining this, too, I hope."

A trail of cloven hoof prints began at the Guardian's back lot, crossed the train yard, and stopped at what appeared to be an opening in the largest pyramid. All of the prints were left-footed, too. I knelt down next to Craig.

"No. They're real."

"Another thing I don't get is pigs can weigh up to five hundred pounds, and these prints are half an inch deep."

A gust of wind stirred up a mist of blinding snowflakes. I shielded my eyes when, in a dark, uninhabited landscape of my mind, I felt a pounding sensation, like an army breaking through an ancient city's walls.

"I'll call animal control," Craig said. "Sometimes a farmer's pig can get on the loose. Be careful, though. Sometimes they can turn violent."

At the hotel, I took down my uniform from the rack as Avery fooled around on Facebook.

"So I'm banging this chick last night," he said, which was enough for me to tune him out. I had to. Not only was Jenna back, but also a mysterious pig was on the loose.

Avery said something that broke through and registered. "So what's new with Jenna?"

"How should I know?"

"So you two are done?"

"Since Thanksgiving, yeah."

Michael appeared in the doorway, Starbucks cup in one hand and a plate of strawberry cheesecake in the other. "Welcome back, Mr. Man. Did you enjoy a tall skinny latte for me while you were away?"

"Dozens."

"My, you look nice. You've showered, shaved, and your uniform is clean and pressed. I'm impressed. Your hair is getting long, though. I wonder what our guests think?"

And with that passive-aggressive comment, Michael disappeared into his office.

"So do I have a shot with Jenna?" Avery said.

"Who doesn't?"

"Is she experienced?"

"Times ten."

"Can I have a preview?"

I granted Avery's request.

"That's hot," he said.

"In a strange way, but what kind of girl talks like that during sex? It was darkly pleasurable but creepy as hell." I shoved my Colt .45s into a holster as Avery slid his sunglasses on. "What's so funny?"

He shouldered his backpack and lowering his shades, said, "The way she was talking? That's what happens when daddy fucks you."

40

There were only six guests checked in and they were low maintenance, so I hung out in the bell closet, studying Nietzsche's *Beyond Good and Evil*. There he spoke about "the new philosophers" who'd arrive in the future. As I wondered about what they'd be like, *Gods' Man* caught my eye and, unable to resist the temptation, I began to look through the book's black-and-white pictures.

Page after page, a sinister man in a long black overcoat followed a young man around town as if trying to tempt him with the allures of big-city life, such as good-looking women.

By midnight, the storyline was clear: The young man had sold his soul to the devil.

On Monday, I told Rob about *Gods' Man* as we walked the snowy trails of the Black Forest. He chuckled.

"I'm serious."

"I never thought I'd say this, but Dr. Parsons is right. Anybody with a good philosophical and scientific education can't believe in gods and devils anymore."

We pounded our shoes against the Greek columns of Bryan Hall, then walked in, Rob tearing off his wool cap and shaking off the snowflakes. The classroom doors began to bang open as students wandered into the lobby, looking at their phones. Liz was in the lead, phone in hand.

She stopped and looked at us both. "What's wrong?"

"Carl's lecturing me about the devil."

She took Rob's scarf. "You're a Catholic. You're supposed to believe in the devil."

"You could become a Methodist," I said. "Fewer rules."

"Carl's right. The Pope doesn't want a bunch of liberal Catholics running his church." She handed Rob the folded scarf, then winked at me. "So what were you guys talking about?"

After I told her, Liz hugged Rob and laid her cheek on his chest.

"It's a common theme in fiction, back at least to *Doctor Faustus*?"

"Chh," Rob said. "Note the key word there: fiction."

"It's also in the gospels, when the devil tempted Jesus in the desert."

"That's fiction, too, although people were meant to believe it. All of the gospels are. That's what Dr. Parsons says, and he's a member of the Academy for Biblical Studies."

Liz smooched Rob's cheek, but he wiped the kiss off with the back of his hand.

"He's fed up with the Catholic church," she said.

"Who isn't?"

"He's right about the Pope having a lot of repairs to do."

"True that."

"So, you're really confident that those Bible scholars have it right?" She assumed a spooky voice. "The devil might actually exist, modern thinkers be damned. And they would, too."

"Wouldn't it be ironic," I said, "if the modern Westerners were wrong about the devil, while the more ignorant and savage men, as Bertrand Russell might have called them, were right all along?"

"Yeah," Rob said, "and then we'd have to figure out how many angels can dance on the head of a pin."

"Pay him no mind," Liz said. "I'm sure my husband-to-be got his superior attitude from Dr. Parsons. Have you read his new book debunking Christianity? Oh my God, how could such a smart man mistake ridicule for reasoned argument?"

Liz reached for Rob's hands, but he pulled them behind his back.

"Rob's fretting about his senior thesis," she said, "the topic for which he's yet to choose. But that's what you're going to figure out tonight, right?" She pushed him toward the front doors. "After we look at wedding dresses, of course."

At midnight, I lay on my mattress in my black robe and studied the dark water stains on the ceiling. They no longer looked like blood-soaked continents, but bloodstained bodies. Before I went to bed, Rob sent me an email.

> loisy@bfu.edu
> to
> zarathustra@bfu.edu
>
> Hey, man. I wasn't trying to be rude today. I'm just stressed out. My thesis. My wedding. Grad school. Speaking of which, if grad school is a bad bet, what am I going to do with my bachelor's degree in religion? Flip burgers?
> I also forgot to tell you something. Before the devil possesses a person, he finds their flaw. As in character flaw. It's a weak spot where the devil wedges his crowbar in and tries to pry his way inside. According to the case studies, the flaws are things like a skeptical mind, loneliness, tampering with the occult, stuff like that.
> So, yeah. Maybe the devil took advantage of Jenna. Maybe he found her flaw.
>
> Rob

zarathustra@bfu.edu
to
loisy@bfu.edu

Hi, Rob. What are you doing up so late? Are you on Facebook getting a solid humanistic education? ha ha

If I were you, I'd write on demonic possession. You've read enough about it, plus graduation is near.

Jenna's flaw? That's interesting. I'll have to think about what it might be.

CS

41

It was about then that the black squirrels invaded the campus. They infiltrated the Black Forest like a cavalry, spying on me from behind tree trunks and creek stones or sneaking up behind me, emerging out of a blanket of gray fog. Sometimes, when the black squirrels were missing, a black-suited man would appear. He'd be walking parallel to me, about a football's throw away, barely visible in the fog, often in places where I didn't even know there was a trail.

I began to see him regularly. It was as though he knew my schedule. One time, he leered at me and waved. I slowed my pace, hiding behind a tall, aged pine as I watched him dissolve in the occluded light. I almost thought it was the Man, Jenna's Man, but I'd severed my ties with Jenna.

Suddenly I felt a smashing sensation in my brain—bam, bam, like a battering ram.

Squatting down, I looked between my knees at the iron-red pine needles. I recalled the apparition at Jenna's on Thanksgiving and then an earlier one, in the late summer, just before harvest had ended. I'd forgotten about this one. I'd been riding down Old Farm Road, shifting gears, when, in a distant field, a black-coated man stepped out of the yellow corn leaves. He stood there as if watching me, a black dot in the coming dark. He waved. I kept pedaling, stealing a glace or two, thinking how a guy like that had no earthly business in a Nebraska cornfield.

The internal pounding in my head subsided. I rose up slowly, the sap from the pine's trunk assaulting my nostrils. Was the Man a flesh and blood being or a spirit? Or was he a

Jungian archetype, the darker side of my personality? My eyes scoured the forest, inspecting the spaces between the trunks that loomed large in the fog. Then my phone chimed.

It was Jenna.

So Carl refuses to be a star? Okay, then. Enjoy being poor in your future rock band Adjunctslave.

Clever, but I wouldn't get dragged back into this.

I left the Black Forest and went to my seminar on existentialism. At the break, I fetched Dr. Parsons a hot green tea, which he took cautiously and blew lightly on.

"Carl, I need you to proofread something for me. Do you remember my talk on Kenny Winslow's suicide?" He told me the news: Oxford University Press had asked him to submit his Kenny essay for inclusion in a scholarly book of essays on suicide. "Thank you again, Carl. I really do appreciate it."

After class, I went to the Blue Note. I eased into Kenny's booth and kept my coat on until my bones thawed. A new sign hung in the window—a neon green shamrock that cast an emerald glow on Dr. Parson's paper.

"Boy, it looks like the bottom's about to fall out from under youse. In that case, I got the perfect solution, boyo, me boy." He threw his chin toward the Guinness sign. "Innarested?"

"Sure."

He brought over a mug. "On the house."

I drank slowly and deeply, savoring the taste of the Irish beer. Then I started in on Dr. Parsons' paper. It was . . . incomprehensible, with dense prose and unnecessary verbiage that rivaled Hegel's. I didn't imagine many attendees at the symposium understood it, except maybe for the other scholars on the panel. But then, he probably had given it for their benefit.

When Tony started in about an upcoming blues festival, I was glad for the distraction and went to join him by the stage.

"It's gonna be a big event, too. Problem is, we don't have a full PA system." He rummaged through a blue milk crate, inside of which were microphone stands and cables. "When lotsa musicians come through the bar, things go missing, you know? A cable here, a microphone there. I like to think mosta them walk off with things by mistake. Their gear looks like ours."

I set my mug on the stage. On the carpet were small strips of black tape, guitar picks, and thin red drinking straws. A setlist was taped at its four corners to the floor next to a stage monitor. On it, were songs from the Rolling Stones, off of their albums *Goats Head Soup* and *Their Satanic Majesties Request*. Picking up a guitar pick, I read the logo. "Woody Woodson and the Renegade Sons."

"So what's eating you?" Tony said, instrument cable in hand.

"Remember that girl who used to come in here with Kenny, the smoking hot babe with the black hair and eyes?"

"The eleven? I sure do. I remember this one night, the gal walked into the bar and made Woody Woodson loose his spot on the guitar."

I described Jenna some more, focusing mostly on her eyes and their dark, intelligent vibe. "Do you think it was her?"

"Now that you mention those spooky eyes, I'd say it was. I'll never forget those eyes. They had an energy to them, a superhuman energy, like you said."

"How many times did they come in, her and Kenny?"

"Two or three. Then I didn't see them no more. They were gone. Poof."

"And when you didn't see her anymore, you still saw Kenny but with other girls, right?"

"By the truckload. A new gal each week, right up to the kid's death."

I looked at the guitar pick and took several huge, satisfying sips of beer. I told Tony about my new diabolical theory about God and the devil, about Jenna and Kenny.

"That's out of this world, kid."

"I know, it sounds stupid."

"So you think she's possessed?"

"Six months ago, a year ago, I would have said that was nonsense. Now . . . I'm not so sure."

"And she got Kenny Winslow possessed, too?"

"Or helped to. I think he was prone."

"And alla them guys she's got a shoe box for are dead?"

"Or alive but screwed up."

Tony leaned his big arms on the railing that ran around the edge of the stage. "It feels like something out of the middle ages. But, okay, if the devil's real, it makes a whole lotta sense." Tony came slowly down the steps, holding onto the railing. "Two summers ago, I saw those two lean over the table you was sitting at and kiss. That was right before he became a star. It was a special kiss, too. There was a meaning behind it, you could tell by looking. A big one." He walked slowly up to me and, breathing heavily, crossed his big, black-haired arms. "So you ain't dating her too, I hope."

"Not anymore."

"Because if Kenny was still alive and I saw those two together, I'd pull him outta that booth and say, 'Eh, Kenny, run like the Sooners are chasing you down the field.' He coulda done it, too. The kid had wheels. God only knows where he got them from."

I was beginning to think I knew, though, and it had nothing to do with God.

42

Rob stopped by the hotel, talking passionately about *The Dirt*. I wasn't thrilled to be dabbling in the world of witchcraft again, but Rob was excited—he had decided to write about possession—and I tried to share his enthusiasm.

"The Crüe fooled around with the occult," he said. "Like this one day at their apartment, when they watched a knife lift up off the table all by itself. Then it rose up higher and stuck into the ceiling. Forks also flew across the room. When their manager told them to knock it off, the paranormal activity stopped."

He also listed more of the devil's favorite flaws and victims, including abused kids, and then left for Liz's parents' house for dinner. A few minutes later, he sent a text.

By the way, have you found Jenna's flaw?

I tried not to think about it. Instead, I chose to study for my existentialism seminar, reading up on those mysterious "new philosophers" about whom Nietzsche spoke, but I soon shelved it when they began to seem . . . shallow and out of touch. I was beginning to think that the real philosophers of the future might have more in common with the superstitious priesthood of the dark ages where God and the devil were the topics of the day. I began to pace the lobby.

Jenna could have any of the flaws I knew about. She was skeptical, lonely, and dabbled in the occult. And I was having serious doubts about her childhood, too.

At midnight, I changed in the bell closet. Sometime during the evening, I'd come to a decision. If Jenna had a flaw, I'd help her find it, but that was it. I wouldn't stick around. I wasn't everybody's Jesus.

On the way home, I stopped by her duplex with a letter in hand and put my ear to the door. Inside, Jenna and an older man were laughing and dancing to salsa rhythms. I brushed a pretty snowflake off the letter, then unfolded it.

"Here you go, pretty girl. Good luck."

> Dear Jenna,
>
> I'll pass on becoming a star. I'm glad you're concerned about me, though. I happen to be concerned about you, too. You've actually got me thinking about the paranormal again, which is hard to believe for a guy like me.
>
> So . . . are you consorting with demons? If so, why? I've also wondered if you've been traumatized in some way, perhaps as a young girl or even more recently—or both. A huge, horrible event has weakened you, both morally and spiritually, and you've been seeking help in all the wrong places.
>
> If my aim is on target, I hope you renounce your "friends" and get the help you need to heal.
>
> Sincerely,
> Carl

In the morning, a loud noise pulled me out of a sound sleep. I opened my cell's door and found Rich and Bubba in the hallway, bare-chested and with sweatpants on.

"What happened?" I said.

"Somebody slammed the fire escape door," Rich said. "It sounded like a gunshot."

On my door was a note, held by two foot-long strips of black tape, and on the doormat lay my copy of the book *Theory of Knowledge* plus three items which weren't mine: a doll of one of the members of the band Kiss with a long, pink tongue; the Beatles' album *Yellow Submarine*; and a long strand of cattle rope.

Later that day, I told all this to Rob, and he suggested I talk to Liz. When I walked into the Newman Center, Liz was sitting in her office chair, reading *Bride* magazine. I slid the six pages of lined grade-school paper onto her desk. I sat down on a brown leather couch and toyed with Jenna's rubber band.

Liz put down the magazine and began reading. "Oh my god, she's screaming at you." When Liz finished, she said, "What'd you say to her?"

I held the pink triangle up to my left eye. "That she's possessed by demons and needs help."

"Carl . . ."

I lowered the rubber band. "What?"

"Setting aside the wisdom of just hitting her with this, whatever you said in your letter, you hit something deep." Liz held the letter with both hands and looked closely at it. "What a long, rambling, incoherent mess, particularly the last three pages." She held up the pages written in a large, uneven block letters. "Rob's little niece writes like that."

I slipped the rubber band around my wrist and webbed my hands behind my neck, looking at the note's last lines:

YOU HORRIBLE PERSON. STOP WRITING ME ALL OF YOUR FUCKING LETTERS. I'M SICK OF IT!!

"What'd I say to deserve such vitriol?"

"What'd you say in your other letters?"

"What other letters? I've only written one."

"Then why does she say letters?"

"I don't know. She's nuts."

Liz spread the pages out on her desk. "Oh my God, look at this. It's like two different people wrote this—a woman and a small girl." She peered out into the hallway, thumbing the ends of the pages. "So if you've only written her one letter, who else is writing them to her?"

43

The March winds blew through Sleepy Hollow, and I was making progress, not only as a teaching assistant but also as an adjunct. I'd gotten to know my colleagues at Nebraska Methodist University—it wasn't hard with all four of us crammed into the same office, sharing horror stories of adjunct life. The culture in Adjunct-ville was apparently the same everywhere—Lincoln, Omaha, and Council Bluffs, Iowa. While a majority of adjuncts had remained on board the sinking ship, treading water to stay afloat in the hopes of landing a tenure-track job, a brave few had abandoned ship, choosing to leave academia instead.

Then there was Paul. One day, when he gave me a lift back to the BFU campus, he told me about his financial struggles and how he was forced to apply for government aid. We'd been talking about his *Adjunct's Survival Guide*, which had grown in length, and I shared my own survival tactics, which he approved and fine-tuned. Then I asked about "the adjunct trap," Dr. Parsons' ominous phrase.

Paul said it was real. If you applied for tenure-track jobs and had been an adjunct for too long, the search committee might toss your application out of hand. You were old news, and they wanted fresh blood, a newly minted PhD with a published dissertation by a serious academic press, like Cambridge.

"That's Eric's problem," Paul said. "He's not marketable anymore. He's busy teaching at four colleges and hasn't had time to publish."

When we pulled into the Haymarket, Paul must have sensed my inner gloom. "Look, I've got some more news for you, but it can wait until you've cheered up. I'll email you."

"Thanks. Something to look forward to."

"Just don't shoot the messenger," he said as I climbed out of the van.

Inside the Loft, I logged on to the Internet to preview the courses offered in the fall when, across the street, Jenna pulled up in the bus. I ducked down, hiding behind an old wagon wheel against the café window, next to a stack of *Prairie Schooners*.

Between the wheel's spokes, I watched the side of Jenna's face, which turned slowly and locked eyes with me, even though she couldn't possibly see me. It was a look of the purest hatred I've ever seen.

I scooted back in my chair. *God, I didn't sign up for this. What does she want?*

My blood was pounding hard in my temples, and as the beats grew quieter, I looked between the wagon wheel's spokes. Jenna looked like a grade-schooler sitting in the bus. She wore a pink tank top and wound-red lipstick, her hair parted in the middle and pulled into pigtails. She stuck her head out the window and looked behind the bus, biting down on her lips as though afraid and escaping from an enemy.

I moved back in my chair for a minute, and when I inched forward, Jenna was gone. I kept a watchful eye on the street, but when my inbox chimed, I clicked on Paul's message, followed by the link to an article he'd sent, and when I clicked it, the title leapt onto the screen.

"The Death of the Humanities?"

I read the article and then swiped up my Mac, dumping my coffee cup into a plastic tub by the front door and startling the customers nearby.

Under a bruise-purple sky, a trail of blazing stars was appearing above the train yard. One huge star burned above the largest pyramid. I walked parallel to a mile-long freight train and threw a rock as hard as I could, striking a telephone pole.

Great. Colleges were looking for ways to cut costs, and humanities degrees were a prime target. In Pennsylvania, a college had axed their philosophy program; in Arizona, it was French and German language programs; and in Minnesota, their music program. A follow-up article would be written next week. More bad news for humanities programs.

When the last boxcar had passed, I rested my shoe on the iron track. Philosophy and religion, literature and history, art and music, they taught us how to live and how to die. They taught us what to value in life and what to let pass by. Socrates said that the unexamined life wasn't worth living and that philosophy was a preparation for death. Did the college administrators know this? Did they know anything besides money? Did they even care?

I was still fuming the next day. At the break, I smoked half a cigarette and then flung it into the pond as the mallards paddled over to investigate.

Nietzsche may have been wrong on the metaphysics, but he saw the value of the humanities, especially the classics of Greece and Rome. Their great plays and poems were like mirrors in which we can see ourselves, by which we can judge our lives and become better men and women.

I looked up at Mr. Bryan, a man known for fighting the secularization of his age—evolution, sure, but also eugenics and social Darwinism. He fought for a life of meaning, a life with values. Suddenly, he seemed a lot more like an ally.

"I wish you were alive, Mr. Bryan," I said softly. "We could use a leader like you. You'd secure a better wage for us adjuncts, but how exactly would you save the humanities from oblivion?"

I turned away from the Great Commoner, trying to ignore the far-off thwacks of hammers, the spinning of drills, and the beeps of Bobcats backing up. The STEM buildings were growing loftier on campus as though part of a minimetropolis, while the humanities buildings seemed far away, old and forgotten and irrelevant.

Then I heard a different noise. Beautiful birdcalls were coming from the sky. I stepped out from under the honey locust as a phalanx of huge, gray-blue birds soared over the Black Forest. They were like baby pterodactyls with long, thin beaks and incredible wingspans, their stilt-like legs behind them.

Migrating sandhill cranes.

I walked to the pond's shore, looking up at the long-beaked birds, listening to the beautiful music they made just as a way of keeping the flock together. I pictured this patch of land in a time before there were humans: these birds in this ageless sky and the woolly mammoths grazing the plains.

I walked back to Bryan Hall with an eye on the migratory birds flying westward with confidence and grace until they were silhouettes in the orange splash of sky. Opening the door, I walked in and felt sad to see the birds go.

*   *   *

At the hotel, Quentin was leaning against the bell desk, arms crossed, toothpick in mouth, rolling it from side to side. He said Jenna had been driving around the block for the last forty minutes. I asked if she was looking for me, and he said he didn't ask her.

She didn't show up during my shift. Just after midnight, I was still reading in the bell closet when, in the lobby, the glass doors slid open, and a pair of high heels clicked across the tiles. I lay down in a covered wagon and turned my phone off.

Somebody opened the bell closet door. Through the slats of the wagon's side, I saw the front desk girl's black nylons and pumps. Soon, I heard voices at the front desk, followed by the click of high heels, and then a mighty rush of wind blowing into the lobby. When I turned on my phone, Jenna had sent me a text.

☹

I texted back: ☺

After work, I sneaked by her duplex. Half of her door had been painted red, the other half pink. The purple-striped, nylon serpent had been cut in half, so that its long cotton entrails streamed down. A shadowy figure moved behind the shuttered window, as if in a hurry. I wanted to knock on the door, but felt that doing so would be counterproductive. I didn't need the drama. Besides, if I wanted to succeed in graduate school, I had to get rid of my women. Many had sworn by this advice. It worked. And it was going to work for me, too.

Next day, Rob and I met at Frampton's Diner in Sleepy Hollow's business district, and then went back to the union for coffee. I recommended that he hold off on divinity school, since the job prospects for teaching weren't good. I didn't want to lead him on, saying there were jobs when there weren't. Too many professors had been doing that to their students—saying there were jobs when there really weren't any. After all, the professors needed students in order to keep their own jobs. When the conversation turned to Jenna, I told him about the stalking, plus her newly painted door.

"That sounds like possession," he said. "She could be fighting the demon off and crying out for help. Your help."

I saw a group of businessmen emerge from the STEM area with Dr. Parsons in the lead. All of them had sunglasses on and briefcases in hand. They stopped in the quad, looking at their phones or turning to take pictures of the STEM buildings, while Dr. Parsons spoke to the tallest, a man with tar-colored hair. When the men shook hands and went their separate ways, Dr. Parsons lingered for a bit, making a second phone call. He'd set his briefcase down, and the eye in the triangle winked in the sunshine. Then, punching a few digits into his Blackberry, he sighed contentedly and sauntered into the union.

Rob and I watched him go, passing through the food court in a satin black workout suit and whistling a song from *The Wizard of Oz*.

Rob stroked his goatee. "I'm really glad Parsons isn't my thesis reader."

"Why, because he'd fail you?"

"He'd never even approve of my topic." Rob sat up ramrod straight and, in a passable British accent, said, "It's impossible to believe in angels and demons in the age of the electric light bulb."

"Bultmann, right? You know, it was a running joke in divinity school—what if Bultmann's wrong?"

"Well, even a lot of Catholic priests and bishops agree with him nowadays. Many dioceses don't even have an exorcist. Which makes you wonder where a possessed person goes for help. But we're in luck. We live in the Diocese of Lincoln. They believe in the devil here."

44

Jenna had sent more text messages. They ranged from *Why are you ignoring me?* to *How's Adjunctslave going? Any gigs yet?* It was tempting to text her back, but I didn't, choosing to plough ahead instead, tilling the academic soil in the hopes of a bountiful harvest. Teaching was still going well, and I at least had outlines of my final papers, the paragraphs sketched more and more fully as the weekdays wore on, my arguments growing more focused and detailed. I'd also bonded more with my fellow adjuncts at Nebraska Methodist University, all of us worried about our futures. Though we saw a ray of hope after Paul had sent me a second article, which, to my surprise, offered us good news.

Unions. That's what adjuncts on the East coast were doing—forming unions in their fight for fair wages. Talk of unions didn't help us, though. To form a union was to rock the boat, something we didn't dare do, not in this economy. At least we had jobs, we said as a joke, although there were dozens of unemployed PhDs all too ready to step into our positions.

One day in early March, I dismissed class and wandered through the historic area of Havelock, where I found a new coffee shop, The Academic Grind. After making fast friends with the baristas, I got a latte at no charge, following which I went for a walk with no destination in mind. A public park was up ahead, and I found a bench under the black branches of an elm. It was sunny and warm, with no wind, though one of the kids' swings was moving slowly above the sand.

For the next hour I reread Nietzsche. I took a yellow marker and lined those passages in *Beyond Good and Evil* dealing with the new philosophers, those self-legislators, those creators of new values. I began to view them as the doctors of culture, the agents of cultural change, bearing the weight of humankind's future by transforming it into to a healthy community.

Not poorly paid adjuncts with no futures.

When I looked up from my book, the middle swing's rubber seat was still moving, its shadow passing eerily over the sand. Just the middle one. Suddenly, an icy wind blew over my lap as a chorus of children's voices washed over me, singing in unison as if jumping rope. But there were no kids, just a large, empty playground with white, eye-hurting sunlight in the trees.

"Pick up and read," the children said. "Pick up and read."

A copy of *Zarathustra* lay on the bench and, picking it up, I read the first passage my eyes fell upon:

"O my brothers, am I cruel? But I say: what is falling, we should still push. Everything today falls and decays: who would check it? But I—I even want to push it."

A tall shadow fell over the book's pages as if somebody was looking over my shoulder. Then I heard a man's voice, reading the passage I'd just read. His words were spoken in a clear, ageless tone, calm and commanding. Then the man went on, reciting the same fragment, over and over, until my vision blurred and my eyeballs grew hot in their sockets. *Everything today falls and decays, falls and decays, falls and decays . . .*

I raised my eyes and gazed into an old man's face, which peered through a veil of pale, ill-looking sunlight, his teeth like mushrooms blackening in rain.

"You must push what is falling," he said.

Along the park's fence, a mother knelt down next to a baby stroller, watching us carefully, while two teenage girls crossed the street in a hurry, looking over their shoulders with large, frightened eyes. On my lap, the book's pages continued to turn, snapping against my hand, and when I looked over my shoulder again, there, walking across the baseball diamond, was a lone man in Sunday black, strolling with his hands behind his back.

Later that evening, when I walked into my cell, I saw my black robe in the bathroom and shut the door so I didn't have to look at it. Then I threw myself on my mattress and, closing my eyes, listened to my heartbeat. I tried to read. I couldn't. I tried to work on a term paper. Nothing. Finally, I rolled over and webbed my fingers behind my head, studying the human shapes on my ceiling, their bloodstains darker.

Liz texted me.

I've checked with my sources, and I'm more sure now. Jenna's letter is a cry for help.

I can't deal with this now, I texted back.

I'm going into social work. I help people. I just have to let you know. Things could get interesting.

They're already more interesting than I'd like.

I know you didn't ask for this, Carl, but maybe it's your fate?

I stared at the screen. I didn't answer. Before I went to bed, Liz sent an email.

liz.oreilly@bfu.edu
to
zarathustra@bfu.edu

Hi, Carl.

I'm sorry to bother you again, but I can't stop thinking about Jenna's letter. I talked to my mom, she works with at-risk girls at the crisis center in Omaha, and she asked if you've ever met Jenna's parents. Have you? If so, it might shed some light on her past and current behavior.

Liz

45

Next day, I stopped by the student lounge, and, seeing it was free of graduate students, checked my email at a computer. My students had sent several messages, but I responded to Liz's first.

zarathustra@bfu.edu
to
liz.oreilly@bfu.edu

Hi, Liz

No, I've never met her parents, nor do I want to. I've asked about them, but Jenna always dodged the subject.

I've been trying not to think about the letter she wrote to me. I started to feel a negative energy attached to it, and so I threw it out.

Still, I'm interested to hear what your mom says. I'm glad Rob has a thesis topic, too. It's about time. He's been helping me out with my research, so I'll try to help him out, too, if I can.

Carl

Then I clicked through my students' messages. Some had offered brilliant excuses for missing class, while others inquired about the next reading assignment, to which I replied, "Read the syllabus." Then I got up and checked my student mailbox, pulling out catalogs from Oxford University Press, and then left quickly as a throng of graduate students entered and grew quiet as they watched me leave.

*   *   *

Back in town, I stopped at St. Michael's. I don't know why I stopped. I just did. A flock of purple pigeons was flying over the cathedral's tower. I looked up, watching the birds as they turned left and then swooped over the street, almost disappearing, until they came into view again as they turned right. I walked my bike up to a stone statue of the virgin Mary housed in a stone grotto lined with baby-blue and white tiles. Bouquets of white carnations had been set before her bare feet.

Please go inside.

I was becoming disturbingly used to hearing voices.

"In where, the rectory?"

Jenna needs help.

"Yeah, from a psychiatrist."

I stared at the virgin Mary, the first disciple who had agreed to bring the Savior into the world, thus allowing it to be redeemed. I soon thought of the church's teachings, especially those laid out in the Apostles' Creed—twelve improbable propositions we had to believe in. Or else.

I sighed. Maybe Bultmann was right. Who could believe in that nonsense nowadays? But as a future advice columnist, I'd have to consult with medical professionals and social workers, law enforcement and clergy, so why not start with the clergy now?

Besides, I could help Rob with his thesis.

I walked my bike down a stone path to a limestone cottage clad in webs of bare ivy branches. I rang the bell, and a dog began to bark and skitter across the floor. The door opened a crack, and a sad-faced man in a baggy red sweater stared back at me.

"May I help you?"

"Is Father Owens here?"

"No, Father's not here."

"Okay, do you know when he'll be in?"

"No, Father didn't say."

A wiener dog pushed its snout through the crack, sniffing my shoe. I would have petted it, but if it were anything like its owner, it would have bitten me.

"Okay, I'll try later."

At five o'clock, I called the rectory. "Father Owens, please."

"Father's in a meeting."

"Okay, do you—"

"No."

I shut my eyes. "Okay, I'll try tomorrow."

Next day, Rob and I walked to the library with a black squirrel in tow as I spoke about my encounter with the parish secretary.

"The little weasel didn't give me the time of day," I said. "He hardly looked at me."

"It was your hair and sideburns."

"My what?"

"You look like a liberal."

"So they lock the church doors against liberals? What do they think I'll do, hold them down and force them to watch Bill Maher?"

"Welcome to the Diocese of Lincoln. It's one of the most conservative in the country. Liz can tell you stories about it— she's from Omaha. The archdiocese up there laughs at this diocese. Everybody does."

* * *

Two hours later, Paul dropped me off at St. Michael's. The male secretary answered the door. He opened it a little wider, so that I could see his sad, wrinkly face. He was nibbling on a chicken leg with a napkin tucked into his shirt.

"Hello, is Father—"

"No." He chewed with grease on his lips as the wiener dog sniffed at my pant leg and then looked up with mean little eyes, baring its teeth.

"May I leave a note, then?"

The dog looked at the secretary, who looked at the dog, and together they seemed to reach an agreement. "Oh, I suppose."

I went inside and wrote a note and then brought it to the secretary at his desk. He was cutting out coupons for a variety of fresh fruits.

"If Father Owens can call me soon, that'd be great."

"Will do."

Three hours later, Father Owens called. He was running late for a dinner but would be glad to meet with me in the morning. When I hung up, Rob sent me an email.

loisy@bfu.edu
to
zarathustra@bfu.edu

Hey, man. I checked out a book called *Hostage to the Devil*. It's by a Father Malachi Martin. I couldn't put it down. I'm totally excited about my thesis now. Now I need to get some firsthand field experience. Any ideas?

In the book, a girl named Marianne was a philosophy major in college. Know what the scariest part is? This guy helped to get her possessed. She called him "the Man." Isn't that who Jenna wanted you to meet? It was scary. I even started to pray. Can you believe it, me praying? The Man helped Marianne to enter into "a marriage to nothingness." That's the phrase she used. She said it was like falling in love with the jaws of an alligator.

If you've got other books for me to read, send them my way. I'm totally using them as sources ☺

Rob

zarathustra@bfu.edu
to
loisy@bfu.edu

Hi, Rob.

Father Martin talks about the Man? I need to read this book. But since I don't have time to read it, can you send me a summary of it when you're done? Also, did Marianne say if the Man was a human being, a demon, or the darker side of her own personality? I still have some Jungian suspicions.

Carl

46

I woke up at 3:15 a.m., my breath puffing white above the bed. Outside in the hallway, I heard slow, heavy-booted footsteps. As they got louder, I sat up and peeled the covers off. There, in the hallway, visible through the crack in my door's bottom, stood a pair of huge, mud-caked boots. Heavy breathing could be heard behind the door, and the intruder seemed to know I was awake. Then the yells of men, like generals in battle, could be heard in the sky, along with the gallop of warhorses, their halter chains jangling in the night.

Then it was quiet. I could make out the refrigerator's buzz, then a train's whistle. Beneath the door, the boots were gone.

In the morning, I woke with a headache. I looked for the questions I'd written out for Father Owens but couldn't find them, so, after I took some aspirin, I rewrote my questions and then exited my cell, pulling the fire escape door shut as I left.

Father Owens opened the rectory door right on time, holding a calculator in his hand. He was a big, imposing man with a shell of hard black hair combed over a bald spot. I introduced myself and we shook hands, after which he led me to his office.

"Busy day?" I said.

"Just paying the bills." He sat down with a sigh and stared at his desk, as though he didn't know where he was. "Have a seat."

I picked up a pillow up off the chair and then sat down. Atop his desk were piles of dirty green bills and personal checks in neat rows—typical offering plate stuff, I supposed.

He reached out and with a finger evened out a pile of tens. "So you had a question?"

"Is now a good time?"

"Believe me, I could use a break." He leaned slowly back in his chair with the calculator resting on his large stomach as his fingers began to drum on the desk.

As I explained my situation, Father Owens listened. He'd sometimes press a digit on the calculator or look beyond me to the rectory's entrance. When I finished, he sat forward and picked up a pile of twenties and looked at them.

"I'll say a few things," he said and leafed through the bills.

According to Father Owens, demonic possession was remarkably rare, and before the church could proceed with an exorcism, the patient had to be given a thorough psychological evaluation. Then, if the church couldn't find a natural cause for the patient's strange behavior, she felt justified in assuming a supernatural cause—that is, a demonic one. Only then would the church proceed with the rite of exorcism. It was a more elaborate vetting process than I expected, but I found the skepticism built into it oddly comforting.

Father Owens looked up from the bills. "Is your friend a Catholic?"

"I don't think so. If she is, she isn't a practicing one."

"Is she the recipient of pastoral care?"

"She won't go near a church."

He curled the corners of the bills. "Hmm."

"Jenna can't even stand the sound of church bells. She closes the windows when they go off, and if she still hears them, she blasts the stereo."

"Hmm."

The wiener dog walked in and sneezed. Father Owens picked it up and set it in his lap and stroked it. It looked kinder in his care.

"Does she have anybody she can talk to?" he said. "Friends? Parents? Relatives?"

"I'm the only one around here she knows." Who was still alive.

He rubbed the dog's ears. "Hmm."

"What if the church did an exorcism anyway, just to be on the safe side? I mean, Jenna has nothing to lose, right? If she's possessed, then you cast the demons out. If there are no demons, then she needs a psychologist. What about that?"

He leaned back as the dog found his footing and curled up in his lap.

"It's more complicated than that. If you perform the rite on your friend and she isn't genuinely possessed, her problems could get worse."

"How so?"

"If she needs psychiatric care—if she's schizophrenic, for instance—telling her there are demons inside of her could be psychologically traumatic." He reached for the calculator and the dog looked up. "Would she agree to see a psychologist?"

"She wouldn't agree anything's wrong with her. And if she does get some help, if she finds out there's a priest at the end of the line, she won't go for it."

"Have you tried praying for her? Or asking the blessed virgin for her intercession? It might open up some doors."

We talked a bit longer, and I thanked Father Owens for his time. As I left, the secretary was cutting out more coupons. I said goodbye. He didn't.

*   *   *

I stopped by the cathedral on my way out. In the foyer, I peeked through the windows of the huge oak doors. At the podium, a nun stood next to a young girl dressed in a navy-blue-and-white uniform. "Try to slow down a bit more. Give the words time to project."

The girl took a deep breath. "And now a reading from Saint Paul's letter to the Corinthians . . ."

A statue of the virgin Mary, clad in a white-and-baby-blue gown, stood in the opposite corner, her bare foot crushing the serpent's head. I dialed up Rob and studied the apple in the snake's fangs.

He picked up.

"Apparently, the process will take forever," I said, "and that assumes Jenna will see a psychologist first. This could take months, years even."

"That's how the church works. If you've been around for two thousand years, you feel you can take your time."

A pucker-lipped old woman with a purple headscarf entered the foyer. She hobbled by on chunky legs and, without looking at me, entered the sanctuary.

I said quietly, "Do you think it's a dead end, in this diocese?"

"Chh, yeah."

"What should I do?"

"Try Omaha. It's your best bet. You'll have to jump through a million hoops here."

47

Dr. Parsons told us the bad news. Black Forest University had voted for budget cuts, and the Department of Philosophy and Religious Studies had taken the brunt. Fewer courses would be offered in the fall as well as fewer teaching assistantships. The logic? There weren't enough students majoring in philosophy and religion to justify all of the courses offered, as if cutting down the offerings wouldn't also cut down the number of students. Plus, the STEM majors would no longer be required to take as many humanities courses, which were seen as a burden to getting their degrees.

And Dr. Parsons agreed! He told us so, making his case in a department-wide email. The American economy was hurting, he'd said, and a growing concern of our students, their parents, and the worried, head-scratching administrators was the rising costs of a college education in a poor job market. It was argued that STEM degrees could land you a better-paying job. Humanities degrees couldn't.

But that wasn't all. Something else was going on, something sinister, and Parsons was in on it. Paul suggested that our own advisor had voted to downsize his own department. I asked how that worked, and Paul replied that anything was possible, especially with Parsons.

So Parsons was in on it, too. He was an investor, just like those cryptic, blue-suited men whom I'd seen roaming the STEM section of campus. No wonder he could afford a church in the English countryside.

During my existentialism seminar, I could hardly pay attention. I was too busy thinking about the fall. Would my assistantship also be cut? As Dr. Parsons circled the seminar table, off on one of his usual tangents—this one on Martin Heidegger and his notion of being-towards-death—I opened my notebook and sketched a portrait of the Man. I was shading in the black preacher's hat when a wave of peppermint breath swept over the notebook's pages, and I sensed a presence behind me. I froze.

The Man stared at me from my notebook page, his eyes like overcooked light bulbs.

"Amusing," Dr. Parsons said, looking over my shoulder. "It seems to me, class, that Mr. Sorensen has been so gracious as to provide us with a visual aid." He walked down the length of the table, beret on, tapping a music baton in hand, or perhaps it was a magic wand. "You are quite the artist, Mr. Sorensen. Are you taking Dr. Himes' aesthetics seminar?"

He circled the table, tapping the magic wand on a finger, remarking how some Christian theologians believed, stupidly, that Hitler was possessed by demons. I looked at my drawing of the Man, whose impish grin seemed to mock me.

"Hitler was possessed," the Man on the page said. "And quite an achievement that was, too."

Dr. Parsons stopped and faced me, his fingers opening and closing on the wand. "These theologians, I must concur, are being quite obtuse and, dare I say, childish. In fact, a contemporary novelist, who is often called an existentialist, has also suggested that Hitler was a victim of demonic possession." He walked away to the podium, picked up his cup of green tea, and, surveying the class, said, "And the writer to whom I'm referring is?"

The eleven graduate students turned toward me, glad I'd been put on the spot.

I closed my notebook, my eyes roaming from student to student, some grinning, others whispering, as I turned to face Dr. Parsons. "That would be Norman Mailer. *The Castle in the Forest.*"

Dr. Parsons rolled the wand between his fingertips and smiled thinly. "I must say, Carl, you are quite an aficionado of the literary scene. And do you happen to know what Mailer's book is about?"

"Hitler's childhood. A demon named Dieter had been put in charge of the young Hitler with the goal of schooling him in the ways of evil, so that by the time Hitler was a grown man, he'd wreak havoc on God's creation."

Dr. Parsons sipped his green tea. "You know, Mr. Sorensen, perhaps you'd like Dr. McBride's 'Philosophy and Literature' class. Oh, wait, I'm afraid that course will no longer be offered at BFU." He brought the cup to his lips and held it there. "It saddens me that a thinker of Mailer's caliber should resort to such theological lunacy. As I recall, Mailer was Jewish, and even the most orthodox Jews don't believe in fallen angels, only good angels." Dr. Parsons finished his tea and, raising the magic wand, said, "Mr. Sorensen, would you like to comment on this apparent inconsistency?"

I was surprised to find myself so prepared. "Actually there are some ancient Jewish groups who did believe in evil angels." I listed off the various Jewish sects, offering a commentary on each one, until the students were all looking at the table. Two guys living in Philosophy House covered their mouths as their shoulders moved up and down.

"Plus," I said. "Even if there were no Jews who believed in evil angels, Norman Mailer never cared what anybody else thought. He had balls. He did what he wanted and said and believed whatever—"

"Thank you, Mr. Sorensen, for your wonderful lecture on theology. Let us meet back in fifteen minutes, instead of our usual ten, shall we?"

Walking outside, I tore off my blazer under the sun and walked in the fields in back of Bryan Hall and then returned to chill with Mr. Bryan.

"I'm starting to know how you felt," I said. "Beat up. Ridiculed. Now we've got budget cuts on the way, and I might be feeling them in the fall."

A black squirrel came out from behind the honey locust tree, sniffing the chips of red bark and turning a large one over.

My phone chimed.

loisy@bfu.edu
to
zarathustra@bfu.edu

Hey, Liz talked to her mom, who works in Omaha at the crisis center. She's pretty sure Jenna is the victim of abuse. Maybe that could be her flaw? Also, there's a priest you should talk to. He's in Omaha, too. His name is Father Myles Conley. He's a visiting professor from Ireland who's teaching at Saint Anne's College. He's the coolest priest you'll ever meet. He loves rock music, especially U2, and he likes Cuban cigars. He's in the philosophy department. Liz said he has weird psychic powers, too. By the way, he's also an exorcist. His number is (402) 608-0315.

You should call him up!
Rob

I looked at the Great Commoner, sensing he had more to say, and when I looked behind me, I knew what it was. There on the other side of the pond, a family of crows was perched on the iron gates of the Black Forest. They cawed loudly and lunged at each other as the biggest bird flapped upward, its wings big and heavy as newspapers.

"All right," I said to Bryan. "I'm taking this on faith." I dialed up Father Myles and closed my eyes.

"Hello, Father Myles?"

"Yes, m'boy, I've been waiting for your call. How's the crack?"

My eyes sprung open. "Excuse me?"

He asked it again, and it still sounded like he was asking about the crack.

I switched the phone to my other ear. "I'm sorry, Father, you'll have to repeat that. The wind is howling here and—"

"Story horse?"

I observed Mr. Bryan, who seemed to grin. "I'm sorry, Father, I didn't get that, either."

"I'm sure m'Irish slang has twisted you into a pretzel, eh? No worries, lad, no worries. Soon you'll carry the gospel of Irish slang to every corner of God's green earth. I don't care where you're from. Paraguay or South Africa, Kazakhstan or Uzbekistan. If you want m'honest opinion, the gospel of Irish slang is the fourth member of the holy trinity. We'd all be better off speaking like the Irish. Until then, I'll speak plain English. How are you?"

"I'm fine, Father. I'm on break at the moment, and so I thought I'd give you a—"

"Smashing. So I've here an email from Liz O'Reilly. You know Liz?"

"Her fiancé and I are—"

"She tells me you're a doctoral student?"

"That's right, Father. I'm studying—"

"So, tell me, are you getting a good dose of Aristotle down there?"

I stood next to the Great Commoner, whose overcoat tail seemed to brush against my knee. "Yes, Father. Aristotle's big at BFU."

"You know, a college education isn't complete without a foundation in the Greeks, especially in the marvelous world of Aristotle. Just ask St. Thomas Aquinas, he'll tell you."

"I'm sure he would."

Father Myles went on about Aristotle's influence on Christian theology, how the philosophy departments at St. Anne's and BFU differed, and other minutiae of academic life.

Draping my blazer cape-like over my shoulder, I walked into the sun's golden rays, light and warm on my face.

"So you've had a run in with Old Nick, eh?"

It came completely out of the blue and was said with the same nonchalance he'd used when he asked if I'd read Aristotle. "You mean the devil?"

"He's got many names, that fella."

"Yeah, I guess so."

"How're you holding up?"

I stopped at the shoreline and swept my shoe over a lump of sand, smoothing it out.

"Still kind of in shock," I said. "Sometimes I wonder if what I experienced was real or not. Last semester, strange things happened." I remembered the seminar room, just moments ago. "They're still happening, I think."

The six crows stood guard atop the gates. One of the birds walked clumsily along, its beak opening and closing.

"It's left a mark on you," Father Myles said. "I can hear it in your words, in your voice."

I knelt down and drew a quarter-moon in the wet sand and then another one—a set of diabolical eyes. A psychic and a clairvoyant? Great. More impossible things to believe.

"I'd be careful if I were you," Father Myles said. "Old Nick and his henchmen have moved inland, bringing with them the ultimate love removal machine. That's not Irish slang either, just plain fact. But anyway, they've done their work in Western Europe and a decent job on the States, especially the coasts. Now they've moved to the Midwest. You see, lad, the Satanic realm sees your country as a cherry pie. The middle part, the Midwest, is soft and chewy, nutritious and sweet. But the coasts? They're crusts."

Atop the gates, two crows fussed and thrust at each other, while the other birds lifted off the gate and sailed over the Black Forest, their bodies growing smaller in the north.

"So," Father Myles said, "what are your plans for tomorrow?"

"Read, write, and teach."

"Stop by Ignatius Hall, why don't you. I've got here a fine Cuban cigar and one for you, if that's your thing. Cigars and spirit possession were made for each other, you know."

"Yeah, I think Aristotle said that." I stood up. "What time?"

"How's two o'clock? I'd chat with you now, but I've got a meeting in that god-awful committee room. I wish the chairman would cancel the bloody thing. Oh, well. At least at St. Anne's we're strong in the humanities. I've got an inkling you already know where I'm going with this topic but more on that later."

48

I pulled Quentin's Silverado up to the ticket booth. I turned on the radio, set to a country station, and listened to the brass shell casings on the dashboard rattle rhythmically to a Brad Paisley song. Just above the gun rack in back was a sticker: "IF IT'S BROWN, IT'S GOING DOWN."

"Good lord," Quentin said. "You ain't never gon' make it like that. You need a boost. Hop on down."

I climbed down and Quentin slammed a telephone book onto the seat, covering the slits in the sagging upholstery, and topped it with a camouflage pillow. I climbed in, and my eyes now comfortably cleared the dashboard.

Quentin patted me on the shoulder. "You a man now. Now go on and get a little mud on the tires."

Thirty minutes later, I crossed over the Platte River. The sandhill cranes were roosting in the flat, sparkling water, while a flock circled peacefully above the woods near the river bottom. The Silverado growled over the bridge, as the water seemed to rise up on either side of the truck, like brilliant, sparkling walls.

I pulled into St. Anne's College, then killed the engine. Its thunder still seemed to echo in the quiet of the cab. I let my forehead fall onto the steering wheel. How'd I end up here? So far from campus, from my studies, and from my beliefs. But something good will come of it. Somehow. I listened to the engine's hot ticking noises and then rolled my forehead along the wheel, looking left. Through the window, a phalanx of sandhill cranes was flying over the football field, and I listened to their birdcalls until they faded away.

Pushing the door open to Ignatius Hall, I continued down the quiet hallway, past the faculty offices, listening to my squeaky shoes, the air rich and clean with the odor of vintage books. I arrived at Father Myles' office and, seeing the priest by a water tank of Japanese koi, I stood in the doorway and knocked on the wall.

"Father Myles?"

"G'day, lad. How's she cutting?"

"Is that Irish slang for how are you doing?"

"You're catching on. How's she cutting? How's the crack? 'Tis the same."

"In that case, she's cutting well."

Father Myles set the fish food down and turned to face me with a lion-headed cane at his side. He had long flaming red hair and a prophet's beard with a touch of gray. His large, energizing eyes were the color of bourbon whiskey, and he had a scarred-up face and a chip out of his nose, making me think of those Roman statues plundered by barbarians.

"You're just as I imagined," he said. "A pull through for a rifle. Skin and bones. You should be fattened up by now." He pointed the cane at a bamboo chair as I walked in. "So you're from the Diocese of Lincoln, eh?"

"Not originally."

"It's one of the few dioceses in the States that still believes in the devil. You've even got an exorcist down there. And with the way your bishop runs the place, I wouldn't be surprised if you've got an emergency backup exorcist as well." He walked slowly to his desk. "So Liz tells me you're a PhD student?"

"It's my first year." I took off my bag and sat down.

"Modern philosophy?"

"With a focus on existentialism."

He sat down and inspected me carefully. "Yes, but tell me one thing. Are you getting a good dose of Aristotle down there? Too many think the ancients and medievals have nothing to teach us."

"They're not exactly pushed, but I've been reading a lot on my own. I'm teaching introductory courses, and we're lingering over the earlier stuff. We're up to Anselm."

"Whose textbooks are you using?"

I listed off the authors and learned they were friends of Father Myles.

"'Tis swell to know that your students are enjoying those books. Magee, Warburton, and Young have the rare ability to speak plain English, a skill that's sorely missing in the academy. I can tell you also have the ability to write clearly and intelligently for a lay audience, unlike most scholars, who couldn't write their way out of a paper bag. But I'm getting ahead of myself. One topic at a time, eh?"

We left the office. Father Myles stopped by a few faculty offices, poking his head in and chatting with the other priests. Thirty minutes later, I pushed the door open and held it as Father Myles walked carefully outside with his cane. It was a partly cloudy day with no wind, and we walked side by side slowly and found a bench in the shade next to the campus cathedral. A statue of St. Ignatius, the founder of the Jesuit order, looked on as a pigeon was feeding in the gravel at the saint's sandals.

Father Myles lit up his cigar. "So tell me about your run in with Old Scratch. I've got the general picture in my mind, but you'll have to help me with the specifics."

Thirty minutes later, I'd finished my story. It sounded less crazy with a priest by my side and a monk looking down.

Father Myles blew out perfect rings of smoke. One. Two. Three.

"What we've got here," he said, looking at the widening white rings, "is an open and shut case of demonic possession."

"But the Lincoln diocese wants her to go through all of these psychological tests."

"Of course they do, and good on them. You see, Carl, the church has to be sure the girl isn't mentally ill. Most times, a mental illness is the culprit, not demonic possession."

I held up *Hostage to the Devil*. "Have you read this?"

"Oh, yes. Malachi was a friend of mine."

"Do exorcisms happen the way he says they do?"

"Not in my experience. The ones I've performed have been relatively mild. Lots of coughing and sneezing, an insult here and there, but no head twisting or vomiting like you've got in *The Exorcist*. That's not real life. That's Hollywood."

A brown squirrel poked its head out from behind St. Ignatius' sandals, twitching its nose, its whiskers shiny in the sunshine. The squirrel walked up to the bench, looked at us, and then jumped up onto it as I leaned away. Father Myles whistled at the squirrel.

"Joey, get down. Come on, off."

"You know this squirrel?"

"Joey's a friend of mine. Here, watch." Father Myles dug into his black blazer and then tossed a peanut onto the gravel. Joey hopped down, seized the peanut, and chewed away the outer shell.

"So back to Malachi's exorcisms. They might have been violent or he might have embellished them—we don't know. He has the storyteller's gift—he was a novelist, too—so perhaps he made his exorcisms a tad more theatrical. It does sell books, after all. But Malachi's overall thesis is correct: God and the devil are at war, and many Catholic dioceses don't take disembodied, intelligent evil seriously. The result? Untold numbers of men and women are suffering from demonic possession with nobody to help them."

Joey dropped his peanut, picked it up, and resumed his nibbling.

"Father Martin says that one of the devil's biggest tricks is to get the world to think he doesn't exist," I said.

"Old Scratch is very intelligent. He doesn't reveal himself too often. If the Amityville horror occurred on every street corner in America, everybody would believe in the devil and, by extension, God. And if most of us ended up believing in God, then the devil would have fewer souls to take with him in the end. So he hides."

Joey returned. He clawed his way up Father Myles' pant leg, sniffing as he went, and then perched on the priest's knee. Father Myles handed me a peanut and pointed the cigar at my knee. When I set the peanut down, Joey snatched it away and leapt off the bench.

"Speaking of Old Nick . . ." Father Myles took a few powerful puffs, and as the halos of smoke began to rise and widen and thin out, he said, "Can I interest you in a tale or two from my field work?"

"Sure."

"Follow me."

49

I couldn't believe the tales he told. They made what I'd seen and heard with Jenna look mild by comparison, stories that began to sound like something from the comics. Father Myles spun out his tales of demons with ridiculous names committing unspeakable horrors on innocent people as we walked through various locations on campus—at the track and field stadium in the bleachers; in the botanical garden; and in the cafeteria, where he stopped to use the restroom and then talk to lunching priests, not for a few minutes, but for twenty. When we finally resumed our walk, he continued on with his supernatural tales, spinning each yarn with meticulous detail, making it seem as though I were there. It was as if I had been an assistant at his side, watching the fight between good and evil, between the priest and the demon, until there was a victor and a vanquished. I'd gotten several text messages during our walk, but I ignored them. I was too embarrassed by the nonsense my ears were hearing but, even more embarrassingly, I couldn't stop listening.

There was something else, too. It wasn't the barely believable tales of supernatural evil. It was a look in Father Myles's eyes. I'd only seen the look twice in my life: on Market Street in San Francisco and at Boston Common. It was those huge, soul-searching eyes of his. I'd heard that psychics could "read" your aura, that field of energy around your eyes, and I soon began to wonder if Father Myles was reading me and learning more about me than I was comfortable with. During those moments, when he got that look that so disturbed me, he'd nod off to the right as if going to sleep. But he wasn't going to sleep. He was having a vision, a vision of my life, fanned out before his eyes, like playing cards.

As we walked into St. Anne's Cathedral, the tales continued, this time in whispers.

"This one time in Dublin, it was a girl, fourteen years old, tiny little thing, one hundred pounds at most, who lifted a three-hundred-pound bishop's throne and flung it into the pews like a rag doll. Normally it took three priests to lift that bloody chair. Or another girl in West Africa, eight years old, who began to speak in Coptic, a language in ancient Egypt. Explain that, why don't you?"

We lowered our bodies into seats in the front pew. Father Myles took off his blazer and leaned back with his cane between his legs.

"Only a handful of people in the world know Coptic anymore," I said, "and they're all scholars."

"That's m'point. The eight-year-old girl certainly didn't go to university to learn it. Nor did her mother, who'd lived her entire life in a West African village." Father Myles turned the cane with his fingers and looked up at the cathedral's ceiling. "Or tell me, if you can, how a young man in Belfast could rise up off the chair in which I was exorcising him and then float up to the dome of Trinity Cathedral?"

That was enough. "Because . . . somebody made it up?"

"When you see it, you'll believe."

"What happened, then?"

"I commanded the demon to bring the young man down. Very gently, of course."

"Did it?"

"If I give the command in Christ's name, the demon must obey. Or the demons, if you've got more'n one."

232

On the back wall, a fly buzzed around Christ's crown of thorns, then from knee to blood-spattered knee. Father Myles got a text but ignored it, speaking instead of other tricks the devil used to distract the exorcist, like having the possessed person cough up foreign objects, such as rose petals, shards of glass, and railroad spikes.

"Railroad spikes?" I said.

"Happens all the time."

The fly crawled up into Christ's nostril and then out again, while Father Myles turned the cane, which hissed on the carpet. "So this friend of yours, what's her name?"

"Jenna McMaster."

"No relation to John McMaster, I suppose?"

"I've asked her several times, but she always got annoyed and changed the subject."

"The simple mention of John's name provoked the evil entity inside of her. You know, John's a good friend of mine. Once in Rome, I invited him along to an exorcism. I said, 'Now, John, I know you think all of this is perfectly medieval and all-out rubbish, but when you see the real thing, you'll believe.' 'Twas exactly what happened, too. After the demon revealed to John a few shameful things about his personal life, including what he'd done in his father's basement as a teenager, John was a believer. An instant conversion, just like in the movies."

After he told me another case, this one from the Pine Ridge Indian Reservation, we left the cathedral, the air suddenly colder, so that Father Myles put his blazer back on.

"Some weather, eh?"

"It was spring just an hour ago. Now it's winter."

"Nebraska weather is like an exorcism: calm one minute, tempestuous the next."

"Or like postmodern fads."

"Oy, is it ever."

We entered the parking lot, side by side. We stopped at the Silverado, and Father Myles leaned on his cane with both hands and watched me put the key in the door. I set my satchel inside, while he gave me one of his steady, soul-searching looks.

"Next time we'll talk philosophy. Speaking of which, you'd better hope your dissertation is still relevant when you go on the job market."

I was aware of this problem, but Father Myles said not to worry about it, that I'd cross that channel when I got there, and that my main task at the moment was to get my schoolwork done and to stay away from Jenna.

"I know you want to help the girl," he said, nodding off to the right, "but she's a doorway to the demonic realm, something for which you aren't entirely ready. And pay no attention to Kenny Winslow, either. His ghost is out there by the Platte River." He perked up and adjusted his hands atop the cane. "Besides, you've got bigger targets to shoot for."

50

liz.oreilly@bfu.edu
to
zarathustra@bfu.edu

Hi, Carl

Rob said you were meeting with Father Myles. How'd it go?

I did an Internet search on Jenna McMaster. Did you know she's moved ten times in the past ten years? Yet every address is in Lincoln.

Lincoln is barely ten miles in any direction. Why would you move so often without really moving? Would she be trying to get away from somebody? If so, maybe that's the person she's venting at in your letter?

Liz

zarathustra@bfu.edu
to
liz.oreilly@bfu.edu

Hi, Liz.

I met with Father Myles today. The Enlightenment seemed to have passed right over that guy. He kept falling asleep on me, too. What's that about?

Jenna's moved ten times? Doesn't surprise me. You should see her current place. It's a mausoleum. She won't be there for long, either.

That's all. Back to my books.

Carl

liz.oreilly@bfu.edu
to
zarathustra@bfu.edu

You know that Father Myles is a psychic, right? So when he has visions of a person's life, it looks like he's sleeping. He was probably trying to "read" you, so he could get a better idea of the kind of person you are. You might want to keep a watch on him next time, since he's known to fall over and injure himself. That's why he walks with a cane. He's had so many injuries over the years that he needs the support.

I'll be at the Newman Center tomorrow.

Liz

Next day, Liz was in her office chair, placing an online order from a wedding store. I walked in, sprawled out on the leather sofa, and got out Jenna's rubber band.

"Ten times?" I said.

"I've bookmarked her addresses. So you've never met her parents?"

"Nope."

"Has she mentioned them?"

"Briefly."

"Good or bad?"

"They're still married and her dad's a swell guy."

"Yeah, sure. What else?"

I poked a finger through the rubber band, then pulled it out. "She didn't say much about them. She'd always think long and hard before she answered a question about them, especially her dad. It was like she didn't know how to talk about them and had to puzzle it out, first."

"Go on."

"That's it."

"Carl, you dated Jenna for four months."

"Yeah, but we didn't do much talking. If we did, it was all about me."

"You're a philosopher. Think."

I stretched the rubber band and raised the pink triangle to my eye. "You want something else? Okay, fine. Jenna's parents are passionate lovers, and in addition to her dad being a great guy, he's a rebel, too."

"She said that?"

"Yup."

"Okay, so let's say Jenna's father violated her. I could see that the most she could say about him was that he's a rebel. Confessing anything more, like intimate details of their secret relationship could be deadly, and death threats aren't uncommon in these circumstances."

Liz bit her lower lip and turned in half circles in the chair. "I'll bet that letter she wrote to you was really meant for her dad. All those feelings of rage she's kept buried deep inside finally came bursting out. Who knows how long the abuse has been going on? It could still be happening."

I lowered the rubber band, warm and sticky in my fingers. "So Jenna's letter is a cry for help?"

"A big one. What else do you know? Think hard."

"Hmm, let's see. She was married once."

"Older man?"

"By twenty years, I think."

"Sounds like a father figure. Does he live in town?"

"The guy walks around aimlessly with his dogs. He's as whacked as she is."

Liz plucked at the gold heart necklace on her blouse and turned in the chair. "If the divorce was recent, that'd rule out the ex-husband as the one who's chased her for ten years." Liz touched her forehead as though she had a headache. "Okay," she said, standing up. "My mom and I are going to look at wedding cakes now. We'll discuss this later."

We went down the stairs together. A priest stuck his head out of his office, and I pushed the rectory door open for Liz and then threw on my shades.

"I can't believe this stuff really happens," I said.

"Oh my God, more often than you can imagine. You should meet the girls my mom works with. You wouldn't believe what they've been through."

51

Inside St. Michael's, I dipped my fingertip into the stone jar of holy water, crossed myself, and then stood and took in the atmosphere. Two nuns were praying the rosary, while the statue of the mother of God stood quietly in the corner. A vase of pink carnations lay at her bare feet.

I pulled the kneeler down with my foot and knelt on it. Closing my eyes, I prayed with the nuns, but soon got distracted. *If Jenna's father is so great, and if her parents are so in love, then why is she so screwed up? No respectable job, no decent relationships, no marriage or kids.*

I was listening to the sincere words of the nuns when the chapel doors of my heart opened up slowly, and I found myself petitioning the virgin.

"Holy mother of God, could you please pray for Jenna? And if the fairy tale world of the Bible is true, could you also ask the saints in heaven to pray for her, too? And if there's a Satanic influence in her life, then please give me a sign, so that I can take this pre-modern theology crap seriously. Please don't let me blow it. Please help Jenna. Help me, too. If Nietzsche, Marx, and Freud are wrong, please give me a sign. Any sign."

My phone lit up.

Liz texted, *My mom thinks Jenna's father is the pursuer. I did a Google search on him. Lyman McMaster. Say that ten times in a row. Doesn't it make you afraid?*

I shut off my phone. Lyman McMaster. My bones grew suddenly cold as I repeated his name, and I got to my feet without putting the kneeler back up and, forgetting to cross, left the cathedral.

Riding to the university with the dark wind in my shoulder-length hair, I stopped at the gates of the Garden. Through the black iron bars, I stared at the tangles of dead flowers and clumps of bluestem, speculating about Jenna's childhood and of her growing up on a farm with nothing to do but watch the corn grow taller and stay at home with Lyman McMaster, a rebel, for a father.

"Lyman McMaster," I whispered.

Two Muslim girls passed by in brown pea coats and headscarves, their eyes cast down as they moved quickly and purposefully. I looked through the bars again, reading the small nameplates of the dead plants. "Basket of Gold." "Baby's Breath." "Rapeseed."

My eyes roamed back to the last nameplate. I looked at each of the eight letters carefully, just to make sure I was seeing right. I took hold of the iron bars, then bit down hard on my lips. That was Jenna's flaw.

I went to Walgreens and bought a box of envelopes along with postage stamps with the Liberty Bell on them, and then rode to the Loft. In the café's dim light I wrote a few drafts of a letter until I got the words right.

Dear Mr. McMaster,

Hello, sir. I was curious to know if you're the father of Jenna McMaster. She lives in Lincoln and drives a bus for the train depot.

If Jenna is your daughter, I'd like you to know that I was dating her but had to cut it off.

You see, sir, your daughter lives in darkness and filth. She also can't hold a steady relationship, she's hooked on drugs, she deals them, and I'm fairly certain she's consorting with demons. I've also heard that she's a prostitute.

Furthermore, I have reason to believe she was sexually abused.

Mr. McMaster, would you know anything about that?

After I found the McMasters' address online, I rode to a Wells Fargo down the street. I pulled up to a blue mailbox and pulled the lid open.

Drop it in, Sorensen. Jenna needs help.

"We'll see if that asshole's guilty," I said and dropped it in.

At the hotel, Avery was watching *Hannity*, who began to interrogate a gun control advocate. Avery said Jenna had been by, asking for me.

"What'd she say?"

"Nothing."

"She just asked for me and then left?"

"Yeah, to seek out her next victim. You're ancient history. How does it feel?"

I walked into the lobby. Ancient history? No, I'd be remembered forever. Dear Jenna and family, have fun stepping on that land mine I've sent you. I hope it blasts you so high you'll land in a new zip code. Trust me, you need it. Yes. You. Do.

Later that night, I woke up in bed but couldn't move. Something invisible and foul smelling was sitting on my chest. In the hallway, I heard footsteps, slow and heavy-booted, each one growing louder and more foreboding, until a figure stood at my door with big, mud-caked combat boots on. The distant gallops of warhorses could be heard, along with the wheel and crash of chariots, above which came the shouts of a strange race of men.

I squeezed my eyes into knots, gasping for breath, trying to turn sideways, to break free from whatever had seized me. I couldn't. Then I began to pray. Soon the unbearable pressure on my chest began to ease up, and when I opened my eyes, the figure behind my door was gone.

At noon, I walked to St. Michael's. A mass was in progress, and Father Owens stood at the marble altar, hands spread wide as he consecrated the bread and wine. I sat down in the last pew and pulled the kneeler down. People stared. My forehead was throbbing like mad, and my eyeballs felt sore and strained in my skull. Closing my eyes, I pretended I was invisible.

After the service, I called Father Myles.

"Talk to me, Carl."

"Do you believe in witchcraft?"

"Of course."

"Do witches case spells?"

"Since the beginning of time."

I told him about the visitor in my hallway and then something else that happened an hour later, after I'd fallen asleep and had woken up again. Half a dozen black pigs had gathered under the crucifix on my wall. The pigs had poked their noses at the Savior's feet, snorting and squealing, while an even larger red-eyed animal looked inside my cell from the window.

"There's a priest I'd like you to meet," Father Myles said. "Father Gabriel Sanchez is an expert on the occult and paranormal activity. Chat him up, why don't you. And since you're covering early modern philosophy in your classes—a time that coincided with the witch craze in Europe—you should invite him to speak to your class. You'll have a smashing time."

52

Father Gabriel Sanchez was from Mexico City via Omaha. He ran a Spanish-speaking ministry in the inner city and also taught at St. Joseph's High School. On Monday, I walked into Bryan Hall, wearing all black, ready to meet Father Sanchez as I passed by the busts of the Western philosophers, saying hello to Socrates, Plato, and Aristotle, and then giving a nod to Augustine, Anselm, and Aquinas. Down the hallway, I saw a tall, dark-skinned priest with huge black circles around his eyes, like a raccoon's. He held a tan folder at his side and smiled.

"Father Sanchez?"

"Ah, yes, Mr. Sorensen. It is pleasure to meet you."

"Did you find the building okay?"

"Yes, I have new GPS."

"Technology is amazing, isn't it?"

"Yes, gadget have good side as well as bad side. I say more on technology during today's lecture."

We walked in. Father Sanchez took off a black leather jacket and draped it around a chair by the podium.

"I hope student can understand my accent," he said. "Sometimes when I speak of Trinity, student not know if I say three or tree."

"I'm sure you'll get along fine."

The students trailed into the lecture hall, shaking water off their umbrellas and falling silent at the sight of the priest. I gave my students a look they all knew: sit down and shut it.

"Father Myles told me that you were once a medical doctor," I said.

"This is true. Before I become priest, I study medicine at university in Mexico. I was doctor for ten years. Then I have encounter with evil spirit, and that is when I decide to become priest."

The lecture hall filled up, smelling of hazelnut coffee and wet coats. I introduced Father Sanchez to general applause and took a seat in the back row.

"Thank you, class," Father Sanchez said. "And thanks also to you, Mr. Sorensen, for having me as guest speaker. It is great honor to speak at the University of the Black Forest."

The baseball players inched down in their seats and chuckled; when they looked back at me, I scolded them with my eyes.

"Today I speak to you on modern world. But first I speak on medieval world. Because why? Because medieval world have very different attitude toward supernatural realm."

Father Sanchez launched into a minilecture on Medieval Europe, noting that most Europeans believed in God and the devil, in angels and demons, and in possession and exorcism. The spiritual world was the air they breathed, he said, but in the modern era, things changed.

"In modern era, belief in the authority of Catholic church begin to lose steam. Is that how you say? Lose steam?"

A small wave of giggles washed over the rows of seated students, and I pressed my pencil's eraser to my lips, hoping they would behave themselves.

"So why big attitude change in modern era? Why so many stop believing in God of Abraham, Isaac, and Jacob and the Lord Jesus Christ? Because Europe experience paradigm shift. I now speak of several things that shift intellectual climate in Europe."

Father Sanchez spoke of modern thinkers who broke from the authority of a parental church in favor of the autonomous individual, who followed his or her own thoughts wherever they led. He discussed Newton and Copernicus, Descartes and Kant, and then moved on to Charles Darwin and David Friedrich Strauss, the first great Biblical critic. Then he ended with the masters of suspicion—Nietzsche, Marx, and Freud.

"All of these modern intellectual development help to weaken belief in God," Father Sanchez said. "They also weaken belief in devil, angels and demons, and possession and exorcism."

After the lecture, we took a break, and when I went to fetch a pop at the machine in the hallway, I found Paul had been standing there, listening in.

"I'm surprised Parsons gave you permission to have a speaker," he said.

"I didn't realize I needed it."

"He likes to know about these things. The department is low on funds. How's your week been?"

I wasn't ready to talk about demonic attacks while standing in the hallway. "Interesting. Yours?"

"I have two job interviews in Iowa. Two hundred applicants. Wish me luck."

I got my pop and went back in the lecture hall, walking down the center aisle, with can in hand and my clipboard at my side. It was time for the Q & A session.

I thought I'd lead it off, if only to set a respectful tone. "Father Sanchez, though belief in witchcraft died off in the Enlightenment era, is witchcraft still prevalent today?"

Father Sanchez raised a finger. "Ah, Mr. Sorensen, you ask good question. Yes, witchcraft still exist today." He summarized the various types of witchcraft today—from Wicca, which teaches not to harm others, to Satanic witchcraft, for which harm to others is kind of the point.

Rob stood up, notepad in hand. "Hi, Father. Okay, so in third world countries, a lot of people believe that demons are literal beings. But in modern Western nations, like France and Germany, people tend to believe that demons are just symbols, at best. Why is that?"

"Young man, you ask good question. I summarize this way: In third world country, you have supernatural explanation for everything because Enlightenment thinking has yet to come to that land. In third world country, Jesus Christ is not pot-smoking hippie or liberal university professor. He is risen Lord who defeat Satan and his demons."

"But what about America?" a baseball player—a jock who thought he was taking a gut course, then got interested in spite of himself—said. "We're a modern Western country, we've been influenced by the Enlightenment, and we're still super religious. What's up with that?"

"Mr. Sorensen, I am very pleased with student inquiries. Unlike other modern Western country, America does not fit secularization trend. America is called anomaly—is that how you say? Anomaly? Perhaps America is very young nation, unlike those in Europe, and therefore does not have existential experience that European nation have. Maybe one day, America will."

As Rob's ballpoint pen raced across on his notepad, I felt satisfied with my students' performance. But when I looked up the center aisle, my heart crawled up into my throat. There, standing in the doorway, was a black trench-coated, turtle-necked man stroking his goatee. Dr. Parsons.

The question and answer period resumed, and I stepped out of the lecture hall. Dr. Parsons backed up, eyeing me steadily, gym bag on the floor, with his cheek cradled in his palm.

"Hi, Dr. Parsons."

"Your speaker forgot his necklace made of monkey bones and bongos for a drum circle. And I assume his witch doctor friend couldn't make it today? Or maybe he's on his way, crossing the Atlantic by boat? Shall I check back in two weeks?"

"That's Dr. Sanchez, our guest speaker." I figured Father Sanchez's old title would give him some weight. "He's talking about secularization. I wanted to put a real face to today's topic."

"Yes, but I don't recall a guest speaker appearing on your syllabus. I do, however, recall five lectures on Medieval philosophy, a crime on any philosophy syllabus, to put it mildly. But to throw in a guest speaker on top of it, which includes a small stipend? The department can't afford it."

"Dr. Sanchez refused the honorarium."

"He did? Well, that's the first time I've heard of a Catholic priest doing something for free."

Down below, a lively discussion was going on as Dr. Parsons listened in.

"Carl, the department is paying you to teach this class, not the head of the Spanish Inquisition. Next you'll be flying Ed and Lorraine Warren out to talk about the Amityville horror. Goodness only knows we don't need any more kooks in America, especially on the lecture circuit. Thankfully, modern philosophy and science have come to our rescue and will soon exorcise the world of superstition and nonsense, such as what your students are witnessing right now." He picked up his gym bag. "Don't forget to clean up the chicken blood when you're done. I have class in an hour."

53

After class, I spoke to Father Sanchez about Jenna. As a medical doctor and also a priest, he could speak to her personally and decide if she was possessed or not. If the possibility were strong, he'd ask the local bishop for permission to perform the rite of exorcism.

This was the best news I'd heard so far, and I could think about little else all next day in class and then at the hotel. I was at the bell desk, reading a book about the various inquisitions in Europe—there were three, against Christian heretics, the Jews, and witches—when the phone rang.

"Bell desk," I said.

"Just seen Drive-by-Jenna," Quentin said. "She's looking for you, and she don't look happy."

Perfect. My letter arrived. "Okay, thanks." I hung up. Thirty minutes later, the phone rang again.

"Bell desk."

"Carl, it's me."

"Jenna?"

"Yeah, hi."

"What are you doing?"

"At the moment, calling you."

I knelt down and took the phone with me, the closest I could get to privacy without leaving my post. "Jenna, what's wrong?"

She hung up. I called her back but there was no answer. Then I called Liz from the bell closet and told her the latest news.

"You wrote Lyman a letter?" she said.

"I had to do something."

"Carl?"

"What?"

"Okay, don't write any more letters." There was a long pause, then a sigh. "Oh my God, I feel so awful making this comparison, but if your hunch about Lyman is right, then your letter to that family had an enormous impact, almost as though it were Christ's second coming."

54

What Liz said about not writing letters made perfect sense. So, of course, I didn't listen. I sent a second letter, and a third. In my fourth letter, I included a photo of an old, drunk-looking man sneaking up on a puppy dog playing with a red ball on a day bed. I had just dropped it in the mailbox and returned to the bell closet, where I was grading my students' quizzes, when Avery came in.

"You have a visitor," he said.

"Send them in."

A police officer in a dark-blue uniform appeared in the doorway. Short and stocky, she looked like a Rottweiler with braided brown hair.

"Mr. Sorensen?"

"Yes?"

"We got a call from your ex-girlfriend. She informed us that you've been writing her unwanted letters. Is that true?"

I looked at my computer's screen and then lowered it.

"Mr. Sorensen?"

"They were to her father, not her."

"But you have been writing letters, correct?"

"A few, yes."

The bell desk phone rang, but the officer's eyes never left mine. "Your ex-girlfriend wants the letters to stop."

"Officer, this is going to sound crazy, but I need to tell you something."

The walkie-talkie on her belt crackled as she turned the volume down, her eyes on mine. "Go ahead."

"I have good reason to believe this guy molested his daughter. I won't go into details, but I'm trying to help her."

She inhaled deeply so that her nostrils widened, but her eyes never left mine.

"She wants the letters to stop, and what she says, goes." She held my gaze. "Understood?"

"Okay, no more letters."

She left. I waited ten minutes and then went outside where Avery stood at the curb.

"Fill me in," he said.

"I'd rather not."

"Is it about Jenna?"

"I wish it wasn't."

"God, you're still hitting that?"

"Not anymore. The bigger question is, 'Who's hitting her?'"

When I got home, I mixed a drink and sent Liz a message.

zarathustra@bfu.edu
to
liz.oreilly@bfu.edu

Hi, Liz.

You're never going to believe this, but the cops showed up at work today. Jenna called them. She wants me to stop writing her dad letters. How do you interpret this?

liz.oreilly@bfu.edu
to
zarathustra@bfu.edu

OMG, you're going to get yourself into trouble. Now you've got Rob talking about this, and it's starting to worry me.

My interpretation based on wild guesses? Jenna's mother got your letters and left them in the kitchen for Lyman to find. He called Jenna and gave her hell. He called the police, not Jenna. Lyman's trying to play the good guy in this—help me, an aimless, unreliable graduate student is harassing my daughter. Then he told Jenna to stop all communication with you. He's got her under the gun, so don't be surprised if you don't hear from her for a while, if ever.

I need to study and Rob does, too. He's obsessed with demonic possession now. We haven't been talking a lot, since he's so wrapped up on those books you had him read. But at least he's motivated to write his thesis and will graduate in May. I guess I have you to thank for that ☺

55

Jenna's phone had been disconnected, so I went to her duplex to scope things out. The window shades were drawn to a close. The toy snake had been removed, and I ran a finger over the nail, which had been hammered deep into the door. Then, lifting the mailbox lid, I saw an envelope from Planned Parenthood.

I slunk around to the duplex's side. A pink bicycle was chained to a split-rail fence, and raindrops glistened on the white handle grips. The scent of pinecones swept down the path. In the back, I found a dartboard hanging on the wall. Taped to the dartboard was the front cover of the *Southern Nebraska Register* showing the Pope, his face mutilated by a hundred dart holes. A single red dart stuck in his left eye.

"Whatcha lookin' for?" a girl said.

I looked up and stepped back. "A friend."

"Ever try knocking?"

"I did."

"Then you must be looking for Jenna."

I pulled the dart out. "Yeah."

"I don't think she's here anymore. She come by an hour ago. Took a bunch of stuff, too."

I pushed my fingertip into the dart's point as I stared at the Pope's right eye. "Did she say where she was going?"

"Naw. She was in a hurry, though. Hold on."

The girl—the owner of the bike, apparently—came outside. She wore a white tank top, cutoff blue jeans, and a Pennzoil cap with a brown ponytail pulled through the back.

"Hey, I know you," she said. "Aren't you and Jenna going out?"

"Were."

"Forget something?"

"Fortunately, no."

"Why'd you stop by, then?"

A breeze lifted the newspaper out, and I stuck the dart in, pinning it down without sticking the Pope in the face.

"I don't really know," I said.

The girl lifted a bare heel and picked out a small pebble. "My name's Dawn."

"Nice to meet you. I'm Carl."

"If you forgot something, you better get it soon because I'm pretty sure Jenna's moved."

I moved my finger down the Pope's robe, feeling the tiny, mutilating holes, while Dawn walked up next to me and crossed her arms.

"That's Jenna's."

"What's it for?"

"Every time she takes out the trash, she takes a few practice throws."

"At the Pope?"

"Yup. Said the death of the Pope was a holy event. Scared the shit outta me when she said it, too. She said that in the place she comes from, stabbing the Pope's face is a holy thing. A sacrament."

"Where she comes from?"

"Yup."

"She's from Nebraska, though."

"Far as I know. But she was talking about some other place. Like another world." She picked off the edge of the newspaper and looked at it. "Half the time I never knew what she was talking about. Jenna's kinda nutty, in case you didn't know."

"This other world of hers—did she say anything specific about it?"

"Naw, but I coulda swore she called it the kingdom." Dawn raised a foot and picked out another pebble. "You shoulda seen her eyes when she said it, too. Looked like she was in love with the place, like she was gonna marry it or something."

"When was this?"

"Last year, in her room. I went downstairs to deliver a package we got by mistake, and she got some ritual going on. Even had a Bible on the table. Incense cones, too. Said she was asking the spirits for help."

"And you've seen her do these rituals?"

"Yeah, a couple times, but I always left before she started."

"How come?"

"Because Jenna creeps me out, that's how come."

"Did anything out of the ordinary happen?"

"Not while I was there. But I could feel stuff passing through my room at night. Gave me goose bumps."

"Do you and Jenna hang out much?"

"Huh?"

"Hang out. Did you see a lot of her?"

"She ain't home much. When she is, she mostly has dudes over. I didn't know any of 'em. Except Kenny Winslow."

"He was here?"

"A few times, yeah. Three, maybe four."

"And you're sure it was him?"

"I got two eyes, don't I?" Dawn threw the pebble over the fence and leaned against the house, crossing her arms so that her biceps bulged out. "Even saw the tattoo he was getting. The razorblade. He come over one night after getting it worked on. Showed it to me, even. But he wouldn't ever stay long. Nobody did, not even you. In and out." She gave me a look older than her years. "And you can take that any way you want."

56

Back at my cell, half a dozen houseflies were buzzing against the sunny window. I rolled up an old newspaper with Kenny Winslow on the cover and began to smash them against the glass. No sooner had I killed the flies than more would appear as if out of nowhere. Finally, I threw up the window for them to escape and then locked myself in the bathroom to study.

It happened there, too. A dark, semi-invisible cloud of flies was buzzing around by the showerhead, and I wondered if they'd come in through the ceiling fan or had materialized out of thin air. A funny-looking face seemed to stare back at me from within the swirling cloud of flies. I went out to get the newspaper, and when I came back, the flies had vanished.

Next day in class, I was secretly reading an article on paranormal activity when Dr. Parsons stopped at the podium. "Isn't that correct, Mr. Sorensen?"

I looked up. "Um . . . absolutely."

He smiled skeptically as he wrapped and unwrapped his fingers over the magic wand.

"I must say, Carl. That was quite a spectacle you played host to last week in your class. Fortunately, I was not present for your witch-tribunal, nor thank goodness were your colleagues. However, I do hope that you took liberties to balance the intellectual scales a tad. Did you also teach your students about modern accounts of evil and the demonic, many of which are naturalistic in origin and thus have no recourse to supernatural agencies? Thomas Hobbes, say, who argued that the devil was a symbol of evil rather than a literal being? Or Benedict Spinoza, who claimed that good and evil don't exist in any literal sense? And then, of course, there's the great Voltaire, who poked fun at the folly of the Middle Ages, the Renaissance, and the Reformation with its superstitious beliefs in magic and witchcraft. And let us not forget those pioneers of the human psyche, Sigmund Freud and Carl Jung, both of whom asserted that those who believed in the demonic were the victims of a disturbed mind. The demonic is within us, not from without." He gripped the wand tightly. "I trust you are exposing your students to these important modern thinkers?"

"Of course."

"I don't know how men and women in the twenty-first century could live as though the Enlightenment had never happened. Instead, such individuals seem to prefer the enchanted world of the Abrahamic faiths. The insufferable William Jennings Bryan is a case in point. Hopefully by next year the last traces of his personage will have vanished from this campus."

During the break, I went downstairs and ducked under the stairwell, next to a yellow janitor's cart, and dialed up Dawn whose number I'd gotten before I left.

"Jenna come by and got a garbage bag of clothes," she said.

"When?"

"Like, ten minutes ago."

"Did you say anything?"

"I tried to, but she gone out the back door and into the back yard. Then she threw her bag over the fence and climbed after it. Next thing I know, her dad pulls up in front of the house in a flatbed truck. Guy was banging on the door and snooping around."

The bottles of cleaning solvent made my eyes water, and I walked out from the stairwell. "Did you talk to him?"

"Hell, no."

"What's he look like?"

"I don't know. Had sunglasses on. A ball cap, too."

"Are you sure it's her dad?"

"He's been over to the house before. Always got the same thing on—big old sunglasses and a baseball cap."

The logic professor walked by and tipped his fedora in greeting.

"All right," I said and rubbed the back of my neck. "Call me if you see anything else. And see if you can find out where she's going."

"Yeah, I will. Oh, and I didn't mean to talk bad about Jenna last time. She done a lot of good things, too. Like buy me a bike. Paid for it in cash, even. She even let a homeless kid live with her for two months, early last year. So, yeah, Jenna done good things, too. But I ain't gonna lie, she's scary. Ask the landlord. He won't go near her."

When class resumed, Dr. Parsons buried us under an avalanche of scholarly minutia and polysyllabic words. Irritated and bored, I texted Liz.

Jenna bought her friend a bike. Interpretation?

She's probably helped out dozens of people over the years. She's atoning for her sins. But they're not hers. She just thinks they are.

So her dad's gotten her to think it was her fault?

I'm sure nothing is ever his fault.

Dr. Parsons prattled on, often pausing to improve upon his witch trial comment. It got old fast. When several guys from Philosophy House began to join in, snickering and offering jabs of their own, I tuned out and texted Father Myles, who said I could stop by later in the afternoon.

The rest of the seminar was every bit as painful. I found it difficult to concentrate or to even look at Dr. Parsons or my colleagues at the table. I even began to loathe them. They weren't really my friends; they were the enemy, guys against whom I'd be competing for jobs, assuming there were any left.

After class, I left the seminar room with my head held high, and when I rode back to the hotel, Quentin stepped out of the parking ticket booth, guitar in hand, and handed me the Silverado's keys.

57

Father Myles stood in his office at the fish tank, feeding his blue-and-white koi.

"Story horse?" he said.

"Things could be better, I guess."

"How about a coffee?"

"Let's go."

At Starbucks, we stood in a line ten-people deep, all of them with their fingers scrolling phone screens. The cash register clattered with coins, while a barista with a strip of hot-pink hair called out a customer's drink. I stood next to Father Myles, who had his hands atop his cane, and whose wild bright-red hair and beard were like a burning bush.

"So how does a person become possessed?" I said. "Malachi talks about character flaws the devil takes advantage of, which is how he works his way into your life. Is that true?"

Father Myles grew thoughtful. "You know, possession is a funny thing. Demons don't just jump out from behind a bush and grab a hold of you and say 'Ah, now you're mine.' That's Hollywood's version, not the church's. Rather, a person must invite a demon in. Possession is voluntary, cooperative, and it's also a process. It can take months, even years for a person to become genuinely possessed."

The line moved forward.

"But yes, Malachi is basically correct. Old Nick knows our flaws and uses them to his advantage. Speaking of Malachi, he had a friend once, the famous psychologist M. Scott Peck. You've heard of Peck, *The Road Less Travelled*? He also wrote a book on demonic possession. In one case, Peck tells about a father who abused his daughter, which made the girl a target for possession. Her name was Jersey, and for almost forty years, the devil was her only friend. A sadder state of affairs I cannot imagine."

After Father Myles gave me a more realistic commentary on possession, we got our coffees and sat down by a sunny window. A young family was sitting nearby, a mother and father plus two small girls. The parents wore jogging suits and looked at their phones; the two girls did the same. One of the girls texted the other and both giggled.

I told Father Myles about Jenna's father and my hunch about him.

"Ever met the fella?"

"No, but she says he's a real swell guy."

"I'm sure she does. Where's she from?"

"Central Nebraska."

"Find out which diocese she's in. I'm seeing the Diocese of Grand Island, but get me the specifics, if you can."

I sipped my coffee, wondering about his use of the word "seeing." The small girls had moved on to video games, their blonde heads touching over the table, like two suns. Father Myles poured in cream and stirred his coffee.

"You know, there's a myth about the American small town. We think they're so quiet, so peaceful. Far from it." He spoke of Sherwood Anderson, the author of *Winesburg, Ohio*, which had blown the myth of the American small town to smithereens, showing its inhabitants to be full of outcasts, perverts, the lonely, and the like. "Some of those small town fathers are as innocent as nuns doing squats in a cornfield."

I asked about the rite of exorcism and if Father Myles thought Jenna was possessed. He told me it was highly likely, but he needed a photo of her first, allowing him to read her and to glimpse her spiritual state.

We walked back to campus. I felt drained by the conversation, but Father Myles was still going strong, hobbling merrily along with his cane.

"Did I tell you that after an exorcism I like to stop off at Starbucks? It's a ritual of mine. Every exorcist I know has a ritual after the ritual. For some it's Dairy Queen, for others McDonald's. Often it's the nearest tavern. Nobody knows that we've just come from an exorcism. 'Tis quite funny, actually."

I opened the Silverado's door with barely enough energy to drive back to Lincoln. I threw my satchel inside and turned to Father Myles, who seemed ready for another round of conversation.

"So if I send you a picture of Jenna, you'll know if she's possessed?"

"I can usually tell, yes."

"But if you're a psychic, wouldn't you already know?"

"It doesn't quite work that way. I need to see the girl first, either in person or in a photo."

"So you know about my life?"

He looked away and smiled. "I've got an inkling."

"What about my future?"

"The more we get to know each another, the clearer it'll become."

I thought of Dr. Parsons and our confrontation in the seminar room. I didn't have much respect for him left, but I did respect the thinkers he'd listed. "Can you tell me something about myself? I'm still a little skeptical about this paranormal stuff."

He lowered his head as his beard blew in the breeze, and when he looked up, his eyes were . . . different. I flinched at the sight of them.

"Are you sure?" he said.

I swallowed. A dreamy, all-knowing look had come into his eyes, and suddenly I feared what he knew about me. I almost didn't want to know.

But my interest in truth won out. I nodded.

"You're a drinker, for starters," he said.

"Every now and then, sure."

"Try every other day. You must contain your drinking before it contains you. It could impede your academic performance." He looked at his hands. "May I tell you something else?"

"Sure."

"I'm seeing cutbacks in your school's strategic plan. Big ones. This will spell disaster for your teaching assistantship."

"That could be . . . that's . . . Tell me something else."

"How about later?"

"How about now? This is my academic future we're talking about."

Father Myles looked away at the ball fields. "There will be plenty of time for talk. Until then, I'd advise you to lay off the hard stuff. Drink more coffees, if you can. I wouldn't be surprised if Old Nick tried to use the bottle against you. And send me a picture of the girl, if you can. Just don't get too close to her. If you do, the demons will attack you with more of a vengeance and they could very well succeed."

58

Betty the secretary was waiting for me. She stood outside the lecture hall, glaring at me above her rimless spectacles, like a bison ready to charge.

"Hi, there," I said.

"Dr. Parsons wants a word with you."

"Now?"

"As soon as humanly possible. His words, not mine."

I walked in, and Dr. Parsons looked up from a book and told me to sit down.

"Carl, did I not specifically tell you to have no more guest speakers? The department can't afford it. I see that you've also invited the Reverend Bill Blitzer to speak to your class?"

"That's right. And, again, he's doing it without charge."

"I didn't know Protestants believed in the devil, at least the few I know. So tell me, what is your reason for having a second speaker?"

"Actually, I'd booked Reverend Blitzer before you spoke to me in the hallway." This was a lie but it seemed like the right thing to say. "And I wanted to keep my word. I won't have any more speakers, though. I haven't booked anybody else, nor will I."

"Fair enough. But I must ask you something, Carl. What is your sudden fascination with demon possession? We do philosophy here, not theology, and certainly not magic. If you'd like to teach theology, perhaps you can adjunct at a local college. There you'll find no shortage of students from the four corners of Nebraska who'd be glad to discuss spiritual warfare with you. Now I'd better see you and only you teaching your class from now on. You are highly valued as a teaching assistant, though I can think of many a graduate student who'd love, love, *love* to be in your shoes. Understood?"

Without waiting for a response, he stood up, and I did, too.

"Now I must be off to the gym. That piece of rum cake I had for lunch was delicious but—whew—it made me dizzy. Plus, I feel fat." He put on his beret and black leather jacket. "Oh, and by the way, the department will undergo some budget cuts in the fall, with fewer teaching assistantships being offered. However, I shall see to it that you keep yours, assuming your teaching performance is back up to par."

He kept talking, but I wasn't listening. I just watched his lips move as he rubbed lip balm on them, hearing only two words: budget cuts. Father Myles had seen it.

He wrapped a black silk scarf around his neck and then looked at his watch. "And did I tell you that I'm flying to England soon? There's a lovely old Norman church in the rural county of Northumberland, which, ironically, is known as 'the cradle of Christianity.' I might make my big purchase and have several fabulous ideas for its restoration. I really hope it becomes our second home. Otherwise, it'll be converted into a mosque. So wish me luck. Cheerio."

59

Outside, groundskeepers in light-blue T-shirts and denim were spreading red mulch in the flowerbeds along Bryan Hall. High clouds, thin and wispy, like check marks on a student's paper, were streaked across the blue sky as a private airplane droned faintly over campus. I stood next to Mr. Bryan, who gave me a thumbs-up and told me not to fret. He seemed to know what had just happened in Dr. Parsons' office. I set my phone in the Great Commoner's hand and fumbled for my smokes, when my phone rang. I picked up.

"Yeah?"

"Jenna's dad's here now," Dawn said. "He banged on her front door, and Jenna flew out the back one. She's got her car parked on a backstreet. Got a garbage bag of clothes with her. Boxes, too."

"Is she going to a friend's house?"

"She ain't got friends. Prolly the city mission."

"Where else would she go?"

A black squirrel sniffed its way over the red mulch and turned over a chip.

"Only other place I know of is a church."

"A church?"

"Yeah. I can't remember which one, but Jenna took me by it once. Said it was her favorite place."

The squirrel rose up on its back legs and, turning, watched me with a single, black eye.

A church, of course. "Is it on top of a hill?"

"That's it."

"Why does she go there?"

"To get away from her crazy life. I think some bad things happened to her when she was a kid. That's why she does them rituals in her room—for power."

The squirrel began to chatter loudly, and I pushed a fingertip into my ear, focusing to hear. "Well, keep me posted if you see her again. And call me if her dad tries to pull anything funny."

"I got my eye on him now."

"What's he doing?"

"Just sitting in his flatbed truck, looking creepy. But yeah, I'll call you if something happens."

60

After I lectured on Kant's ethical maxims, I rode to the church on the hill. The cottonwood had been struck by lightning since I'd been there last, split right down the middle, the two halves of the trunk spread out grossly on the grass. The moist inner meat was exposed, glowing pink in the half-dark; the west wind carried off its aroma, perfuming the air, along with the odor of wet, dead leaves. At the bottom of the hill on a white gravel road, a large deer appeared and then a smaller one, their large gentle eyes the color of syrup in a pan.

Inside the church, the rows of pews were dark and silent. Atop the altar, red candles were burning dimly in their wine bottles, while a demonic face with "X"s for eyes had been spray-painted on the back wall. An army-surplus sleeping bag lay spread out in the corner with boxes on top of it.

One of them was a shoe box with my name on it.

I walked over and stared at it. Then I knelt down and lifted the lid. My psychological report was inside. Jenna had edited the front page, adding words and sentences, these additions in blue ink, penned in her irregular scrawl.

Lowering the lid, I moved to the next box, a cigar box. Inside was a stack of driver's licenses, held together by a pink rubber band. I pulled it off and thumbed out the licenses. All of them belonged to male drivers, young and old, and all of them were from the Midwest—Nebraska and Iowa, South Dakota and Missouri. One guy was from Illinois.

Jenna's other victims? Probably. I wanted to do an Internet search to see who these guys were, to see if they'd come up as missing persons, until, at the end of the batch of licenses, I held a college ID card in my hand.

> Kenny Winslow
> DOB: March 15, 1986
> Major: Sports Medicine
> Home Town: Red Cloud, Nebraska

Outside, a crow cawed. I got up and walked to the side window. The meadow was quiet, the grass still, and the stars looked new and huge overhead. Through the line of black pines, the headlights of a fast car bounded over the speed bumps in the parking lot. I was tempted to take my box and burn its contents, but I didn't want to give any hints I'd been there. So I put the boxes back, then left.

Walking my bike past the felled cottonwood, I advanced down the hill as the family of deer fled one by one into the forest. I stopped by the white gravel road, fresh with dozens of deer tracks, and crept low behind a green oil drum.

Jenna appeared. She was holding two brown shopping bags of clothes, a pink scarf dragged behind her in the grass as she scrambled to the safety of the church. I snapped a few photos with my phone and then recorded a small video, planning to send them to Father Myles.

I stood guard for an hour, watching the entrance to the forest and, once I felt sure that she was safe for the night, I left.

61

Next time we met at Starbucks, Father Myles told me something else about myself: I was on the brink of a major discovery. It would happen over spring break, too. I asked him about it, but the specifics were unclear in his mind, though the general outline was there. "There's a fella who's going to help you solve the Kenny Winslow mystery, a college football player, someone Kenny had played against. A Husker." I'd texted Rich Richardson asking who it could be. *Darnell James*, he texted back.

The days passed. One night at the hotel, Avery and I were in the kitchen, while Robert the cook dished up our runzas. Larry the Cable Guy was on TV, telling jokes about Nebraskans.

"Larry rules," Avery said. "He's from Nebraska, too. He rips on us big time, but you just have to laugh. Everybody loves Larry."

Robert the cook swaggered by the deep fryers, gobbling up stray French fries and listening to Snoop Dogg on the radio.

"So who's Darnell James?" I said.

"You mean DJ? He's the biggest, baddest defensive lineman to ever play for the Huskers."

"So he's a Blackshirt?"

"Since his freshman year. He could've gone pro after his freshman year, too, but he wanted to finish his degree. Why do you ask?"

"Just curious."

"DJ's from Oakland, California. When he walks onto the field, the medics get the stretchers ready. Just watch us against Colorado from two seasons ago. Brutal."

Robert called out the orders and put the plates under the heating rack. He ate a stray fry and then walked away.

"Nebraska's getting in your DNA," Avery said and picked up his dinner plate. "Soon you'll be wearing scarlet and cream. You might even start going to the games."

We chomped down in the bell closet, as I asked for more about Darnell James. Did he live in town? What were the key plays and tackles he'd made as a Husker? Avery told me the facts, but also warned me that if I ever speak to Darnell, there was one topic I should never bring up: Kenny Winslow.

"Bad blood?" I said.

"Log onto YouTube."

We watched some old game footage, including a clip where Kenny ran right over Darnell for a touchdown.

"Darnell got steamrolled," I said.

"Did you see the comments? They're hilarious."

"So two years have gone by, and people are still talking about this play?"

"DJ's still embarrassed by it, too, which is why you shouldn't bring up Kenny."

62

On Saturday, I walked to the University of Nebraska. I'd devised a clever way to bring up Kenny Winslow to Darnell James. I walked through the gates of the Garden in black shorts and a black tank top with black running shoes on, the patches of grass on either side of me freshly cut with silver lawnmower lines still visible. I walked into Love Library and spoke to the girl at the circulation desk.

"Hey, have you seen Darnell?"

"Um, I haven't seen him today. Have you tried the periodical section? He studies in there."

I checked, then came back. "No luck."

"Oh, then you might try the rec center. If he's not here, he's there."

"Is that a gym?"

"Um, yeah. Just go toward Memorial Stadium and then turn right. You'll see a bronze mammoth. The rec center is right across from the mammoth."

I walked into the rec center, which echoed with the hollow thunder of basketballs. I passed the front desk and entered a weight room. It didn't take long to spot Darnell—he was the big one sitting on a weight bench in the corner, elbows on knees, head down. Tattoos in what looked like Arabic spiraled up and down his arms, and his large fingers were wrapped in athletic tape, shredded up, and powdery. I walked up to the weight bench and stared at the black do-rag atop his head. He looked at his palms, pink and smooth like the insides of seashells.

"Mr. James?"

He looked toward me, though not actually at me. "This him."

"Hello, sir. My name's Carl Sorensen. I go to BFU. I realize you're busy, but I was hoping I could ask you a few questions. If you don't mind."

Darnell pulled at a loose thread of tape on his index finger. "'Bout what?"

I put my hands on my hips. "Kenny Winslow."

He pulled at the thread, only more slowly, and then curled it around his finger and snapped it off. "Kenny dead."

I moved my shoe over a strip of athletic tape on the floor. "I realize that but—"

"Read the papers."

"I have."

"Do it again."

"They don't tell the full story, do they? The reporters missed something. And I believe I've got a better theory. I also know where Kenny got his superhuman strength from."

Darnell lifted his head a little but still didn't look at me.

"I'd like to run my theory by you, but I need to know a few things first."

Darnell balled up the piece of thread and let it fall to the mat. He clasped his pink palms together and began to rock slowly from side to side.

"It won't take long," I said.

Darnell opened his palms and looked at them. I looked into the mirror above him and then down at Darnell, now motionless on the bench. Then he reached for his gym bag and rose to his feet, our eyes briefly meeting.

"Out front," he said.

63

I waited in the rec center's lobby. I was dying for a cigarette but didn't dare go outside to light one. A campus police car was circling in the parking lot, and I tried not to look at Mr. Crushfoot, the bronze mammoth, towering above the rows of shiny cars.

I checked my calendar on my phone. All those term papers to write. I sent Rob a text.

Need you to check out books. Game?

I'll have free time coming up. I'm flying through my thesis. What are you up to today?

Meeting with Darnell James.

No way.

We're closing in.

On?

Kenny Winslow, Jenna, the whole shebang. Gotta run.

Darnell walked out in a black tank top and shorts and black shoes. His arms were as large as my legs, thick and sinewy and smelling of soap.

"Let's go," he said. "We'll talk on the way."

We walked outside and crossed the parking lot, so that I passed under Mr. Crushfoot's big, upraised foot.

"So what do you want to ask me about?" Darnell said.

"A girl. Kenny knew her and you might have, too. How much time do you have?"

"I've got books to check out, but you can come with me, if you want."

An hour later, Darnell and I walked out of Love Library and into a sunny day.

"What you say sounds crazy," he said, "but it makes sense, too. You and I, we got away. But Kenny, he went all the way. He met the Man."

"I had trouble believing it, too. I still do at times, but if God and the devil are real . . ."

A gray-headed man in khakis and a pink polo shirt, backpack on, shot by on a skateboard.

"How much time you got?" Darnell said.

"As much as you need."

"I'll tell you something else. Let's go."

We left the campus, following a pair of train tracks to the north, past Memorial Stadium; our shadows shifted back and forth on the red rocks of the bedding that was scattered with occasional rusty railroad spikes. Darnell joked about his infamous meeting with Kenny in the end zone, a meeting the sportscasters had dubbed "the Hit." They had compared it to Bo Jackson slamming on through Brian Bosworth in the end zone, but then adding that Kenny's hit on Darnell was worse.

"So after Kenny scored that touchdown, I said to him, 'Man, how'd you do that?' and he said to friend him on Facebook, so I did. Then, on a bye week, a bunch of us guys were down by the river. Me, Kenny, guys from both teams. Had us a barbecue. So there I was, in the middle of the river, just chilling on a sandbar with my biology books on one side and a *Sports Illustrated* on the other, when I saw Kenny on the shore, just tossing a football up and catching it. He texted me, *Watch this.* Next thing I know, that football he was holding went flying over the river to the other side and knocked some bark off a tree.

"So I texted him back, *Ain't no way.* Then he texted back, *Show you again.* Next thing I know he did it again—the longest, most perfect throw you ever saw. It hit the same tree, in the exact same spot. Next thing after that, I saw Kenny walking on the water. He came right up to me with his cross-trainers on, bone dry. He said, 'What you thinking about?' And I go 'Are you for real?' And he went, 'You can do it, too. Just ask and I tell you how.'"

We stopped at a train crossing and stepped to the side. The red warning lights were flashing, and the bar dropped down over the tracks. Soon, a line of sea-green boxcars drifted on by, and Darnell set the book bags down and began to massage his upper arm.

"I saw that girl a while back, too," he said. "She was downtown at a café. She just looked at me with that look she got, like nobody was home."

A police cruiser pulled up at the crossing. The driver's side window went down and the officer said hello. As they talked about the upcoming Husker scrimmage game, I lost myself in the monotony of the boxcars, yearning for a cigarette as I decoded the graffiti on the padlocked doors, scrawled in Jenna-like letters: *Lost Boys of the Corn Belt Club.*

The final car—cabooses were apparently a thing of the past—rattled by, and Darnell picked up the book bags. "Okay, so what else was I gon' say?"

"Something about Kenny and how his personality changed?"

"Oh, yeah. So besides Kenny getting super strong and all, it also seemed like, when you were trying to talk to the brother, you weren't talking to Kenny anymore. You were talking to somebody else."

We crossed the tracks, wandering deeper into the North Bottoms, a haven for college students. Darnell revealed that

Kenny had gotten into fistfights just before his death. One night, the two of them had been walking through the campus, discussing the NFL draft because scouts had been in town that week.

"So Kenny and I were walking through campus, minding our own business, when some frat boy said, 'Get a haircut.' So Kenny, he got all upset, and I said to be cool, but he pushed my hand away and started walking across the street. 'Turning the other cheek is for sissies,' he said."

Kenny had walked into the frat house, and when he came out, his shirt was off. "So I just looked at Kenny with scratch marks on his arms and chest. 'You look like you killed a man,' I said. And he replied, 'What makes you think I didn't?' and kept on walking. So I went inside to see, do I need to call an ambulance? When I got up to the room, frat boy lying on the floor with a big old dresser on his head. So I helped the brother up, but he said not to call the police, because whoever does is gon' get beat ten times worse. That's what Kenny said."

We arrived at a tiny white house with unkempt grass and a sofa on the porch. We walked up the steps and sat on the sofa, which I thought would break under Darnell's weight. Through the window behind us, the voice of Christopher Hitchens could be heard on the TV. He spoke of how sinister old virgins ran the Catholic Church.

"What'd you say to Kenny after he roughed that frat boy up?"

"Not one single word. Like I said, Kenny became somebody else, like it wasn't Kenny you were talking to. A lot of us guys were afraid of him then, even us linemen, cos' he acting like he got magical powers, plus all the fights he was getting into. But yeah, there was something 'bout Kenny you didn't want to mess with."

Hitchens switched topics, saying the Qur'an was fiction, just like the Bible. Darnell looked at me.

"So deep inside of you, what do you think 'bout Kenny? Do you think he was possessed by the devil?"

"I hope not. I hope all that stuff's fiction. But . . . I'm not sure."

"Yeah, but what you say 'bout the devil makes sense of it all."

"That's what I keep saying, too. But I don't know what's real anymore and what's not. I mean, the idea is just flat-out crazy—evil incarnate taking people over and destroying them for fun? Who can believe it? But at the same time, it makes the most sense out of the facts of anything that I've heard."

The early dark descended on the North Bottoms, and the neon-blue of TVs could be seen through the front windows of houses across the street. On the screens, football players in red and white jerseys chased each other down the field. I got out my phone and Darnell got out his.

"You want to eat with us, cos' we talk more, if you want."

"Thanks, but I've heard enough for the night."

Hitchens ranted on, insisting that the tale of an illiterate Arabian man receiving divine revelations from an angel was nonsense. No thinking person could believe it, Hitchens said, and that was that.

"Dude's funny," Darnell said.

"I like him, too."

"Just read *God Is Not Great*. He speaks the truth. I respect that. You read it?"

"It's in my pile, under a dozen other books."

We looked at our phones and scrolled through our messages as Hitchens warned the West about the coming Islamic caliphate.

"Something else you want to ask?"

"Was Kenny from Red Cloud?"

"'Bout three hours away. Only two people I know from Red Cloud. One's a writer, the other's Kenny."

64

Darnell had given me a bottle of water for the road, and I wandered the North Bottoms, moving past a sports arena and the state fairgrounds and then back to the university where I stopped to rest in the Cather Gardens. Sitting atop a large rock, I took thoughtful sips of water and sent Father Myles a text.

I'm sure Kenny was possessed.

As am I.

And Jenna helped?

She did.

I'm writing a letter to Kenny's parents. I need to know about his last months on earth.

His mother would be glad to talk to you.

Am I right in writing this letter?

There was a long pause. Then, *It's your fate.*

Perfect.

Back at the Guardian, Rich and Bubba were pitching horseshoes in the sandlot, while I took refuge in a sanctuary of cottonwoods where the grass was beginning to green by the tracks. I logged onto the Internet and ran a search on "Winslow" and "Nebraska." When I found a Cindy Winslow of Red Cloud, Nebraska (population 1,003), I opened up a Word document and wrote her a letter.

Dear Ms. Winslow,

My name is Carl Sorensen. I'm a doctoral student in philosophy at Black Forest University.

I'm writing to you because I've taken an interest in your son, Kenny. Contrary to what the medical community has stated, I believe there was another factor involved in his death, something the health professionals missed.

If you'd like to meet for coffee sometime, I'd be glad to share what my research has revealed. I'd also be interested to learn more about Kenny—about his childhood, his religious beliefs, and so on. Doing so will help me to get a clearer picture of what I believe happened to your son.

Sincerely,
Carl Sorensen

After I proofread my letter several times, I dropped it into the Guardian's mailbox and tried my best to forget about it.

April arrived. All during that first week, I ditched my phone, the Internet, and the squabble of philosophers at First Friday. I'd drafted my existentialism paper on Clarence Darrow, the great agnostic, mostly to appease Dr. Parsons in the hopes of securing my assistantship in the fall—which, I'd heard from Paul, was already on the chopping block.

By Friday, I was caught up. All my papers had been drafted and my students' midterms graded. I rode out to Quentin's ranch to celebrate, both of us munching on pork sandwiches smothered in baked beans, followed by a jam session on the guitar. He'd upgraded to a better instrument and had broadened his musical horizons; instead of country music, he was playing recent popular hits, especially by The Killers. After he gave me a tour of his bow and arrow collection, and offered up a top-ten list as to why he dropped out of graduate school, he took me back to the Guardian.

As he sped away, I looked at the Guardian's mailbox. I had a hunch something was in there, something essential, and I wanted to be completely alone to witness it. Once the Silverado was out of sight, I opened my slot.

An envelope glowed in the dark cave of the mailbox. It was from Cindy Winslow. Both addresses were handwritten in pencil, and I opened it carefully and turned my back on the fiercely setting sun.

Dear Carl,

Thank you so much for your letter. It would be nice to have you down sometime. I'm looking forward to hearing from you.

Regards,
Cindy

On Monday, I called her. We agreed to meet on Wednesday, the day of my existentialism seminar. What would I tell Dr. Parsons? Turns out I didn't have to. He'd cancelled class and I wasn't complaining. With the way things had gone between us lately, not seeing him or my classmates was something to be celebrated.

The day before I left for Red Cloud, I stopped into Bryan Hall to inquire about my paper on Clarence Darrow, only to find Dr. Parsons standing up in his office, facing the window, wearing a black suit with his hands behind his back. The stereo played softly on the bookcase—Gregorian chant, I think. I leaned against the doorframe, listening to the monks' voices, deep and mournful and sinister. I knocked.

"Dr. Parsons?"

He didn't answer. His briefcase lay open on his desk, and the eye in the triangle observed me. The atmosphere was thicker and harder to breathe in, and though the window shades were up, the office was darker than usual.

I stepped inside. "Dr. Parsons?"

He didn't move. The monks' voices began to swell, louder and louder, until they washed over me like a huge wave of menacing sound, and from every corner of the office I could hear the sound of heavy, impatient breathing. Feeling dizzy, I touched my forehead as big beats of blood began to beat inside my skull, and I backed out of the office and left the building.

65

I pulled up to the Winslow house, then killed the Silverado's engine. In the shade of a giant sycamore, I shut my eyes as the snapshots of my long trip began to scroll by: the plains and plateaus of greening grass, the pink gravel roads galloping up and over the hills, the empty miles of blue sky, and the great flocks of sandhill cranes flying over the fields.

On the Winslows' porch, the wind chimes began to ring like a choir of angels bursting out in song. The notes grew louder until they were absorbed into one harmonious note and then began to separate into various tinkling sounds. I got out and walked up the driveway. Through the screen door, a woman in a long flower-print dress appeared. Her hair was long and brown and pulled up on the sides by hair clips.

"Hi, Carl."

"Ms. Winslow?"

"Yes, please come in." She pushed the screen door open and I wiped my shoes on the mat. "Did you find the house okay?"

"I drove right to it. It was a nice drive down. I've never seen this part of America before."

"Yes, springtime is a nice time of year, all two weeks of it, as we often say."

She led me into the living room. The thin white curtains, like brilliant robes, were on either side of the window, and they blew out gracefully and then fell back and were still. On the sofa were three cardboard boxes with envelopes, both regular and manila, sticking up.

"You'll have to excuse this mess," she said. "Those boxes you see are full of letters. They're still pouring in. I haven't had time to read them all. Other boxes are in the garage. Those I've read."

A coffee table stood in front of the window. She offered me a chair, and I took off my satchel and sat down.

"I haven't had much time for reading," she said, sitting down across from me, "though I must confess that when I got your letter, I just knew I had to open it." She began to rub the knuckles of her hand. "It was so unlike the others."

I looked around the room. Three portraits hung above the fireplace mantle. Ms. Winslow looked up and then at the fireplace.

"That's Kenny at his high school graduation. And that's Trish, his twin sister. And the big German shepherd is Lester—he was Kenny's dog." Ms. Winslow picked up a Catholic Bible off the coffee table and pulled a white envelope from between its pages. "When I read your letter, I thought to myself, Carl's right. There must be more to what happened to my son."

"That's why I'm here today—to discuss some things with you."

"Yes, that'd be nice. Would you like to go to the café now?"

66

We walked along the sidewalk, through the speckled shade of the oaks and sycamores. The white houses stood quietly behind neatly manicured lawns, and on the other side of the street, a girl pulled a wagon with a young boy inside, eating an ice cream cone. The treetops whispered softly as the great gray clouds sailed slowly over the town, like prairie schooners in the sky.

"Didn't Willa Cather grow up here?" I said.

"Her childhood home is down the street. It's a museum now. They give tours, if you're interested."

"I've read *O, Pioneers*."

"I've read several of her novels and some of her poetry as well. A lot of scholars and students visit the museum, especially in the summer and fall."

We walked into the small business district and entered Cutter's Café, taking a sunny table by the window. A payphone was behind me and next to it a jukebox. The machine made a clicking sound as if starting all by itself, and an old Hank Williams song began to play.

"You know," Ms. Winslow said. "I almost wasn't going to open your letter. But I'm really glad I did." She picked up a menu and opened it. "So you've discovered something nobody else on the case has?"

A waitress walked up, took our drink orders, and then left.

"Yes, I believe so," I said. "Do you think losing your faith in God could lead a person to depression, madness, or even suicide?"

"I suppose in some people it could."

"But you don't think that was the case with Kenny?"

"You mean taking his own life because he lost his faith in God? I don't buy that at all, not a bit. Members of my own church are unsure about their faith at times, and they're doing just fine. And Kenny, well . . . I'm sure he'd lost his faith already, even before he'd left for college." She turned a page of the menu. "He often joked that twelve years of Catholic school can do that to a person."

The waitress brought our drinks, a glass of Coke and an iced tea.

I picked up my Coke and took a sip. "My advisor made that argument, at a panel discussion trying to make sense out of his death—about Kenny losing his faith in God and how it was too great a burden to bear. But there's something else I'd like to suggest to you, another piece of the puzzle. It's going to sound pretty unbelievable—it does even to me, if you want my honest opinion—but it makes more sense than anything else I've heard."

Ms. Winslow frowned and, tearing open a sugar packet, said, "And what's that?"

By the time we'd finished our sandwiches, I'd told Ms. Winslow everything about Jenna, her plans to make me a star, the funny-looking faces, the Man, everything. The waitress had brought us coffee by then, and I leaned over my cup.

"So you don't remember if Kenny dated a girl named Jenna?"

"He was dating a lot of girls, then."

"Do you remember any big changes in him, like in his lifestyle or personality?"

Ms. Winslow looked out the window. A red truck pulled up with bales of hay stacked up in the back.

"I suppose the first change was in the way Kenny looked. I'm sure you've seen the pictures, of his long hair and those tattoos he got? Plus all of that muscle he put on? He must have gained twenty pounds. And that's what I don't understand. He'd stopped running and lifting weights around that time. He'd always get up before sunup and go running on the backcountry roads with Lester. But during Kenny's last season as a Bison, he would sleep in late. He went to the gym less and less, and yet he put on all of that muscle, all that weight. Then he became a big star."

A man in a camouflage T-shirt and blue jeans entered the café and took off his hat.

"What was the second big change?" I said.

She looked at her coffee cup. "Well . . . not long after his appearance began to change, Kenny began to isolate himself. The warmth between Kenny, Trish, and myself just kind of went away. But it wasn't just his family, it was happening with everybody. Like this one time when Father Farrell stopped by the house, Kenny wouldn't come out of his room. Father had to speak to Kenny through the bedroom door. After Father left the house, I went into Kenny's room, and there he was just lying on his bed and facing the wall. He ordered me out of his room, which startled me, because Kenny had never spoken to me like that before." She tilted the coffee cup, then looked up. "Does that make sense?"

"Yes, it does."

"There's something else that scared me, too. When we get back to the house, I'll show you."

67

On the walk home, Ms. Winslow told me a few more things about Kenny. Every time he'd come home from college, he'd act a little more distant, a little bit less like the Kenny she knew. And a few months before he died, she hardly knew Kenny at all.

Walking up the porch, Ms. Winslow pushed open the screen door.

"It happened on Easter weekend," she said, and set her purse on the dining room chair. "I'd just come home from work on Saturday, and that's when the religious figurines went missing."

"The figurines?"

She walked into the living room to the fireplace where a row of statues of various saints, with Jesus in the middle, stood on a mantle.

"When I got home, these figurines had been turned around. They were facing the wall. And Our Lord, he was missing. Can you guess where I found him? In the fireplace, lying facedown in the ashes. I asked Kenny if he knew anything about it. He didn't. He seemed irritated that I brought it up." She sat down and began to tap my letter on her knee. "You know, come to think of it, I bet Kenny was dating a girl named Jenna."

"You do?"

"Yes, I'm remembering more clearly now. It was two summers ago, I think. I'd woken up late one night because Lester was barking at the coyotes. I went down the hallway to shush him when I heard Kenny in his room. He was talking on the phone, but it didn't sound like Kenny. That's why I stopped to listen. I stood outside the door with my hand on the knob. He said something like, 'I like the sound of that, Jenny. I really like the sound of that.' But I'll bet you anything it was Jenna."

I took a seat across from her. "Do you know where he met this girl?"

"Kenny didn't talk much by then. Like I said, the warmth between us was dissolving. Where did you meet her, if I may ask?"

"At the Lincoln depot. I think a lot of guys did, including Darnell James."

"You mean DJ?"

"Do you know him?"

"He's been over to the house before, DJ and some other boys. Please don't tell me that Darnell is involved, too."

I set my satchel on it and took a seat. "Not like Kenny and I were, which leads me to my next question. Do you know if Kenny ever rode the Amtrak into the Lincoln depot?"

She tapped the letter on her thigh slowly and thoughtfully until she looked down and closed her eyes.

"Yes . . . it was for a field trip to Iowa. There was a conference on sports medicine, and Kenny and his classmates went."

"That must be where he met Jenna. It's her hunting ground."

"Do you really believe that?"

"Jenna's a vortex, a doorway into the demonic realm. She preys on people who come to Lincoln, mostly athletes and students, or anybody with big dreams and high hopes. She hooks them like fish with her promises of stardom and begins to reel them in until they're in the net."

Ms. Winslow bit down on her lips, and I looked at my hands and folded them in my lap.

"I want to show you something." She rose up quickly, and when she returned, she inserted a disc into the DVD player atop the TV. "I'm sure you've seen what Kenny did to DJ? Well, watch this." The old footage blipped on the screen, and there was Kenny, dragging six Miami Hurricane players into the end zone for a touchdown. She paused the disc. "That's never happened before, at least not when you're Kenny's size. And from almost the fifty-yard line?"

"It's hard to believe."

"But it makes sense if what you said about Jenna is true."

The curtains blew in and a soft breeze entered the room.

"So Easter Sunday was the last time you saw him?" I said.

"Yes, it was. I remember it well because of the way Lester was behaving. He was sitting by Kenny's bedroom door, just moaning and growling. Finally, when Lester started barking, Kenny got so upset that he stormed out of the house and drove back to Lincoln. I even made his favorite dish for supper, but he didn't stay for it. As Kenny backed out of the driveway, Lester ran to the front window and stood up on his hind legs with his front paws on the sill. The sound that dog made as Kenny raced down the street, I'm not sure you could call it barking. It was screaming."

Outside, a school bus went by, rattling the front window as it passed, and a young mother and her kids began to walk down the street.

"Lester lay in his doghouse for days after that. A few days later, he was dead." She came back and sat down. "Carl, I don't know what else you can you do at this point. Kenny's gone. Do you think you'll see this Jenna again?"

"It's likely."

"Hold on." She left and came back. "Before he died, Pope John Paul II blessed it, and I'd like you to have it for protection."

She opened the small maroon box with a rosary inside. I took it carefully from the box and thanked her for having me down.

We walked outside as the cool winds began to blow.

"I hope the drive down didn't inconvenience you at all," she said. "Red Cloud is quite a long way from Lincoln."

"In more ways than one," I said. "But I'm glad I came. I had a lot to think about on the drive, so it worked out."

I opened the Silverado's door as Ms. Winslow raised a hand up to block the sun.

"If you discover anything else, will you let me know?"

"That's the plan."

"Thank you so much, Carl. I hope school is going well for you and that what happened to my son hasn't been too much of a burden for you."

"I think I'd call it an adventure, actually. When I first moved here, I thought Nebraska was just flyover country, something you look down on from a jet plane. I thought nothing of interest ever happened here. I've changed my mind, though. There's no place like Nebraska."

68

I was ready to celebrate my detective work. I drove back to Quentin's, stopping first at the grocery store for T-bone steaks, a sack of potatoes, and fresh green beans, plus a bottle of Jesse James whiskey and Coke. After we fixed a hearty meal and talked about Kenny's developing story, we drank heavily in Quentin's man cave. Taxidermy kits were spread out on various tables, while the heads of elk and deer watched us from the walls as if listening to our talk. I poured a third drink, emptying the bottle of Jesse James, while Quentin picked up a rifle off the workbench.

"I saw Drive-by-Jenna," he said. "Saw her daddy, too. He's looking for her, and she's looking for you. Soon they're both gon' be looking for you."

"I'm living dangerously."

"You ain't scared?"

"Whatever doesn't kill me makes me stronger."

Quentin inspected the rifle's barrel. "It's the stuff that does kill you that you've gotta watch for. You gon' need to switch up your routine. Change is good. Now go on and get her done. And don't be getting no funny ideas, either."

Quentin drove me into the Haymarket, pulling into a parking stall under the pedestrian bridge. I got out and looked at the row of pigeons eying me from the heights.

"Now you just take yourself a walk," Quentin said with both hands on the wheel. "Get you some fresh air until you figure things out."

I began to walk the blocks, first one, then the other, making figure eights as I pondered ways to avoid the McMasters, of new spots I could frequent—bars, cafés, and the like. I kept wandering the same two blocks, when I stopped at a storefront and, cupping my palm to the glass, looked inside.

A copy of *Ink Magazine* lay on a table. On the front cover, a girl straddled a Harley, wearing a black bikini and smiling coyly for the camera.

I looked deeper into the shop. Poster boards hung on the walls with various designs on them: human skulls and roses, Japanese characters and koi fish, dragons and serpents along with nooses, guillotines and other instruments of torture. At a workbench, colorful bottles of ink stood silently in rows along with several small gun-like instruments covered in clear plastic bags, glittering like sacraments on a church altar.

I backed up. In the window, I saw my pale face and my large, worried eyes. Then I saw the Blue Note with its cloth awning flapping in the wind. Turning, I walked toward it, deciding to finish the night there.

"Holy moley, you're alive."

"Hey, Tony."

"Long time, no see."

I slid into Kenny's booth. "I'm closing in on the mystery."

"Are you gonna gimme the inside story?"

"Yeah, but I need to throw one down first."

At two a.m., when the Renegade Sons were hauling their guitar cases out to the back alley, I'd told Tony about Darnell, Ms. Winslow, and the supernatural aspects of Kenny Winslow's story. Tony listened carefully behind the bar, smoothing out dollar bills on the countertop.

"It makes sense," he said. "Trust me when I say these things to youse."

"So you believe in the supernatural?"

"Boy, do I. I moved halfway across the country because lotsa scary things were happening. Lemme pay the band out, then we'll talk."

An hour later, Tony locked up, and together we walked out to the empty street where a white Cadillac convertible was parked at a meter. He set his briefcase down as he dug into his leather jacket pocket for the keys and then lit a half-smoked cigar.

"It was a family tragedy," he said. "I was living in Brooklyn when some relatives of mine had just bought a house in Long Island. In Amityville. Long story short, one of them kids who moved into the house had a history of getting into trouble. Guy had run-ins with the cops, was shooting lotsa dope, and got into fistfights with his father." He rolled the cigar slowly between his fingers. "Then one night—November 13 of 1974, at three in the morning—he murdered his family with a high-powered rifle. His mother and father, plus his two brothers and two sisters. Guy went from room to room, shooting each member as they slept."

"You're related to the Amityville killer?"

"Distantly, yeah."

"What's his name again?"

Tony puffed on the cigar and then looked away down the street. "Ronald DeFeo Jr."

DeFeo. Yes, I'd heard of him. After he'd murdered his family, a new family had moved in, but they'd moved out twenty-eight days later, claiming the house was infested with demons. Their story became *The Amityville Horror*.

"Ronnie committed the most brutal murders in Suffolk County's history," Tony said. "Before the big massacre, Amityville was just a place. The locals used to call it Sleepy Hollow, because nothing bad ever happened there." Tony picked up the briefcase. He looked down the street, then at the cigar. "Ronnie changed alla that."

I stepped back as Tony unlocked the car's door and squeezed into the soft white leather seat.

"So you moved to Nebraska because of a family tragedy?" I said.

He put the key in the ignition. "That, and I was running with the wrong crowd, too. You gotta remember, this was Brooklyn in the 70s. Drugs, prostitution, extortion—it was all there, in the underworld, and I saw it, too. Demonic activity like you wouldn't believe." He looked at the cigar, then at me. "I just hope you don't get caught up in alla this. Like I said, I got high hopes for youse. I still believe that, I really do."

69

Back at my cell, I logged onto YouTube and typed in "DeFeo." Several clips came up, and I watched a few. The storyline matched what Tony had said. Ronald DeFeo Jr., also known as Butch, was an American mass murderer. All six of his family members had been found dead in bed, lying face down with gunshot wounds to their backs and heads. Ronnie was now serving six life sentences in a New York prison. Before I logged off, I sent the links to Rob in an email, thinking they might be relevant to his thesis.

I got into bed and tried to clear my mind's slate. I couldn't. When Jenna's pink rubber began to glow faintly on the doorknob, I rolled onto my side and faced the bare wall. Then I recalled her scars, on both her wrist and neck. *Accidents, my ass. She tried to kill herself. Twice. Something else to lay at her father's feet, the bastard.*

I was tempted to check up on her, to ride out to the old church, but Father Myles' voice boomed in my ears. "Stay away from the girl."

Then I remembered something: I'd yet to send him the pictures of Jenna I'd taken, the pictures and the video he needed in order to learn more about her. I went into the kitchen, mixed a drink, and then searched my phone for the files as I drank heavily. After I'd sent the pictures, I watched a DeFeo documentary but soon grew drowsy and got back into bed. When the pink rubber band became too luminous to bear, I threw on a faded black sweater and slacks and left my cell.

When I walked into the old church, Jenna was there, sitting in the corner, writing on a yellow notepad by candlelight. I stood in the back of the church, next to a stone jar once used for holy water but now full of dead beetles and black spiders.

"Jenna?" I walked up to the back pew and rested my hands on it. "Can I come in?"

She continued to write and then turned a page.

"I talked to Dawn, your neighbor. She said you'd moved." I moved along the pew, toward the left-hand aisle. "Why did you move? I thought you liked your new place."

"It was okay . . . for a while."

"How come you move so much?"

"It's my life. Always on the move."

"But Lincoln isn't very big. You weren't even in your duplex for a few months. You didn't even decorate it. And what's up with the pink-and-red door?"

Jenna looked up.

"Not only that," I said, "but you move every year, too. It's online. What are you running from?"

"Carl, you move too."

"Yeah, but not every year. So come on, tell me." I entered the left aisle, pink rubber band in hand, having already made my plan. "What, you think I wouldn't understand?"

"You wouldn't."

"Try me. And no more of your cryptic ways. You can't do that anymore, at least with me. I'm not leaving until you tell me the truth."

She bowed her head and seemed to draw longer lines on the paper.

"Look at me," I said, and when she did, her eyes were dark and distrustful. "You think I wouldn't understand? Because it's complicated, right?"

I pressed on, rubber band ready to fire, the rosary coiled up in my pocket. The closer I got, the more I saw Jenna's face, and the more it hurt me to look at her. I slowed, then stopped at the first pew. I didn't go any closer. I just stood there as Jenna picked up a shard of dark red glass, her face pale and sleepy.

"Do you want me to go?"

"I would rather be alone." She looked at the shard of glass. "Another story of my life."

"Okay, fine. But can I give you something first?"

She brought the glass close to her eyes and began to turn it.

"It's something you gave me last year. It gave me a strange kind of power, an ability to focus, to excel, and I want you to have it back. Maybe it'll help you, too."

"What are you talking about?"

I held up the rubber band. "You shot me between the eyes with it, remember? At the hotel? I was on the curb and you were in the bus. I got your number that night."

She squinted at the glass and then looked suspiciously at me. God, that face. It hurt to look at. When she rested her forehead on her knees, I aimed the rubber band at her.

"Look," I said.

She did and I shot her.

I lowered my hands. "Gotcha."

She swept the rubber band across the floor and threw the glass into the pews. "That hurt."

I snatched up the rubber band as Jenna pushed the notepad off and turned away.

"I won't hurt you," I said.

"Why'd you do that?"

I bent down so that my lips touched her head, and I set the rubber band on her knee.

"Because that's where your soul is," I said.

70

Rob, Liz, and I went to an Islamic festival held at the campus's Multicultural Center. Rob and I were in plain clothes, but Liz wore a long dress and green headscarf with a henna tattoo on her hand. We sat down with our plates of Middle Eastern cuisine as Arabic-speakers filed in the room.

"Carl, I keep meaning to tell you about something," Liz said. "It's a vision I've been having, a vision about the McMasters."

"What? That it's all a dream?"

"No, I'm serious. I keep seeing the color green. Does that mean anything to you? The color green?"

"Not really."

She spread out the napkin on her lap and smelled the steaming spicy rice.

"It has to do with the McMasters' house," she said.

"I've never been there, and I never intend to go."

"Gosh, that's so weird."

"With her, everything is."

During the luncheon, the students who'd taken Arabic language classes spoke highly about the Muslim woman who taught them. Soon, it was Liz's turn. She got up in her long dress as Rob and I focused on the cuisine.

"I'm rocking my thesis," he said. "Thanks for sending those Amityville videos. And yeah, those DeFeo murders were brutal. Did you see the youngest girl? Ronnie shot her in the face. She was only thirteen."

I chewed slowly and reached for my cup. "Was there a motive?"

"Ronnie believed that his family was conspiring to kill him. He had to get them before they got him."

"Six human beings is a lot of people to murder. Did anybody help him?"

"A few think so, but most say he acted alone."

"He must have acted fast, then. I mean, the noise should have alerted somebody."

"I know, right? After his family had all gone to bed, Ronnie watched an old World War II movie. He fell asleep, and sometime after three o'clock in the morning, he woke up, and there, standing in front of him, was a black-handed demon, holding Ronnie's rifle."

"A black-handed demon?"

"That's what he said."

Liz was adjusting the green headscarf, giving me a quizzical look.

"And even in prison," Rob said, "Ronnie was ranting and raving that the devil made him do it, but then he denied it later on. Were demonic forces involved? Did his friends help him out? Or did he act alone? We'll never know."

Liz looked at me again as she adjusted the podium's microphone.

"This year's been so interesting," Rob whispered. "Now Liz is interested in Jenna. And by the way, she says to be careful. If the devil found her flaw, he can find yours, too."

As Liz began to speak, I checked my messages. The usual excuses from my students were there, as well as an email from Dr. Parsons. It was listed as urgent, and so I opened it first.

Hi, everyone!

I'd like to inform you all about a wonderful opportunity to adjunct at Southeast College. If you are at all interested, please do contact Dr. Rick Henderson, the division chairperson at Southeast.

Dr. Parsons

I left the Arabic festival early. I stopped by Frampton's Café, ordering a runza which I ate as I dashed through the countryside, speeding into town to Southeast College. There I found Dr. Henderson, lounging in his office chair, legs kicked up on his desk's edge. He wore a pink polo shirt, tan khakis, and brown loafers with no socks. From a clock radio came the sounds of smooth jazz, while he pressed buttons on his smartphone.

Twenty minutes later, I'd landed the job. I was in good spirits, until I arrived at my cell and pulled a sheet of paper off the door. A crude rifle had been drawn with a black magic marker. Next day, there was a second drawing, this one of a fish—a giant marlin—jumping out of the sea. And the following day, there was another drawing—the number thirty-five.

In my cell, I fanned out the drawings on my desk: a rifle, a marlin, and the number thirty-five. I tried to connect the dots—the fish a symbol of Christianity, thirty-five the age near which Jesus died—but with no luck. After I did my laundry in the basement, I came back upstairs and folded my pants and shirts, then my socks. I held up a pair of black dress socks.

"Holy shit, these are kid's socks."

I went through my other pairs of socks, both dress and casual. Every pair had shrunk by two sizes. I emailed Father

Myles about it and copied Father Sanchez. They replied immediately.

> fr.myles@stannes.edu
> to
> zarathustra@bfu.edu
>
> Carl,
>
> You've got a case of demonic infestation. Demonic oppression will follow.
>
> Paranormal events are happening here as well. Does Jenna have a black cat? There's a black cat walking around in my office. It walks on my Persian rug, stops, sits, looks at me, yawns, licks its paws, and then moves on, walking through the wall by the fish tank.
>
> I'm sensing it's her familiar spirit.
>
> Myles

> fr.gabriel@stjosephs.org
> to
> zarathustra@bfu.edu
>
> Hello, Mr. Sorensen.
>
> You have bad case of demonic infestation. I come down to investigate. Until then, I encourage you to ask Blessed Virgin for protection.
>
> Fr. Gabe

71

I woke up in my cell, cold as prison walls. I got dressed, grabbed my satchel, now unbearably heavy, and stepped into the hallway on my way to Starbucks, my new hideout. A poem had been taped on my door.

> Stay for a while
> Until it's time to go
> It happened again
> Will anyone ever know?

Above me, a naked light bulb flicked on and off with a fly-like buzz.

"What happened again?" I said as I rode to Starbucks. When it dawned on me, I wrote Mr. McMaster another letter and dropped it in at the Wells Fargo.

> Stay away from Jenna. This is your final warning.

All afternoon I was unable to teach or read well, and after I'd bought new socks at Walgreens, I went home for lunch, where my cell continued to be unusually cold. I found Craig, who stepped in, and together we watched our breaths roll out like scampering ghosts.

"It's seventy degrees today," he said, "but it's winter in your apartment."

He checked the windows and water heater, neither of which was a problem. The heater was all the way up, but nothing was coming out of it. He would have checked the air conditioner if I'd had one. I still couldn't get warm. The next day, the cold continued. Craig offered to move me into a new studio, but I said no, I didn't have the time or the energy to move, and besides, I had too much work to do. And so, Rich and Bubba took me in.

My problems continued there, too. I'd be jerked out of sleep at three a.m. by a recurring dream: eight blasts from a high-powered rifle. The lack of sleep took its toll on my teaching and term papers. And when I'd meet Rob at the union for lunch, I kept fading in and out as he spoke incessantly about Ed and Lorraine Warren, the famous paranormal investigators who'd been key players in the Amityville case. The Warrens believed that demonic forces had held the DeFeo family down in their beds as Ronnie went from room to room, shooting each of them, execution style.

"Man, what the Warrens say makes sense," Rob said one day at lunch. "How could Ronnie have murdered his entire family without waking anybody up? A Marlin is a super loud rifle, too. You'd think somebody would have heard—"

"Wait, what's it called? The rifle?"

"A Marlin."

Rob continued on, but I wasn't listening. A rifle. A marlin. The number thirty-five.

I got up, ending our lunch. I hurried outside to the pond where the bronze mammoths waded in the sea-green water. I stood alone on the shore as the low, dark, rain-heavy clouds began to stack up mightily over the campus. Zipping my windbreaker up, I dialed up Quentin.

"What's a Marlin?" I said.

"A big fish."

"I mean the rifle. Tell me about it."

"Into guns now, huh?"

"Is it powerful?"

"If it's brown, it's going down. She loads thirty-five calibers. Remingtons. They'll kill a tractor."

My knees hit the sand. "Thirty-five calibers?"

"Got a Marlin in the man cave now. Show it to you sometime."

I hung up, then texted Rob.

What caliber were the bullets in Ronnie's rifle?

I waited as sprinkles of rain began to fall. Off in the west, the Sower stood in the sky, gray and ulcerous, his sowing hand seemingly empty. When Rob didn't reply, I shouldered my satchel, now a dead weight around my neck, and, with an eye on a huge crow preening itself atop the gates, entered the Black Forest.

An hour later, I walked out of the forest's east end and stood alone in a deserted parking lot. I must have walked for miles. High above the treetops, the thunderclouds were blowing away. I dropped my umbrella into my satchel and then walked onto an open two-lane highway and stood on the broken white line. The huge, brain-shaped clouds were drifting low over pastures as the cows came out to graze, and the ponds sparkled fiercely. A road sign glistened green in the wet gravel: "Slippery Rock. Thirty miles."

Slippery Rock. The home of Nebraska State College. The home of Kenny Winslow and the Bison. I never realized the college was so close.

I walked over to the sign to make sure I was seeing it right. Slippery Rock. Thirty miles. A safety pin had been pushed into the wood pole. I pulled it out and then looked down the highway where my eyes followed the broken white line.

Fifty yards up ahead, an old abandoned farmhouse stood on the left, barely visible through the overhang of elm trees. A black cat was on the gallery porch. The cat got up and walked inside, stopping halfway with its tail sticking out, waving it up and down as if to tease me. Fastening the safety pin, I dropped it into my pocket and crossed back over the highway.

I walked toward the old abandoned farmhouse along an irrigation ditch full of black, windblown water. Soon, I entered the gravel drive and passed through the shade of the elms, bony and bare, as big droplets of water fell onto the weed-choked yard. I walked up the rickety front porch, then poked my head inside.

Toy dolls were scattered across the floor. Some of the dolls' faces had been melted off while others had been hacked to pieces, their arms and legs missing. I picked up a blonde doll with a noose of hair and a missing leg and began to inspect the four walls of the room. They were decorated with flies and beetles and various butterflies, all of them crucified by safety pins.

A cat's black face appeared from around the corner. Its green eyes blinked.

"Asmodeus?" I said.

The cat walked into the other room, and when I got there, it was licking its claws with its pink tongue.

"Are you the cat from the used bookstore? If so, what are you doing way out here?" I pushed my fingers into the doll's leg, feeling the small cuts in the hard plastic. *Or are you Jenna's familiar spirit, like Father Myles had suggested? Or perhaps you're both?* My eyes rose to the ceiling for a moment, and when I looked down, the cat was gone. My eyes rose to the ceiling again as I cocked my head to listen.

I walked up the stairwell and entered the first room on the left.

A large doll sat in the corner. She wore a wedding dress and had raggedy red hair falling down her shoulders. A lacy white veil had been pulled back on her head.

I walked into the shuttered bedroom. Beams of sunlight slipped through the thin wood slats as dust particles spun in the dead air. I walked up to the doll. Her small feet were bare, and her red lipstick had been painted on recklessly so that a long smear ran across her cheek. Kneeling down, I stared into her eyes. There were no eyes, just empty sockets.

"So what do you know, Missy?" I don't know how I knew her name but I did. I turned my head to listen. "Yes, I hear the choo-choo train. No, I don't know where your bouncy ball is. Your favorite toy is next door?" I left and came back. "This?" I set the plastic knife down by her hand and then inched my ear toward her dark red mouth. "You want me to have the knife? Sorry, it's too small. I'd need something bigger."

I said goodbye. As I walked down the stairwell, I heard a loud clatter and then hiked back up.

The knife lay in the middle of the floor.

"I told you it's too small." I set the knife by her feet. "Wait, you want us to get married? You're cute, Missy, but I don't think so." I playfully touched her kneecap. "I'd date your older sister, though. I bet she's hot. Can you set me up with her? Okay, good, let's talk later." I turned to leave but stopped under the doorframe. "Yes, Anna can come over to play. Just stay out of trouble."

*   *   *

Back at Bryan Hall, a blanket of gray clouds was spread out above the campus again. I circled the dark waters of Chautauqua Pond, the swans and ducks mysteriously missing, and I held my phone in hand, eagerly waiting for Rob's text. It arrived.

Sorry. Working on my thesis. Can't stop writing. Bullets were .35 calibers

Are you sure?

Very

The rest of my day was shot. I couldn't pay attention, especially in my seminar. It only grew worse when, during the break, Dr. Parsons encouraged me to apply for additional adjunct gigs. He didn't say why, though I knew the answer: my teaching assistantship was gone for good.

When class was over, I went to the student lounge where half a dozen graduate students were playing cards at a table. I sprawled onto a sofa, got out my phone, and logged onto YouTube.

I'd just typed "DeFeo" into the search when the card dealer said, "Did you get the Southeast College gig?"

"I already submitted my syllabus to the chairperson."

"What's your end game—to snatch up every adjunct gig you can?"

I sensed the card dealer's eyes on me as the others rotated in their chairs. "Why not?"

"We'd like some teaching experience, too. Why else do you think we're here—to do nothing?"

I smiled. Sure looked that way to me. "You'll have to be quicker on the draw, then."

Every card player was looking at me now. I couldn't see them physically, though in my mind's eye I could. A short guy wearing a pork pie hat lowered the bill over his eyes, while a gothic-looking guy with eyeliner on gave me the finger.

I lay on the couch a bit longer, listening to their idle chatter, along with the slap of playing cards. When I got up to check my mailbox, I could feel the heat of their eyes on my neck.

I fanned out my textbook catalogs. As I listened to the soft slap of cards on the table, it was as though I could hear the vibrations of their thoughts moving across the lounge. Has Sorensen ever heard of sharing? Does he know that grad students are supposed to stick together? Does Carl even have a heart?

Opening a catalog, I grinned widely. Oh, well. Better me teaching those classes than you fools. You'll make philosophy boring. I won't. You'll ensure the death of the humanities. I won't. So yeah, that's my end game—to be a new kind of philosopher and to ensure the humanities' survival. I'll make damn sure of it. Somehow.

I went down a flight of stairs to the second floor and entered an empty classroom. There, with the lights off, I sat in the back of the room and, getting out my phone, watched a documentary on the Amityville horror. It was true. On the night the DeFeos died, Ronnie had fired eight shots from a .35 caliber Marlin rifle into the bodies of his family members.

On the ride home, I stopped by the Blue Note to talk to Tony.

"High Hopes, howya doing?"

"How many times were the DeFeos shot?"

"Gosh, lemme think." He described each of the murders: Ronald Sr. was shot twice in the back. Louise, his wife, was shot twice. The youngest boys, Mark and John Matthew, were each shot once. "Boy, imagine that, Ronnie standing between their two beds, shooting one brother in the back and then, turning, and shooting the other." Then there was the youngest sister, Alison, who was shot point-blank in the face, while her older sister Dawn was shot in the head.

Eight shots from the Marlin.

When Tony set a tray of bourbon shots down on the table, he stepped back, hands on hips. "What's gotten into youse? First it was philosophy, then Kenny Winslow, and now the DeFeos?"

"It's . . . complicated. I'll tell you about the DeFeo part later on. If I feel like it."

I drank until the shot glasses began to blur on the table, then walked my bike along the main line track back to Rich's pad. Nobody was home. I waited. Nothing. So I entered my cell and fell onto my mattress, my clothes still on, and drifted off into a deep and troublesome sleep.

72

I began to have a recurring dream. I was somewhere in the Middle West, standing outside of a farmhouse at night when, on the second floor, hot flashes of gunfire would light up the windows. Or I'd be inside the farmhouse, asleep in bed and, waking up and turning my head, would see a dark figure in the doorway, rifle in hand.

One morning in mid-April, I woke up after dreaming I'd been murdered in bed, and as I left Rich's pad, I saw a strange object in the hallway, leaning against the wall by my door. There was a six-foot tall garden lamppost with a stuffed squirrel at the top. A small placard hung from the middle of the post. "High Hopes."

I went back in and called Father Sanchez. When he pulled up in the church van later on that day, I was outside, sitting in the sandlot.

"You first," I said.

We went upstairs. Walking down the hallway, Father Sanchez slowed and stuck his hand out across my chest. We stopped.

"Ah, the energy in building is very negative. I already have headache." He made the sign of the cross and whispered words in Spanish. "Squirrel sign was here this morning, yes?"

"As far as I know."

"Did you touch?"

"Heck, no."

He walked cautiously up to the sign. He lowered his glasses and moved in close, inspecting the squirrel at the top. "I take critter back to Omaha and have scientist colleague run test on material. But first, I bless apartment, then you take me to see girl."

Arriving at the church on the hill, I led Father Sanchez down the left aisle, up to where Jenna lay sprawled on the sleeping bag. She sat up suddenly and backed into the corner, clutching a pillow, her eyes like a reptile's, low, hooded, and lurking in the dark cavern of her hair.

"How are you, young lady?"

"None of your business."

"You are not scared to be alone?"

"Who says I'm either?"

"May I ask how come you are here?"

"I don't have to answer your stupid questions."

Father Sanchez asked if she had any place to go, like her parents' house, but Jenna lay down and turned her face to the wall. He looked at me and raised a finger to his lips. Quietly, he brought out a small bottle of water, unscrewed it, and flung a few drops onto Jenna. She lay there as if asleep. Then he unscrewed a second bottle and raised it high when Jenna whirled around with her pillow held up, like a shield.

"Don't even, priest."

Father Sanchez lowered the bottle. He screwed the lid on and spoke softly in Spanish as Jenna plugged her ears and pushed her face into the pillow.

Back in Lincoln, we stopped at Henry's, a secluded bar I'd recently found. I had a couple of shots of bourbon, while Father Sanchez had a Coke.

"Girl is possessed."

"How do you know?"

"The eyes. Girl's eyes are alive. She also have negative reaction to holy water and prayer. I'm sorry to inform you, Mr. Sorensen, but your friend is in danger. She ask demon into her life, and now she must ask demon to leave. But she cannot expel on her own. She will need the help of the exorcist."

I paid for our drinks and went out into the hot windy night. I leaned against the wall and closed my eyes. I could sense Father Sanchez observing me and, to my surprise, he made the sign of the cross.

"You have too much to drink, Mr. Sorensen. Come, I take you back to apartment."

Back home, I got out of the van. I walked to the driver's side window, and Father Sanchez handed me my satchel.

"Oh, thanks."

"You going to make it, Mr. Sorensen?"

"I'll be okay. Anything else I should know?"

"I suggest you live in some other place."

"I already am, at my neighbor's."

"No, some other building. As soon as possible, if you can."

"Really, how come?"

"Because there is small girl looking out of your apartment window right now."

73

I didn't know if it was Missy or not. Maybe it was. Or maybe her older sister had visited my cell, I wasn't sure. At that point, anything was possible. Father Sanchez had called me on the ride up to Omaha, warning me about a spree of demonic oppression that would break out, should I spend more time in my cell. I said I wouldn't. He said I should begin house hunting, too. I said I would.

Walking into the Guardian, I knocked on Rich's door. No answer. Then I sent him a text. Nothing. I paced the hallway for ten minutes, then sat down and waited for thirty. At that point, I put my ear to my cell door, then opened it and flicked on the light.

My cell looked normal. It was cold inside, the window was ajar, and my books on my desk were in three perfect piles. I turned up the heater, which kicked right on, and then closed the window and locked it. Two small handprints were on the dark windowpane. I put my palm up to the left handprint, then the right one. Then I ran my fingers along the floorboards and picked up a few strands of long black hair.

I went into the bathroom and turned on the light. I held the black hairs up to the medicine cabinet mirror. Were they Jenna's? Or were they Missy's older sister's? Or had Craig shown my cell to a potential female renter?

A train's horn blew. I flushed the hairs down the toilet and then looked at my face in the mirror. My black robe hung on the wall. It seemed to change shape—from a robe, to a black suit, and then to a robe again.

So . . . maybe the paranormal was real. If so, it'd prove the humanities were valuable, which meant they had to be taught in college, not replaced by STEM courses. Gods and devils, ghosts and haunted houses, possessed dolls and other phenomena, these things were still relevant, all-too-relevant for the modern world.

I squinted at my robe's arms. Silver cuff links grew at the ends, and large buttons appeared on the lapels. Now it was a black suit. When it transformed back into a robe again, I went out into the hallway to await Rich's arrival.

An hour passed. A spring thunderstorm blew through town, flooding the streets, and the hallway was eerily quiet and cold. Then I heard something like whispers coming from inside my cell. Peeking under the door, I saw what appeared to be a pair of bare feet.

The hallway door opened and there was Rich, carrying two six-packs of Coors Light, one in each hand.

"Bra, sorry I'm late."

"Can I have one of those? Like, now?"

"*Hey, mi casa es su casa.* Been waiting long?" He gave me a six-pack and then opened the door.

"No." I stared across the hall. A scratching noise could be heard from inside of my cell. I went in and closed Rich's door, then opened it again. There, across the hall, came the slow scratching sounds as if a girl's fingernails were being dragged down my door.

Like Dr. Parsons, I also went house hunting. At this point, I'd have even taken an old country church. As Rich and I pounded our six-packs, I called Paul, asking for housing suggestions. The Guardian was out of the question. So was the

North Bottoms—too many college students. Then he suggested Philosophy House. He said I should go and see Dr. Parsons tomorrow, since there might still be vacancies for the fall.

Philosophy House. I wasn't thrilled about living there, but at least I'd be away from downtown Lincoln. No McMasters, no haunted studio apartments, and no football crowds. Just my books, my solitude, and my PhD.

So before class the next day, I met with Dr. Parsons. A Judy Garland song was playing in his office, and he was singing and dancing to it. His black turtleneck and slacks glimmered with a reptilian shine, while a new briefcase made of alligator skin shone on his desk. A golden, eye-like emblem was on the briefcase too, only this eye was the eye of a madman.

He shuffled over to his chair and then rolled it over to mine and sat down. He crossed his legs and put his hands in his lap, and he sat super erect. How were my studies going? How was adjuncting? How was I getting along with the other graduate students? Then he spoke eagerly about campus events, especially the STEM divisions, with more construction scheduled for the fall.

Even though I hadn't had anything to drink in the last couple hours, my bladder felt ready to burst.

"Anyhoo, Carl, you're in luck. We have vacancies at Philosophy House. Several of our graduate students won't be returning, and enrollment in our humanities degrees is low for next fall. In fact, it's nearly nil."

As I filled out the housing application, Dr. Parsons got up, singing and dancing to the oldies, and rearranging the coats, like dark slabs of meat in a butcher shop, on the rack by the door. The housing application took forever to fill out, and I had to go to the bathroom bad. When I finished, I gave him the application, then stood up.

"Congratulations, Carl. You're about to embark on a most wonderful journey at Philosophy House. I'm so excited for you. Just think. A community of philosophers who share the same intellectual vision."

"Yes. Absolutely."

"It's been my hope that Philosophy House will one day be famous. After all, Plato founded the Academy; Aristotle, the Lyceum; Epicurus, the Garden; and Zeno, the Stoa. Suppose you and the other students bring Philosophy House to the world's attention?"

"That'd be nice."

His phone rang. "Oh, it's Peter calling me from England."

My bladder and I thanked him for the interruption.

"I'm so glad you stopped by. You'll have a swell time at Philosophy House. It's such a lovely residence."

Pushing open the bathroom door, I unzipped on my way across to the urinal, then let go. In front of me on the wall, sad looking faces appeared in the tiles. Crying faces, too. Then funny-looking faces, which seemed to mock me. I closed my eyes. *So you guys are back, huh? Okay, fine. But I've got news for you: I've got the courage to challenge my convictions, even my atheistic ones, which, for better or worse, have been dissolving. But I'm ready to go further, if I have to.*

"So bring it on," I said out loud, "and I'll show you how much truth I can handle."

I opened my eyes. The faces were gone.

When I was washing my hands, I overheard two men talking in the hallway. The words "fall semester" and "investors" and "STEM education" could be heard above the splashes of water. When I turned off the faucet, one of them said, "Oh, why don't we invite them to stay at Philosophy House?"

I looked over at the door. Through the smoky glass pane, I saw the black shapes of two slender men. Both wore hats of some kind, and one of them wore eyeglasses. There was a vibe between them, like teacher and disciple. One of them moved closer to the door, but then turned with his back to the glass with the word "PUSH" barely visible on it.

By the time he entered, I was hiding in a stall. He began to whistle an old-timey tune, one I instantly recognized, having heard it only minutes before. After he flushed and thoroughly washed his hands, he stood in front of the mirror for what seemed like five minutes, then left.

Dashing to Philosophy House, I had to find out what was going on. Would nonphilosophers be living there, too? The usual suspects were gathered on the porch, blathering on and on. I coasted by, holding my phone to my ear and looking the other way. Had that been Dr. Parsons in the men's room? And whom else was he inviting to live at Philosophy House, if not graduate students?

Then another thought occurred to me. Had one of the graduate students ratted me out for having guest speakers in class? Probably. They'd do anything to get ahead. I fantasized about socking the snitch in the mouth, but I let it go and, coasting off campus with my head held high, called up Quentin.

"I found a new place to live on campus."

"Already pulled the trigger on it, huh?"

"It's not a life sentence. Besides, the rent is uber cheap, and I'll need to use our library more."

"You gon' be right there."

"That's my point."

Soon, the state penitentiary came into view. Behind the high barbed-wire fence, several dozen inmates in gray sweat pants and shirts were standing on a baseball diamond or sitting in the bleachers. Prison guards were perched in the four stone towers of the prison yard, and when my phone chimed, I pulled into a vacant lot next to a real estate sign. It was Dawn.

Jenna's father is here, she texted.

I called her. "Now?"

"He's looking in her front window."

"Who's he with?"

"His wife. She's in the truck, looking all sad."

"What's she look like?"

"Just like Jenna, but older."

I pedaled back up Old Farm Road. When I got to the old church on the hill, the sanctuary had been destroyed. The red wine bottles had been smashed against the altar, and the four walls had sledgehammer-sized holes in them. On the back wall, foul phrases had been spray-painted in black: *GOD = FAILURE* and *MARY SWALLOWS* and *EAT, FUCK, KILL.* There were pentagrams drawn on the dusty floorboards, in the middle of which was a tree from which hung a noose with the head of a Christ-like figure in it.

I called Father Myles and talked to his answering machine. "Hey, it's Carl. I'm at the church. Jenna smashed the shit out of the place. Or somebody did. I need to talk to you. Call me, please."

I began to feel nauseated, so I stretched out on the front pew with my forearm over my eyes. I was short of breath and had my phone on my chest. It rang and I picked up.

"I saw the entire thing in a vision," Father Myles said. "There was a McMaster family blow out, with full-on screaming, shoving, foul language, and sordid accusations. Quite the show. Lyman even grabbed the candleholders off the kitchen table and threw them at his wife. She's okay, but the dining room walls are in bad shape." He offered a few more details, saying that Jenna, in a demonic-inspired rage, had vandalized the church, and then added that I wasn't dealing with Jenna anymore. I was dealing with Lyman. I was even going to meet him, too.

I sat up. "No, no I'm not."

"I'm afraid you are, and when it happens, stay calm. Let him say what he has to say, and don't be fooled by his charm. This fella is the smooth flavor of criminal. Remember, the devil comes as an angel of light. Lyman does, too."

I stood up and walked to the window. "So do you think Jenna's possessed?"

"I'm quite certain of that. Those pictures of her that you sent to me, did you notice how blurry she is? Not the background, just her. That's what happens when you've got demons attached to you. And the way she was walking up that hill—good Lord, she looks like an old woman. What's inside of her is very ancient, very cold, crafty, and calculating, and it's been roaming all over the earth since the beginning of time. And when you add Father Gabe's report into the mix, I'd say we have a genuine case of demonic possession."

I was feeling so sick that I cut the talk short, saying I'd call him later on.

For an hour, I lay on the pew, waiting for my stomach to settle. Bats darted in and out of the sanctuary with their quick, impatient flaps. Soon my body began to feel weightless, like it was floating and moving off the pew. I tried to call Father Myles and tell him about my minilevitations but I couldn't.

My phone was dead.

74

I wasn't about to meet Lyman McMaster. Instead of drinking at the Blue Note, I drank at Henry's. Instead of studying at the Loft, I went to Starbucks. Even though I'd switched up my routine, I still saw the sulfur-white bus passing by wherever I happened to be.

Then one day, Jenna walked into Starbucks and dropped my letters to her family on the table, her eyes instantly capturing mine. An older, similar-looking woman with short red hair walked up beside her.

Lyman walked in last. He wore a baseball cap and sunglasses, and as he approached the table, Jenna sat down and then kicked an empty chair toward him. He looked at the chair and then slowly sat on it, hat and sunglasses still on. The mother sat down with her hands atop her purse, but Jenna's haughty eyes were still on her father.

Finally she turned to me. "Hi."

"What's going on?"

"We should be asking you that." She picked up the letters and fanned them out.

"What about them?"

"Carl, why are you writing them?"

The mother looked up and gave me a disapproving look. She was a Jenna look-alike, wearing a tan blouse and brown pants that looked like they came from a church rummage sale.

"Because I'm worried about you," I said.

"He's worried, daddy, did you hear that?"

I wondered for a second how Jenna could talk without moving her lips. But then I realized the mother had said this.

Lyman looked down and then slowly took off his sunglasses. When he opened his eyes, I winced. They were the color of cement, with small, red lightning-bolt cracks in the whites. I wondered if he lived in a basement with a computer screen as his only source of light.

Lyman smiled but his eyes didn't. "Hi, Carl." He held out his hand and I shook it. Cold, dead weight. "You know, now that I've seen you with my own eyes, it really amazes me that a smart, good-looking guy like you would be capable of this."

I swallowed hard. I knew this was a trap, intended to win me over. But if I just listened and spoke the truth, he wouldn't be able to stand it.

"I just don't get it, Carl. Why are you doing this?"

I looked deep into those cold, menacing eyes. "Because sometimes, when we dig deep, that's where we find the truth."

As the smile began to fade from Lyman's face, he leaned back and twisted around as if stretching his back muscles. Then he turned and stretched the other side's muscles, too.

"Carl, I can't believe I'm hearing this."

"I never thought I'd write those letters, either, sir, but I have good reasons to believe that every word I said in them is true. And it's high time somebody said it all out loud."

Jenna looked dreamily at the batch of letters, and she began to pick at a liberty bell stamp, peeling it off. "All these letters . . ."

"Yes," the mother said hoarsely.

Lyman glared at her. "I mean, who would have thought that a smart guy like you could ever do this to a family."

"If the letters were false, they wouldn't have an effect."

"I'll have you know I missed work to try to straighten this—"

"Jenna married a guy twenty years older than her," I said. "So did her sister. That isn't normal, sir. And both girls are divorced now, which isn't surprising, and leads me to conclude they've got daddy issues." Leaning forward, I locked eyes with Lyman, who leaned slowly back. "So if you're such a great guy, why are your daughters so screwed up?"

Jenna's lips parted, while her mother's pain-stricken eyes never left her husband, and when he looked at her, their eyes crossed like blades.

Lyman shifted. He stared out of the window with a smile, his leg moving up and down like a motor, as he twirled his sunglasses by the arm, the lenses throwing light. "You know, Carl, this is amusing."

"That's not a term most prosecutors would use."

"I had to miss a day of work."

"So you said."

"I should have called in sick, because that's how you make me feel. Sick."

Outside, a line of grade school children went skipping by under the white oak trees, their moms and dads in tow, holding hands.

"If you're such a great guy," I said, "then explain to me a survey about abused girls that I read. It listed eleven long-term effects of childhood abuse. Jenna showed all of them."

Lyman looked at his favorite spot on the window. When the sun peeked below the café's green awning, he slid his sunglasses on and crossed his arms and grinned.

"Carl, there's a Bible verse I'd like to share with you. Now I know you're a Bible scholar, so I'm sure you'll appreciate this." He leaned forward and rocked from side to side as if trying to remember the verse. Then it came to him. "'Inasmuch as you do this to the least of my disciples, you have done it unto me.'"

I hadn't heard it in years.

"And that's exactly what you've done to me and my family, Carl. You've harmed us, which means you've harmed Jesus."

I stared Lyman down, his eyes lurking behind those sunglasses. I also remembered the temptation in the wilderness, how Satan twisted the scripture to fit his own wicked agenda.

"I see what you're doing, but I'm not falling for it. Neither are they." I rose up and snatched my computer, but Jenna slammed her palm onto the table.

"See, daddy?" she cried. "That's the tone of voice he uses with me. Did you hear him? Did you?" Her eyes pleaded with me to stay.

She pulled her palm back slowly on the tabletop as I lowered my body into the chair, and from under the table she kicked my shoe to make sure I understood.

I stayed for ten more minutes, locked in verbal combat with Lyman McMaster. He dodged my questions, shook his head, snickered, and made long, drawn-out sighs.

I kept hitting him with facts. "Why does Jenna have cut marks on her wrist and neck? Why does she never wear a seat belt when she drives? That's right. Because she has a death wish, and we all know the reason why."

"This is ridiculous."

"No matter how many times you smile and say that, it's still not going to be true."

"You know, Carl. I'm really amazed that—"

I was done. I got up and walked away.

"Do you still want to date my daughter?" he said.

I stopped, turned, marched up to him, and clapped his shoulder three times.

"She's been yours for all these years," I said. "Just keep her."

Then I left.

Outside, I strode under the line of white oaks, breathing hard and feeling full of explosive energy. Lyman had gotten up and stood by the large window with a palm pressed to the glass. His sunglasses were off, and he watched me with a surprised look as if seeing me for the first time. I shot him a thumbs-up, and his eyes turned cold and cruel. He pressed his other palm to the glass now, looking more like an ape than a man. Jenna and her mother sat in their chairs, heads bowed with their backs to me.

75

The spring semester was coming to a close. Outside the Guardian, the baseball players were in the sandlot pitching horseshoes and playing volleyball. Steaks were sizzling on the grills above the barbecue pits, and the picnic benches were covered with red plastic cups and cans of Coors light. I was holed up in Rich's pad, working on my term papers. I didn't go to the cafés, either, not after my run in with the McMasters.

Days passed. When I got bored of Rich's pad, I'd make an occasional visit to my cell. I didn't stay long at first. But the more I'd visit, the longer I stayed, and the longer I stayed, the more comfortable I felt there. Then something happened. The negative energy that once inhabited my cell seemed to have been expelled.

Next thing I knew, I was back at my cell. The old magic had returned. My inner being felt strengthened by an overpowering power, one that helped me to read voraciously and switch paper topics on the fly. No longer was I writing on Clarence Darrow, just to please Dr. Parsons. I was writing on Friedrich Nietzsche.

My topic? The new philosophers. There was a need for them in America, especially in the academy. College students would watch *Survivor* and *American Idol* religiously, learning the intimate details of the contestants' lives, yet were unable to name the Ten Commandments or the Bill of Rights. They could use Facebook and Twitter all day, could hook up at bars and clubs with ease, but they couldn't name the masters of suspicion—Nietzsche, Marx, and Freud, to say nothing of their intellectual achievements. No worries, though. At least the students still had their cell phones, their little silver friends, to provide them with the answers to life's deepest questions. No need to study Plato, Jesus or Kant anymore, either. Everything the students needed nowadays was at their fingertips, lit up on their blue touch screens. Yes, the death of Western civilization was at hand. The barbarians were at the gates once again, and somebody had to emerge to sound the warning siren.

The new philosophers would save the day. They weren't like other philosophers, who were concerned about their academic careers and their barely readable books, with nothing relevant to say about the dreadful plight of our planet. The new philosophers, on the other hand, would be true philosophers once again, lovers of wisdom and helpers of humankind. They'd be the creators of new values, would be the future consciences of humankind, and would aid in its moral and spiritual development.

It was too much to think about, the gravity of it all. During those nearly insane nights at my cell, I felt happy and incredibly hopeful about what these new philosophers would be, about when they'd arrive on the American scene, and about the nature of their philosophizing and the impact it would have, especially in higher education.

As I outlined my paper, I felt as though something else, something external, were doing the writing, guiding my hand over the yellow notebook's pages, dictating my paper's structure, paragraph by paragraph, line by line, word for word.

One late night in my cell, I opened my copy of *Zarathustra*, ready to take additional notes. The aroma of Jenna's hair, like violets, was there on its pages, and I read the first passage my eyes fell upon. *You must push what is falling.*

"Suppose that's what they'd do," I said, sitting down at my desk. Since the new philosophers would be creators of new values and would go beyond traditional morality—beyond good and evil, as Nietzsche put it—suppose they'd think the unthinkable or even act in unthinkable ways? I looked up, and there was an image of Christ crucified on my wall. Then he vanished.

I smelled the book's pages. *Maybe the new philosophers would even act cruelly, if it would rescue us Westerners from our mediocre lives.*

A startling thought. When its gravity became too burdensome to bear, I lay down and stared at the ever-widening water stains on the ceiling.

Hours later, I woke up. Rain was falling softly on the roof, and a locomotive rumbled by, blaring its horn. Something hard and cold stung my chest. A water drop. Then another.

I sat up. My bed sheets were soaking wet. Dark drops of water were dropping from the ceiling onto my mattress.

I stood up. I looked for Craig's number but couldn't find it. Then I shoved my mattress aside, tore off the bed sheets, flipped the mattress over, and ran my palm across it. Dry. Or dry enough.

After I spread out several cooking pots on the floor and sat atop my mattress, listening to the *ping* of water in the pots, a shadowy figure appeared in the corner.

A girl. She seemed to be composed of dark, semi-invisible grains of sand. She smiled, then waved. Her hair was long and black and straight, and she wore a low-cut, tight-fitting black dress with black velvet gloves pulled up to her elbows.

I pulled my knees into my chest. Was this happening? Yes, it was. There was a girl here, in my cell. A spirit.

The girl's gaseous form had materialized fully now, and she had a doll-like look to her, sort of like Missy, but older. She spread her arms wide as if to display her black velvet gloves. Then she peeled one off and, holding up a small hand, revealed a gold watch. She turned her head sideways, observing me with mild interest.

As the water drops splashed into the cooking pots, I fixed my eyes on the gold watch, trying to decipher its mysterious meaning until I felt hypnotized by its barely audible ticks, and the girl gradually fizzled out of sight.

Next day, I asked a crowd at Henry's about local ghost legends. Were there any and, if so, was there one about a teenage girl in a black dress and gloves? There were lots of ghost sightings, they said, but none that fit what I'd told them. When I rose up unsteadily and stepped out for a smoke, a sulfur-white bus dashed down the street. It honked.

When I sobered up, I rode out to the old church and, walking inside, found a note where Jenna's sleeping bag used to be.

> Carl, you need to help me.
> Come this Saturday @ 8:00PM.
> 402 Lone Pine Road
> Battle Creek, Nebraska
> My dad won't be there.
> (Ps. Stay away from Starbucks!)

I found a second note on the altar and a third note on the front pew. All three notes said the same thing, and each one had been folded up with a piece of sea-green glass on top.

I dialed up Father Myles. "Jenna wants our help."

"I told you to stay away from her."

"I haven't talked to her, but she left a note. Three of them, actually." There was static on the other line. "Father, are you there?"

"Yes, of course. It sounds like she's fought the demons off and wants your attention. Stop by tomorrow, if you can. We'll plan for an exorcism." Lots of static and breakup. "Carl?"

"Yeah, I'm here. She says to come by Saturday."

"Then Saturday it is, and not a day later."

"Why the rush?"

"We want to get to her before the possessing demons convince Jenna to try to kill herself. Again."

"Wait, hang on. You mean there might be more than one demon?"

"I'm thinking about half a dozen. I might also add that you're more of a target for a demonic attack now. You've treaded deep into their territory, and they don't like that. You'll be wrestling with these monsters more. Just make sure you don't become one. I'll be praying for you."

We tried to communicate further, but the wall of static was so harsh it hurt my ears. I hung up.

So I was a target now? Fine. I'd fight them off. I'd go deep, deeper than I've ever gone. What doesn't kill me makes me stronger.

I plunked down on the front pew with these new demonic dangers in mind, then got up and went to the corner where Jenna's sleeping bag used to be. The wood crate was still there. So was the AppleJack Festival sticker on the side. I sat down on the crate, elbows on knees, and looked out at the sanctuary. So much had happened here. Our second date, the yellow blanket, the philosophical talk, listening to Blue Oyster Cult and the disco hit "Express." Among other things. I wanted to text Jenna to see how she was doing. I fought off the temptation, but in the end, it won.

Just want to say hi, I texted.

Hi.

Are you okay?

For now.

What's going on?

☹

What do you mean?

It hurts.

What does?

Reality.

I watched my breath blowing up in ghostly gusts, while up in the balcony, beings with gaseous bodies were gathering in the pews, as if for a secret ceremony. The men wore dark suits and hats, the women black dresses and shawls. All of their faces were rubbed out as if by an eraser. Crossing my arms, I looked at my knees and then at the sanctuary floor where Jenna's unholy drawings could be seen in the ever-thickening dust.

76

Riding my bike into town, I passed by the state penitentiary. The guardsmen were standing watch in their high stone towers with their rifles silhouetted against the pink sky. I stopped by Henry's first, then Dawn's place. I rang the doorbell and soon footsteps could be heard coming rapidly down the stairs.

The door swung open. "What the hell?"

"Shh."

"It's one in the morning."

"Interpret this."

Dawn read the note, then gave it back. "That's where Jenna's from. In Custer County." She covered her nose. "Damn, have you been drinking?"

A police car pulled up to a house across the street.

"Dawn, I need a favor."

"You're not dragging me to Jenna's parents' house."

"I'm not asking you to."

"You can borrow my daddy's gun, though."

"We're not dealing with a physical problem."

She crossed her arms. "Whatcha dealing with, then?"

"It's hard to explain."

Across the street, a bald officer walked up to the tree-hidden house. Dawn stepped down onto the porch, and both of us watched his advance. She dug into her robe pocket and pulled out a pack of Winstons. She looked way too young to be a smoker, but these days I guess it didn't surprise me.

"Dawn, I need you to pray. You and Jenna obviously have some kind of connection, so I need you to pray for her safety, for her soul, and for all of us who'll be with her on Saturday night. I don't know if this'll even work, but I need you to do it, okay?"

The officer rang the doorbell, then stepped back. Soon a shirtless man in blue jeans and a moustache appeared in the doorway. He held a gold aluminum can, his face red and tired-looking.

"This Saturday?" Dawn said, lighting up.

"At eight o'clock. You can pray before then, if you want."

She pushed the doormat into place with a big toe and looked at me skeptically. "Can I ask you something?"

"Shoot."

"How'd you get involved with her anyway?"

"It's complicated."

"So you gonna tell me the story sometime?"

"Possibly."

We looked across the street. The bare-chested man stared blankly at the officer, whose arms were crossed and his legs spread out a bit.

Dawn blew out smoke. "Prolly never thought it'd end up like this, huh?" She offered me a smoke, which I took.

"I'm not sure what to think now," I said as a second cop car pulled up, "but I'll just chalk it up to fate and leave it at that."

77

I pulled up to the Platte River, then killed the Silverado's engine. The flat, sparkling water flowed wide and salmon pink, the surface swirling slowly between the tree-lined banks. A train chugged its way over a ledge in the bluffs, its flatcars loaded up with large pipes, and I sat in the quiet for a time, unsure of why I'd stopped here—I'd just felt the urge to pull over.

I got out and walked to a picnic bench, then took out my phone. Rob had sent a link. "First Person Killers: Ronald DeFeo." I pressed play and the footage began. There, on the screen, in a maroon sweater and a brown ponytail, sat Ronald DeFeo, the fifty-seven-year-old Amityville killer.

"Maybe I should have gotten a medal for killing them," DeFeo said.

I took note of his cold, black stare. *Maybe I should have gotten a medal for killing them . . . for killing them . . . for killing them.*

Rob texted, *You know how Nietzsche says that, if there is no God, then we have to become gods?*

Yeah.

At his trial, DeFeo said, "When I've got a gun in my hand, there's no doubt about who I am. I am God." How's that for existentialism?

Wow.

He also said that once he started shooting that night, he couldn't stop. He said something was inside of him, making him commit the murders.

Where'd you learn this stuff?

The prosecuting attorney wrote a book. High Hopes.

"Some weather," a man said.

I dropped my phone. A fisherman was standing there. He seemed to have come out of nowhere. He wore faded blue overalls, a white T-shirt, and a denim cap decorated with fishing lures, mostly flies.

"We weren't expecting you until after dark," he said.

"I was supposed to arrive later?"

"You're not a ghost hunter?"

I picked up my phone. "No. I've got better things to do with my time." I dusted it off when I noticed an old Chevy truck, rusted beyond belief with age, parked next to Quentin's.

The man set a tackle box on the picnic bench, while I tried to fire up my phone.

"Meant no offense," he said. "It's just, a lot of ghost hunters have been here lately, a lot of young folks, just like yourself."

"What for?"

"They're searching for Kenny Winslow. Folks say he comes out at night." He opened the tackle box and several colorful flies fell out. I took note of the man's right hand—only three fingers were on it.

"What's he doing when they see him?" I said.

"It depends. Some folks have seen him walking on the tracks. Others have seen him sitting on them, picking up red stones and throwing them into the river. Or he's wandering in the woods behind us, circling the tree trunks and looking up, like he's searching for something."

On the interstate, across the river, semis barreled by in both directions, while a crow flapped downstream, cawing shrilly. A long line of boxcars snaked its way slowly around a bend in the bluffs when, in the deepening dusk, a ball of blazing orange light rose up from the railroad tracks.

An orb. It shot down the riverbank, spinning in circles over the purple water, growing larger and larger. At first, it was the size of a honeybee, then a meadowlark, then a white-tailed deer, until a young man was walking on the water.

Kenny Winslow.

Kenny moved closer, his body almost transparent. He wore black athletic shorts and a tank top with an Adidas shoe on his left foot. His hair was honey blonde, long and straight and wild, and he stared intently at me through strings of blood on his face.

He stopped twenty yards away, arms at his sides, elbows bent, and watched me. He had fully materialized now. His hair blew across his face and mine did, too. I tucked my locks of hair behind my ears and he did, too. Then he held out his left hand. A tattoo was on his forearm. A razorblade. I stared into his black, lifeless eyes and felt as though my own eyes were looking back at me. Then he dropped to his knees and, like a tree, collapsed on the sandbar, lying facedown, his hair afloat in the slow moving current.

The man next to me was tying a fly to his line. His lips were moving, but no sound was coming out. Then an orange orb rose up off the sandbar and, spinning in circles, shot away in the falling dark.

Somebody was shaking my shoulder. "Bub?"

"Huh?"

"You look like you've seen a ghost." He rested a hand on my shoulder, so that I could feel the three fingers, bony and with black hairs, and I looked down into his huge, unblinking eyes. "Everything okay?"

"I should probably bolt," I said. "Nice talk." I walked away toward the Silverado, still unable to fire up my phone.

"You take care, bub, and don't be a stranger. We could always use your company."

I closed the Silverado's door, then locked it. I looked at my phone. It was dead. I cranked the ignition and put the truck in gear; as I drove away, I looked up into the rearview mirror. The man was gone and the truck was, too.

78

I pulled into St. Anne's College, but I wasn't ready to meet with Father Myles. I was too busy fretting about what I'd seen at the river. Had the fisherman really been there? Had Kenny been there, too? Maybe it was my imagination. Or maybe I needed to see a psychologist. I didn't know. It was hard to say anymore. I just sat in the truck in the empty parking lot, thinking. Soon, the worry in my chest began to grow, so that it went as deep as bullets, and I was no longer certain which viewpoint was more childish: my old atheism or my reemerging belief in the supernatural.

I looked at my phone. Still dead. I looked here and there, trying to find something with which to occupy my mind. Then I opened the glove box. Small gold liquor bottles glowed fiercely inside, like a treasure. Next to them were small, aphoristic books, all of them by obscure publishing houses.

What a godsend. I took a bottle, twisted off the cap, and drank. The whiskey felt like fire on my lips. I took another drink and then another until it felt like the inside of my body was ablaze. When I left the truck, I was consuming a third bottle, which I dumped in a trashcan, just outside of Ignatius Hall.

Walking inside, I peered down the dark paneled hallway. The faculty office doors were closed for the night—all but one. Far down the hallway, a small figure could be seen sitting in a pew, pushed up against the wall. A cane was in his hands. I walked slowly with a hand touching the wall to steady myself. When a men's restroom caught my eye, I moved toward it with my eyes centered on one word: "PUSH."

When I exited, I walked up to Father Myles, who seemed to have dozed off in the pew.

"Father Myles?" He barely opened his eyes. "Father, I'm here." He looked up as if confused, and I sat down while he wiped down his forehead and temples with a red handkerchief. "Busy day in the committee room?"

"Fortunately, no."

"How come you're out here?"

"'Twas cold in my office." He looked at the red handkerchief, coated with dark spots and smears.

"I texted you Jenna's diocese. You were right. She's from the Diocese of Grand Island."

"I've yet to get your text. My phone's out of commission."

"Mine is, too."

He dabbed at his forehead. "'Tis to be expected. We're days away from an all-out spiritual war. The demons are starting their attack on us by draining our electronic devices of their power. There's plenty more of that coming, mark my words." He spread the handkerchief across his lap, and his eyes grew wider and more focused on it.

"Have you had any more visions of Jenna?" He didn't answer, and so I asked again. No answer. "Father?"

He looked up. "I'm sorry, what's this now?"

"Jenna—have you had any more visions of her?"

"Plenty."

"Really? About what?"

"I'll say more about her later on. But to tell you the truth, I've been more concerned about you." He focused his attention on the handkerchief again, as though a vision were occurring there.

I plugged my phone's charger into the wall. "How so?"

Father Myles seemed to nod off. A minute passed. Then he opened his eyes.

"Carl, I see you having serious problems with people in your department next year. Not only will you have conflicts with your fellow students, you'll have bigger problems with that Parsons fella. You and he are worlds apart now, especially after what you've learned this year. You've stumbled upon a spiritual realm few mortals ever see. This gives you insights the others don't have. Believe me, it's a blessing and also a curse." He moved a finger over the dark red spots and smears. "And if you're not careful with your alcohol consumption, it's entirely possible that you won't get your degree at all."

"What?"

"'Tis true."

"But my studies are going well again. Plus, you're a psychic and a clairvoyant. You'll be able to see if something bad is coming my way. If you do, you'll tell me, right?"

"I'm leaving for Nepal in June, on special assignment. You won't always have me here, which is why you must be careful."

"But you'll still know what's going to happen in Nebraska, right?"

Father Myles' forehead was shiny and beady with sweat again. He sidled up in the pew and then ran the handkerchief across his forehead and down each of his temples. He looked at the cloth and opened it, and his eyes were seized by something he saw there.

"Father Myles, if you see anything bad coming, can you tell me?" I grabbed his cane and shook it. "Father?"

Father Myles looked around as though in a daze. He swallowed hard and folded the handkerchief and put it out of sight. He bowed his head. "If I see it coming, yes."

"Did you see something just now about me?" He didn't answer. "Father Myles, did you?"

"I'm afraid so."

"Can you tell me?"

"Do you really want me to go there?"

"I've seen and heard enough this year. Shoot."

He looked at me as if to make sure I was sure. Then he wiped his face again and spread out the handkerchief on his lap and gazed into it. A deadly silence filled the hallway now, and the beats of my heart were increasing in volume and speed.

"I see you becoming a wandering fugitive," he said. He looked at me and his eyes were sad.

"A what?"

"I see you stripping away the blinders from a good many people in academia and beyond. I even see you sparking a national debate."

"What, when I become a . . . fugitive?"

"It'll have far-reaching consequences."

"Tell me this is symbolic."

"I wish it were."

"So it's literal?"

"I'm afraid so."

"That's insane. I'm here to get my degree. I'm here to . . ." I couldn't think anymore. Not after those statements.

"You won't need a doctorate. In fact, you'll do more without one. You'll do far more for humanity than any of your professors and all of the graduate students combined. You belong to a higher rank of order, a new species of philosopher, of which your colleagues know little or nothing. You'll go far beyond anything they could ever do in several lifetimes. You'll even go beyond . . . good and evil." He ran his fingers over the handkerchief, over the splatter of dark red spots, and he bowed his head and closed his eyes.

"What am I going to do, Father?" He didn't answer me, though I could tell he knew the answer. "It must be pretty big, then, if you won't tell me."

He breathed in deeply through his nose, and when he opened up his eyes and turned toward me, I inched back on the pew. "Father Myles?"

Down the hall, the passing winds nudged the double doors open as cold air blew in and chilled my legs.

"Do you want me to leave?" I said. "I can call you later, if you want."

"I want you right here next to me." He moved his hands up the cane and rested his forehead under the lion's head and closed his eyes.

We sat for a time in silence. I looked at my phone. It was apparently charging. I had the urge to press him about his vision, but every time I turned to ask, I held back. I didn't want to disturb him, seeing as his lips were moving as if in deep, serious prayer.

Eventually, we talked about the upcoming exorcism. My phone had charged up by then, and I called Paul, Rob, and Liz, who agreed to be assistants at the rite. Father Sanchez was on board, too. Then we were done.

"I can't wait until all this blows over," I said, checking my email. "Good thing I'll be living on campus in the fall. I can focus on my coursework, my comprehensive exams, and my dissertation. I'll study nonstop. I'll enjoy my solitude, too. After all, nothing ever happens in Sleepy Hollow, right?"

I unplugged my phone's charger and looked at Father Myles, who sat slumped in the pew, staring at the wall.

"Or so they say," he said.

Down the hallway, the double doors opened up on their own again and slammed. Another cold breeze invaded the hallway, this time freezing my face. I leaned forward in the hopes of dodging another icy draft and soon found myself looking intently into my hands as if trying to see a vision of my own.

"You know," Father Myles said with a hand atop the cane. "Nietzsche often looked at his hands. He believed the future of world history lay in them. You, also, will have quite an enormous impact, especially after you become what you're about to become."

I looked deeper at my hands, at the intersecting lines, like upside-down crosses, as I tried to understand the meaning of it all.

"You are a man of destiny," he said, and rose up slowly from the pew. "Your real work as a philosopher is about to begin. Once you start, you won't be able to stop." He began to hobble away, and as I looked intently at my hands, he said, "The future of higher education in the States is entirely in your hands."

79

Pulling into Quentin's ranch, I drove along the gravel drive as gold dust followed the truck, like a sun-lit cape. I went inside the house and descended the stairs to the man cave, where Quentin pulled a black curtain aside and revealed a wall of firearms: rifles, shotguns, pistols, and semi-automatics. I'd never seen anything like it outside of the movies. Quentin toweled off his hands, black and smudged from gun cleaning solvent, and looked at me slyly.

"So which one you think it is?" he said. "Only one gun in this man cave you know of, and you're standing right in front of it."

My eyes dropped down one row, then another, and that's when I saw it—the Amityville rifle.

A .35 Marlin. Eight shots. Six people. Life in prison.

"Wanna hold her?"

"No, I'm cool."

"She ain't loaded. Besides, you in Nebraska now. Guns are mandatory."

He took it off the rack, muzzle pointed up. The rifle seemed twice as big now. I took a drink of my scotch on the rocks and stared at the rifle's lever.

"So that gun can kill a person?" I said.

"Any gun'll do that, even a BB gun if you handle it right. This baby right here loads seven bullets, and if that don't do the job, all you gotta do is reload."

The scent of freshly oiled guns was overpowering. I sipped thoughtfully on my drink as Quentin turned the rifle over, eyeing it carefully as if inspecting the work he'd just done.

"Ready?" he said.

I gulped down the rest of the scotch and set the glass on the workbench and then I went up to Quentin, who lowered the Marlin into my hands.

"Jesus, I didn't know rifles were this heavy."

"There's a lot that you don't know, but that's all right, cuz that's what I'm for. And I'm gon' start by taking you deer hunting come November."

I squeezed the long cold barrel and then loosened my grip on it and slid my hand down the smooth steel.

"Wish you could bring her on Saturday," Quentin said, "but you gon' bring something else, instead."

"I'm bringing a gun?"

He took a handgun off the wall. It was compact and looked efficient. "Sure are."

"I don't think it's necessary."

"Will be if her daddy shows up."

"Jenna said it'd be her and her mom."

Quentin raised the handgun, stubby barrel pointed up. "And what makes you think she's telling the truth? Jenna ain't exactly a truth teller. Now suppose Lyman's hiding out at the house and then walks you across the barnyard with the end of a shotgun pushed into your back. What you gon' do then, huh?" He opened the handgun's chamber, looked inside, and closed it. "Truth is, Lyman's gon' be at a horse auction, and when he's all done, he's gon' be chasing skirts at the saloon. But supposing he comes back to his house, you gon' need protection. And even though he ain't brown, he's still going down, you hear?"

Tilting the rifle, I moved my finger along the inside of the lever.

"Why don't you come with us?" I said. "We need another assistant, somebody strong, and somebody to restrain Jenna in case things get violent. And if Lyman shows up, you can be the one with the handgun, not me. And definitely not Father Myles." I took aim at a deer's head on the wall. "Sorry, but I'm not bringing a gun."

"Oh, we gon' bring it."

"So you're going with us?"

"Damn straight. And if Mr. Molester tries something funny, he gon' get this gun shoved up his asshole. Then he gon' know what it feels like."

For the next hour, we drank and talked about the academic year. At one point, I took the Marlin off the wall again, this time aiming it at a buck's head, its black eyes big and alert.

"So what are your plans for next year?" I said.

"Start a business. Raise my kid. Live the good life. You?"

"Reading and writing. I assume graduate school's out of the question for you?"

Quentin spit an ice cube into the glass. "For now."

I lowered the rifle. "So you might go back?"

"Nothin's impossible."

I looked around the room and saw a black poster with a white outline of a human body on it. "Possible, but not very probable, right?" I aimed at the white outline and wrapped my finger around the cold trigger. Behind me, the splash of scotch could be heard in a liquor glass.

"Don't you worry about me, desperado. You got enough problems of your own to deal with."

I looked over my shoulder. Quentin was looking at me, holding out a liquor glass with his index finger extended. "You about done with that?"

I lowered the Marlin. "Oh, right. Sure." I gave it back to Quentin, who handed me a fresh drink. "That's a work of art right there. I didn't know those Marlins were so beautiful."

"Like I said, when deer hunting season rolls around in November, you gon' go with us. Gon' use the Marlin, too. You two were made for each other."

80

I walked into the Blue Note with Quentin behind me. He went to the corner booth and took off his denim jacket, while I approached the bar, asking Tony for some painkillers.

"Jeez Louise, you look like you're burning up." He set a bottle of Tylenol on the counter and then a shot glass with water. "You doing all right?"

"It's these headaches."

"You're in graduate school, you're supposed to have them. Just ask this guy. Look, there he is now."

Paul walked in, motorcycle helmet in hand.

"Good evening, doctor," Tony said.

"How's it going?"

I swallowed the pills, then wiped my lips. "You finished your degree?"

"Ten years. On the dot."

"Congratulations."

"That's just the first hurdle. The next is finding a tenure-track job in the humanities, assuming they still exist."

"No worries," I said and handed the shot glass back to Tony. "Under my watch, they will."

An hour passed. As we went over the instructions for the exorcism, I stared at the four shot glasses in front of me, my vision so blurry that I saw eight. A funny-looking face kept appearing in the window, its eyes black and bulbous, like the Man's.

"Father Myles says we should be in a state of prayer," Liz said. "We should ask for forgiveness for any wrongs we've done. A clean slate is important, if not essential, at an exorcism."

"Demons see everything we've done," Rob said.

"Sometimes at an exorcism, they'll blurt out our darkest secrets for everybody in the room to hear. Talk about embarrassing."

"So what's that mean for you?" Liz said.

"Uh, go to a confession?"

"You haven't gone in years, so make sure it's a good one. In fact, we'll go together." Liz suggested we all go and do some soul searching, but I wasn't too thrilled about the idea. In fact, I'd done enough soul searching this year.

Then we agreed on a meeting spot: on the west steps of the Nebraska statehouse, just under the Abe Lincoln statue.

"What else?" Rob looked at me as if expecting me to chime in, but I was feeling terrible inside, and my abdomen felt on fire from the whiskey.

Liz turned on her computer. "I've got something."

During the past week, she and her mom had done research on Lyman McMaster, who'd been busted for everything under the sun: drunk and disorderly conduct, writing bad checks, beating his wife, and soliciting underage girls.

"Police report?" Quentin said.

"It's fifty pages long."

"It'd be longer, if he wasn't Mr. Sly."

"That's what my mom said."

As Liz read off additional crimes, the funny-looking face appeared again. It transformed into that of a pig, then a hyena, then to an evil-looking chimp.

"He was even busted for drug possession," Liz said, "and Jenna was busted along with him, too. She was eighteen."

It happened at Jenna's old apartment, in a small town between Lincoln and her parent's farmhouse in Custer County.

"So here's what my mom suggested. She said that when Jenna was eighteen, Lyman didn't want her to move very far from home, so he got her a place in this small town. That way he'd have easy access to her. But then they both got heavily into drugs, and that's when the sheriff ran them out of town."

Liz touched her temples and bowed her head while a sportscaster on TV made predictions about the Bison's upcoming season.

Paul looked at me. "So this is what's occupied you all year?"

"Pretty much."

"How've you been able to focus?"

"Who knows?"

Liz pushed the computer away. "Gosh, I need a drink."

"Me, too," I said. Then my phone rang. It was Father Myles.

"Have you gone over the instructions?" he said.

"Done."

"I'd like to have a word with the others. I'll keep it brief before the enemy drains the power from our phones."

I handed my phone to Quentin and then went to the bar.

The funny-looking faces greeted me there, in the bar mirror just above the cash register. They appeared in rapid succession, like a deck of cards being shuffled—the Man, Kenny Winslow, the other young men for whom Jenna had shoe boxes—they were all there, staring back at me. I was no longer surprised by the visions, but they made me a little dizzy. I put my hands on the bar counter, squeezing my eyes shut, then opening them. I bowed my head and began to experience sudden spells of blindness.

I looked up. In the bar mirror, the Man was grinning at me. He stood in a small boat made of Bible pages and slabs of wood from broken crucifixes, sailing on a lake of hog slop and raging red flames, the flag of defeat waving high on a pole. He beached the boat on a shoreline made of human skulls and leg bones and, like a tour guide, pointed to a mountain range of human corpses in various stages of decomposition.

I saw Tony at the end of the bar. He lowered his copy of *Prairie Fire* and looked at me strangely.

I looked into the mirror. With one of his three fingers, the Man wrote my name on the bar mirror: Dr. Carl Sorensen. The blind spots hammered away at my eyeballs, and when my vision became clear again, Tony was standing next to me, looking like he was about to call me a doctor. When I looked into the mirror again, the Man had erased my name, but left the first two letters there, only this time they were reversed and rewritten in blood: RD.

81

loisy@bfu.edu
to
zarathustra@bfu.edu

Hey, man. Here's the transcript of the exorcism. I gave it a title. "The Exorcism of Jenna McMaster." I'll use it as a case study for my thesis. Can you tighten up the prose and make corrections? That'd super help me out. I've also written it in first person present. The students in my creative writing class are using that point of view a lot. Our instructor says it's hip.

I wrote down a lot of the things you missed during the exorcism. Jenna (or the demon inside of her) punched you pretty hard. I hope your eye is feeling better. It looked awful on the drive home. Father Myles hopes you're doing well, too. He says to be careful, since you're a major target for a demonic attack. He said not to worry, though. It's your fate.

If you want to grab a drink before you leave for California, I'm game.

Rob

The Exorcism of Jenna McMaster.word.doc

zarathustra@bfu.edu
to
loisy@bfu.edu

Sorry about the delay. My eye is healing up. It still looks pretty bad, but my headaches and eyestrain are even worse.

Your journal looks good. I've made a few changes, but overall it was smooth reading.

No time for a drink, but in the fall, sure.

CS

The Exorcism of Jenna McMaster
by Robert Alfred Loisy
Introduction to Cultural Anthropology
Black Forest University

It's been raining all afternoon. Father Myles and Father Sanchez roll up in a St. Anne's van. We're waiting on the west side of the Nebraska statehouse, just below the Abe Lincoln statue. Me, Liz, Paul D'Angelo, Quentin Smith, and Carl. Carl's been having terrible headaches, but after we cram into the van, Father Sanchez prays over him, and his headaches immediately go away.

We hit the interstate. Father Myles tries to call Ms. McMaster, but there's static on the line. Father Sanchez calls her up, too. More static. Father Myles says not to worry and we drive onward to York, Nebraska.

Paul and Carl are talking about school. Paul earned his PhD but hasn't found a teaching job yet. A guy named Eric Tanner just landed a job with the State and so he won't be an adjunct anymore. Paul tells Carl to apply for those adjunct gigs, to which Carl says he will but doesn't sound too excited about it.

Now Liz has headaches, too. She says it feels like an ice pick has been stabbed into her skull, puncturing her left eyeball and making her cheek muscles feel twitchy. Father Sanchez prays over her, and the headaches ease up.

We pull off the interstate in York for gas. In the back lot, Father Myles stands inside a pay phone booth and calls Ms. McMaster, but the connection is bad. Hanging up, he stares out at the ploughed fields. Carl asks what he's seeing, if he's having any visions, to which Father Myles says, "Brown horses in the corral, and a farmhouse with an aqua-green door."

We drive onward to Kearney. It's been quiet for some time. Quentin rolls the window down because we're feeling hot and sick to our stomachs. We stop at a rest area. Soon we're on the interstate again, passing a crew of firefighters putting out a brush fire. When we turn off the interstate at Elm Creek, we push onward to Broken Bow. When we get there, we veer off to the northwest and follow the two-lane highway for miles. There are no houses, just fields and more fields. The sky and prairie are growing darker by the minute as we drive farther out into the boondocks.

We arrive at the McMaster farmstead. The front door is aqua-green, and three brown horses are indeed in the coral, throwing their heads and snorting impatiently. We pray again before getting out, then leave the van and walk up to the farmhouse. Father Myles stops and walks onto the grass. His eyes are serious and look ready to pop out of his head.

"There's another victim—Jenna's older sister." He pokes around in the grass with his cane. "She was eighteen when she ran away from home. Kicked the front door right off its hinges. She had to take care of something, something that nobody else could know about. She was running across this grass here, and Lyman was on the porch and threw something at her. A . . . video cassette tape."

"What tape?" Carl asks.

"'Twas a documentary on the Tasmanian Devil. It landed here, in this spot. Then Lyman . . . cursed at her."

"What'd he say," Carl asks.

"Keep quiet, bitch."

The Six Stages of Exorcism According to Father Malachi Martin's book, Hostage to the Devil

Presence

The basement air is nasty and thick, like somebody has thrown a wet, moldy blanket over us. There's an invisible presence down here, too. It's supernatural to the core, and it wants us dead. Not only that, but it wants God and the holy angels dead, too.

Pretense

Jenna is sitting in a chair, her wrists tied down with leather belts to the chair's arms, with Paul and Quentin on either side of her. She's wearing a white T-shirt and dark blue corduroy pants and no shoes. She looks sleepy. She says she feels okay, that nothing's wrong, that the team can go back to Lincoln, and that this ritual business isn't necessary. "They have to study for finals," she says to Father Myles. "You can go now, Father. No really, you can leave."

Father Myles is wearing a black cassock and a white surplice with a purple stole around his neck. He makes the sign of the cross, the *Roman Ritual* in hand. "In the name of the Father and of the Son and of the Holy Spirit."

Breakpoint

Not much is happening, except for Jenna coughing or yawning or saying we're wasting our time. Then Father Myles unscrews a small jar of water.

Jenna looks up. "Put that shit away," she says in a deep, guttural voice.

"Lovely, eh?" Father Myles says as the spirit-filled drops of water come raining down upon her.

(blank tape)

Voice

Jenna: Beat it, filthy priest.

Father Myles: Time's up, Old Nick.

Jenna: Shut your mouth, faggot. (To Quentin) Is that a gun in your pants, Hicktown, or are you just happy to see us? (To Paul) You didn't read all of the philosophy books you were supposed to read for your exams, did you, "Doctor"? (To Carl) And you, you fool, you thought we were a symbol. Can a symbol do this?

Jenna breaks loose from a leather strap and lunges forward, smashing Carl in the face with her fist.

(blank tape)

Quentin and Paul can barely restrain her. Soon, Father Sanchez is holding her down, too. Jenna has the strength of five men. Ms. McMaster unlocks a dead-bolted door in the corner of the basement and immediately goes upstairs.

Clash

Jenna is chained up against a cement wall, arms spread wide, legs too, all four limbs in leather clamps with Quentin and Paul standing guard. This room looks like a medieval torture chamber or the dungeon where those tourists in the movie *Hostel* were murdered. I don't want to imagine what use it was put to before we arrived.

Father Myles: Tell me your name.
Jenna: No.
FM: Tell me.
J: No.
FM: I command you.
J: Up yours.
FM: I command you.
J: To fuck me.
FM: Tell me your name and the hour at which you will depart.
J: We leave when daddy fucks her.
FM: Your name.

J: S—
FM: Your name.
J: S—
FM: Tell me.
J: Sado—
FM: Say it.
J: Sadomaster.

(blank tape)

FM: I command you once more, Sadomaster, to leave this creature of the Most High at once

S (Jenna): You should see them today, daddy and his little girl, still playing his big, blue-veined flute. How's that for Irish slang, priest?

Something like a gunshot rings out of Carl's phone. He drops it. Six more shots follow and with each blast the phone flips and rattles on the floor. A voice can be heard from the phone.

Operator: Suffolk County Police. May I help you?
Man: Hah?
Operator: This is Suffolk County Police. May I help you?
Man: We have a shooting here. Uh, DeFeo.
Operator: Okay, where you calling from?
Man: It's in Amityville. Ocean Avenue in Amityville.

Father Myles says it's a trap, and he sprays Jenna with drops of water, and she screams for it to stop because it burns like fire. Jenna looks like a young girl now, barely a teenager, with half of her face shot away. A single eye looks at us through a mask of blood.

FM: Sadomaster, you will stop your games.
S: Games, games, games.
FM: Do as I command you and —
S: Daddy commands her to —
FM: Do as I say and leave the girl at once.

Now, a film is showing on the wall, just above Jenna's head. There's no projector in the room, but the image flickers and shakes like an old home movie. We stare. In the film, a twenty-something young man with a brown beard is reloading his hunting rifle inside a big house with eye-like windows. Upstairs, his sister, in a nightgown, walks out of her bedroom and leans over the third-floor guardrail, looking down. "Is that you, Butch?" she says, to which he replies, "Yeah, everything's all right."

Carl's phone chimes. A text message.

S: It's for you, Carl Snarl.
FM: Carl, no. It's a trap. Turn that bloody thing off.
C: It is off.
S: Do it, Carl, do it.
FM: Carl, no.

A rifle's blast is heard from Carl's phone, which flips and settles on the floor.

Operator: What's the problem, sir?
Man: It's a shooting!

Operator: There's a shooting. Anybody hurt?
Man: Hah?
Operator: Anybody hurt?
Man: Yeah, everybody's dead.

(blank tape)

We're driving back to Lincoln. I'm typing out as accurately as I can the last stage of the exorcism—*Expulsion*—before my computer goes dead. The two priests are up front, with Father Myles at the wheel. There isn't much talking. Liz's head is resting on my shoulder and I ask if she's okay.

"Yes," she says, without being convincing.

I ask what she's thinking about, and she says Jenna, especially how she looked as she came up the basement stairs with those tired, extinguished eyes and with Father Sanchez and Father Myles at her sides.

Soon, the priests begin a dialogue.

"'Twas quite a show."

"Let us hope girl stay strong and not invite demon back in."

"If she receives pastoral care, she'll be fine."

"It is hard to believe demon was with girl for twenty-one years."

"'Twas quite a revelation, eh?"

"Or that girl's father helped to get her possessed."

"Introducing her to witchcraft allowed him to continue his evil fantasies."

"Let us hope girl does not give in to father's pressure again or invite demon back in."

"'Tis always possible, though it's not her that I'm presently worried about."

"What do you mean?"

Father Myles looks up into the rearview mirror and then at the highway.

"Yes," Father Sanchez says quietly. "I am worried about him, too."

We stop at the Blue Note. Before we go inside, Father Myles hobbles up to Carl and touches his forearm with the cane. "We need to talk."

Tony rushes out of the bar, dish towel in hand, with his stomach sagging below his belt. "Oh my god, what happened?" Then he says to Carl, "And what happened to your eye?"

The team except for Carl and Tony goes inside, but I linger in the doorway and listen. Tony steps in front of Carl, blocking his path. "You got some explaining to do, mister." When Carl begins to speak softly, Tony wraps the dish towel around his fist and thrusts it into Carl's face. "Didn't I say to stay away from alla this? Hey, you look at me when I'm talking to youse." Carl mutters something and then walks away toward the freight yard. "I had high hopes, but now I ain't sure I got 'em no more. Hey, are you listening? Come back here."

A train's horn rings out in the night as the warning bells at the Sioux Street crossing begin to toll.

82

Michael wouldn't let me on the hotel's lobby floor, not with my super-swollen eye. He made me stand outside, parking cars with aviator sunglasses on. They were bigger than my Ray-Bans and covered the huge mark on my face. During a shift in early May, Avery walked outside to join me. He was whistling a new song by The Killers and playing with a yo-yo.

"You got a haircut," he said.

"Nice observation, Einstein."

"Thanks. You grew a beard, too." Avery studied me. "You look like a philosopher. Very distinguished. Can I see the shiner?"

I lifted my aviators up.

"Holy cow, she slugged you good. It looks like she held a handful of dark purple grapes to your face and crushed them. I've seen my fair share of shiners but, Jesus, that's horrendous."

A lowrider truck, purple and glittery with salsa music playing inside, stopped at a streetlight.

"So what was the demon's name?" he said. "I saw the *Exorcism of Emily Rose,* and the demons who possessed her had names."

"Don't know, nor do I care."

"Oh, that's right. The demon revealed its name after a hundred-pound girl knocked you out."

"Something like that."

"Did you record it? If so, post it on YouTube. It'll go viral and you'll be famous."

"There's no video, just notes a student of mine took."

Avery caught the yo-yo. "Good thing he took notes. You can read them when your vision is back."

"You're in top form today."

"Are you living at the Guardian?"

"I'm moving to campus. I need to get away from this place—the Guardian, the cafés, and the football crowds." I thought of Kenny Winslow. "And trains."

Michael walked outside as the lowrider sped off, the salsa music fading away.

"So what's this bit of news I'm hearing?" he said. "You're leaving us and won't be a part of our team this summer?"

"He'll be in California," Avery said. "Lucky bastard."

I curled my fingers and looked at my long nails. "I'll be back. In the fall."

"Well, I can't blame you," Michael said. "Who wants to live here in July and August? I'd much prefer a strawberry daiquiri and an umbrella at the beach. On a more serious note, you're a highly valued member of our team, you handsome devil, so when you return, be sure to give me a jingle, m'kay?"

Michael and Avery went inside, and I stood at the curbside, looking down the street at the university, its garden in bloom. I wondered about Jenna. I hadn't seen her in a while. I'd heard she'd quit her job at the depot and had hung around for a week or two, then skipped town. Had hopped a train, in fact. I couldn't believe it at first, but the more I thought about it the more it didn't surprise me. Maybe she needed to do some soul-searching or to sever ties with her father. Maybe it was both. As for Lyman, I hadn't seen him around. Nobody had.

My phone chimed.

Grades are submitted, Rob texted.

Good work.

Don't shoot the messenger but I've got bad news.

Go on.

Are you sitting down?

Go on.

Parsons is living at Philosophy House.

I called Rob. "You're shitting me."

"He bought some church in England and had to sell his condo to pay for it. Until he buys and renovates a smaller one in Lincoln, he'll be living at Philosophy House. In fact, he's living there now."

"Jesus Christ."

"You're on different floors, though. He's on second, you're on third."

"How do you know?"

"I saw the housing layout today. It was on Betty's desk when I turned in your grades."

"Who else is living there?"

"I don't know. At least you've got your own room."

A black hawk soared above the Statehouse, hanging suspended above the Sower. Rob began to speak about graduate school, about whether he should go or not. I was annoyed by this change of topics, but I calmly listened and then advised him against it.

"That's what Liz says, too," he said. "She even showed me a lecture on YouTube. The professor was talking about the death of the humanities. I didn't know those degrees were on the rocks."

"That's the current trend, though I have some ideas on how to stop it. What else about Philosophy House?"

"Parsons is super excited. He was in his office today, whistling and dancing to a Patsy Cline song. His cat Thelma was there, too. They're both living on campus."

Great. Cat hair everywhere. "What else?"

"I saw Parsons' movie list for next fall, too. War movies, mostly made in the 50s and 60s. Looks like you guys will be looking at the rise of existentialism in postwar Europe and America." Rob began to list off the movies, but they went in through one ear and out the other.

"Look, just keep me posted on any more developments, okay?" I said at last. "Text me over the summer, if you have to. Or just call me. I mean it."

83

On a Sunday night at the end of May, I left Nebraska. I'd stored my bike and book collections at Rich's pad, then threw open my cell's window and tossed several brown grocery bags of trash into the dumpster below. Then I locked my door, put my keys into Craig's office mailbox, and vacated the property.

Walking down the main line track, I dropped my satchel and blue suitcase onto the red rocks, then torched a Salem to life. I stepped up onto a silver rail and held my arms out for balance, like I'd done as a child. High above, the dark leaves of a cottonwood swelled in the sky, revealing a full moon and a path of shooting stars. Then, as if an invisible god had whispered a suggestion in my ear, I called up a local taxi company, requesting that a cab meet me in the Haymarket. Then I got a text. It was Jenna.

Hi.

Where are you?

On a journey.

Where to?

It's a secret.

Tell me.

It wouldn't be a secret, then.

Fair enough. *How are you feeling?*

Better. You?

This year has taken a toll.

There was a long pause. *How's Adjunctslave?* Then, ☺

I squinted at the screen, then pulled my cigarette out. Was this a joke? I waited for a follow up. There wasn't one.

You're something else, I texted. *Still.*

Something bird-like soared across the sky, over the freight yard, and across the moon, and when I looked at my phone again, she'd texted, *It takes one to know one* ☺

I walked north between the silver tracks, my shoes stepping on the wood planks. I passed under the pedestrian bridge and walked by a tarot shop, followed by an import store with African masks hanging silently in the window. Rain clouds were blowing in fast over town, while a street sweeper was making its rounds, its brooms spinning on the cobbled streets, the windy air smelling of dirt and soap. At the block's end, I stopped at a storefront and, cupping my palm to the glass, looked inside.

A new edition of *Ink Magazine* lay on a table. I looked deeper into the tattoo parlor and then stepped back. In the window, my short hair and beard looked nice. There was something different about me, though. My eyes. They were different now. I searched for traces of my old self, but all I saw were another man's eyes and a strange kind of fire burning in them.

The cab arrived.

Twenty minutes later, the driver pulled up to the old abandoned farmhouse I'd been in once before. The upstairs light was on. I got out and stood in the gravel drive, listening to the waves of tallgrass moving closer in the darkness. A tractor's chug could be heard in the fields behind the house, and I stood there with my head tilted, listening to the engine's monotone through the passage of wind. Then I walked inside and hiked up the stairwell.

Missy was in the corner.

"Hey," I said and sat next to her. A pair of long black velvet gloves and an overturned high heel lay between us. "You're trying on your big sister's clothes? Sounds like fun. Are you going to introduce us soon?" She leaned in and my ears perked up. "You are? Good."

Outside, the cab's door shut. I got up and unclasped the window's shutters and pulled the left panel open. The yellow cab idled in the gravel driveway. Under the black elms, I glimpsed a lone man walking down the open highway. His hands were in his overcoat pockets and his wide-brimmed preacher's hat glowed in the blue light of the moon.

When I turned, Missy was gone, but a gaseous form was beginning to appear. It was a girl, a Missy look-alike, but older. She wore a long black dress and black velvet gloves, and I immediately knew who she was this time.

"Howdy," I said when she'd materialized fully. "You must be Missy's sister."

The girl's cheeks turned bright red and she clasped her hands below her waist and looked away.

"So what brings you here tonight?" I squatted down and tapped out a smoke, this time tearing the filter off. "You want me to hear something? Okay, let's hear it."

She took three steps to the left, then turned on the heels of her bare feet and faced me. The girl's eyes, wild and dangerous, regarded me between her long drapes of straight black hair. Then, peeling off a black glove, she held up a pale arm.

A thin gold watch. Ticking.

In the deepening silence of the upstairs room, I smoked slowly and thoughtfully, listening to the soft ticks grow louder and more ominous, until I had an inkling of what this might mean. Then she gave me a dead-serious look, to which I smirked in reply, and she put a finger to her lips and held it there.

Arriving at the Lincoln depot, I walked onto the station's platform, past the empty benches, above which were ads for a summer writers' conference. Then I passed an old man in an army jacket and faded blue jeans, sitting down with his back slumped against a pole. I sat on a bench and got out my phone, ready to check my texts and voice messages. I'd let dozens go unanswered, so busy was I with paperwork and school.

When I bent over my phone's touch screen, I was startled by my appearance again. I turned my phone on and began to scroll when, off to the right, I saw the old man look up.

"Excuse me."

"Yeah?" I said, still scrolling.

"I was wondering if you could spare a little change."

"Sorry, no money."

"I suppose I could go to the city mission, then."

"Good idea."

"Or to St. Michael's."

"Why don't you go, then?"

Somewhere in the freight yard, an outbuilding's door began to bang, making a loud, otherworldly racket.

"You know," he said. "The Pope is a friend of mine. He even gave me his phone number. Said I could call him, if I want to."

I squeezed my phone and it cracked. Shut up, goddamn it. "That's nice. Congratulations."

"Maybe you'd like to call the Pope?"

Call the Pope? That's insane. "No, thanks. I wouldn't want to disturb him."

A whirlwind of dust and pebbles blew into my suitcase's side, and when I tapped my touch screen, a text message appeared. *You'll have to reload,* it said. An icon of a devil's face ended the sentence. The area code was 666. Lowering my phone, I looked over at the old man, who seemed to have fallen asleep.

Then I saw it. The Amtrak was coming. It charged into the Star City, shaking the long cable of naked light bulbs above me. The rumble of the speeding train began to warm up my body, first my legs and stomach, and then my shoulders and skull, so that one of my canine teeth began to hurt. I stepped into the yellow loading zone, satchel slung over my shoulder and my suitcase in hand, and then looked over my shoulder. To the southeast, the Terminal Building loomed in the sky and beyond it the Sower, its light flashing red, like a siren.

Acknowledgments

I would like to thank all those whose help and advice gave shape to this novel: to my parents for the gift of life; to my former teachers for making philosophy and religion come alive; to my students at Doane College for a fearless, bold learning environment; to Cheryl Ann Fletcher for many talks about paranormal activity and the lives of psychics (extraordinaryconnectionswithcherylann.com); and to my editors Dave King (davekingedits.com) and Lindsey Alexander (lindsey-alexander.com).

CPSIA information can be obtained
at www.ICGtesting.com
Printed in the USA
FSOW01n0109251215
14645FS